DICTATOR OF THE DAMNED

Cold eyes, smiling evilly behind a black silk mask, watched a new murder machine strike terror throughout all New York. A hooded monster of crime had seized the law's weapons, and ruled unchallenged from his secret throne. Richard Wentworth, the fugitive SPIDER, driven from his faithful allies, battles alone against the Dictator's death-grip on a great city.

THE MILL-TOWN MASSACRES

City of steel by day, with nightfall Keystone became the evil den of nameless horror. Into the shops where brawny men toiled over molten metal, along quiet streets, a strange madness erupted, loosed a slaughtering maniac horde, then vanished, blotting out its murder trail. . . . What chance had the SPIDER, sole champion of the despairing townsfolk, against this nebulous death? But Richard Wentworth, playing a lone hand in the murk of madness, answered the call.

Also available from Carroll & Graf:

The Spider #1

THE MASTER OF MEN! ™ #2
SPIDER

Grant Stockbridge

Carroll & Graf Publishers, Inc.
New York

First Carroll & Graf edition 1991

Carroll & Graf Publishers, Inc.
260 Fifth Avenue
New York, NY 10001

ISBN: 0-88184-789-5

Manufactured in the United States of America

This volume is dedicated to
Timothy Truman
whose talent and enthusiasm
brought the dream of
Harry Steeger
into reality.

Dictator of the Damned

With appalling suddenness, a new, hooded monster of crime unleashed swift murder and soul-chilling madness upon Manhattan. His army of assassins struck with wanton savagery to lash terrified millions into a paralysis of fear. The Dictator held sway!— and Richard Wentworth, the avenging SPIDER, driven to the ambuscades of the underworld, faced the vortex of sudden peril alone.

CHAPTER ONE

The Call to Doom

Young Frank Dunning was visibly nervous as he tooled the long limousine expertly in to the curb before his employer's residence on Madison Avenue. He threw a quick glance over his shoulder, as if fearing the quick, deadly burst of a sub-machine gun from somewhere in the obscurity of the shadows across the street.

He slid swiftly out from behind the wheel, and held the door open for the Honorable Howard Appleton to alight. At the same time he carefully scanned the pedestrians who were passing. The Honorable Howard Appleton dismissed him, and hurried up the steps of the old brownstone residence.

Frank Dunning, eyeing his broad back, thought with admiration that his employer was a very brave man. For Howard Appleton was walking in the shadow of death. Only that evening he had accepted the post of police commissioner of the City of New

York—a post which, to Frank Dunning's mind, carried with it the threat of death. Appleton was the third incumbent of that position in the last ten days.

Young Dunning's mind flew back to the first of those two. Patrick Sargent had been found dead of poison two days after being appointed; and there was little reason to suspect that Sargent had taken his own life. Then, Harlan Foote, the second appointee, had suddenly been afflicted with a mental ailment that required his removal to an insane asylum. Now, Howard Appleton, a former fighting district attorney of New York County, had accepted the job.

Dunning's eyes were troubled. But momentarily he forgot his caution as he saw his employer safely on the top step, thumbing the buzzer. He breathed a sigh of relief, got into the limousine, and started away.

Neither he nor Appleton saw the two slowly moving sedans that crawled up Madison Avenue. The first warning they had was the wicked, *spatting* sound of a silenced revolver.

A black hole appeared as if by magic between Appleton's shoulder blades. He uttered a tortured gasp, and clutched at his throat. Blood suddenly flecked his lips. He tried to shout, but no sound came from his throat except a muted gurgle. He staggered, his knees buckled under him, and he collapsed before his own door. He twitched convulsively, stiffened—and lay still.

The Honorable Howard Appleton, formerly District Attorney, and newly appointed Commissioner of Police, was dead.

*   *   *

Several people passing in the street began to shout. Frank Dunning braked the limousine to a stop, and leaped to the pavement. He sprang across the sidewalk and up the three short stairs to kneel beside the body of his employer. The two slowly moving cars which had just passed also pulled up short. Four men emerged from them, two from each.

A large crowd gathered almost at once, miraculously, as if from nowhere. The two men from the first of the two cars pushed confidently through the crowd, making directly for the stoop. The second pair, lost in the crowd for a moment, soon joined their companions beside the body of Appleton.

The door of the brownstone was open now, and Appleton's man-servant, Brock, appeared. Brock was tall, saturnine. No expression of any sort flickered across his face as he saw the dead body of his master. He glanced up, and his eyes flitted from one to the other of the four men who had come from the two sedans. Then his gaze rested on Dunning. He said savagely: "Damn you, Dunning, I didn't think you'd do it!"

The young chauffeur flushed, stepped around the body of Appleton and stood toe to toe with the servant, glaring at him.

His big, capable fists were knotted, and he said hotly: "You say anything like that again, Brock, and I'll shove your teeth down your lying throat!"

Brock smiled thinly and shrugged. "I'll talk at the proper time."

Police were coming from both directions on Madison Avenue now, and a radio car pulled in at the curb. A few minutes later a car from the precinct station house also arrived.

Young Dunning exclaimed: "Damn you, if you think—"

The two men who had descended from the first of the passing sedans moved inconspicuously up on either side of Dunning. "That's all right, Buddy. You just stick around here." Their hands gripped the chauffeur's elbows tightly.

"W-Who are you?" Frank demanded. His face had gone suddenly white.

The two men flipped open their coats, exhibiting shields. "We're Sorenson and Masters of the Five-Star Detective Agency. Appleton hired us to act as bodyguards when he was appointed Commissioner. We got here just a minute too late—but in plenty of time to see enough to fry you, Mr. Chauffeur!"

"You couldn't have seen anything!" Frank Dunning exclaimed with growing consternation. "I swear I didn't kill him—"

He was interrupted by one of the two men who had alighted from the second sedan. This man was dressed in impeccable evening clothes, and he carried himself with an air of great authority. He was in his middle fifties. His name was Hugh Varner, and he was known throughout the City as the attorney for the banking syndicate which floated municipal loans. Varner's companion was Stephen Pelton, the City Comptroller.

Varner glanced sidewise at Pelton as if for confirmation of what he was going to say, then addressed the two detectives, Sorenson and Masters. "I think, if you gentlemen will look in poor Mr.

12

Appleton's limousine, you will find evidence against this young man," he said. "We were coming to visit poor Howard, to congratulate him on his appointment, and the first thing we knew that anything was happening was when Howard fell forward with that hole in his back. Pelton and I glanced toward the limousine, and we saw Dunning here, bending over as if he were doing something at the bottom of his car. I suggest you look there—"

He stopped as Sergeant Thayer, of Homicide, pushed through the crowd. Thayer was a grizzled veteran of twenty years' service in the Department, and he had little respect for wealth or position. It was due to his extreme, brusqueness, and to his dislike for toadying to those in authority, that he had not advanced beyond the position of sergeant. Now he demanded gruffly: "What happened here? Who shot Appleton?"

The two detectives, Sorenson and Masters, retaining their grip on Frank Dunning's elbows, quickly gave the sergeant a resume of what had occurred. Then Hugh Varner repeated his story of having seen Dunning place something in the bottom of the car.

Without a word, Thayer turned brusquely around, and pushed through the crowd to where Dunning had left the limousine. He opened the door, peered in under the wheel, and whistled. The floor board was loose, and the rubber mat that covered it was buckled in several places as if it had been replaced in a hurry. Thayer pulled back the mat, unscrewed the single nut that held the floor board and lifted it up.

There, resting on the battery, was a long-barreled

high-calibre revolver, to the muzzle of which was attached a late model silencer.

Very carefully, Thayer lifted the gun out of the receptacle, his handkerchief wrapped around the barrel. He carried it through the gaping throng, up the steps of the dead man's house, and thrust it under the nose of Frank Dunning.

He growled: "Looks like you rushed yourself a little, Dunning. You might have gotten away with it if you had smoothed out the mat a little better. I guess this will cook you."

Dunning shouted feverishly, desperately: "I didn't put it there, Sergeant. I swear to God I didn't!"

Thayer said softly: "Dunning, I arrest you for the murder of Howard Appleton. I warn you that anything you say may be used against you!"

Ten minutes had elapsed since young Frank Dunning had driven Howard Appleton up to the curb in the limousine. Life and death had marched on inexorably in those ten minutes.

And across at the other end of town, the man who was known as the *Spider* did not as yet know that at that moment there was being woven a weird pattern of murder and madness and fear, which would once more drag him into the vortex of sudden peril upon which he was about to turn his back.

CHAPTER TWO

The Fourth Appointee

In the beautifully appointed penthouse apartment above the small nine-story building which he owned, Richard Wentworth, *alias* the *Spider,* was entertaining friends at a late supper. They were seated about the snowy-white tables, sipping a priceless liqueur which Wentworth himself had brought back from Thibet years before.

Directly opposite him, at the foot of the table, sat Stanley Kirkpatrick, one-time Commissioner of Police. At Wentworth's right hand sat the woman Wentworth loved—Nita Van Sloan, whose fine-textured, copper-bronze hair reflected a hundred facets of light from the brilliant fixtures high up in the ceiling.

At Wentworth's left sat a little girl, golden-haired, demure. She was no more than ten, but she bore herself with all the grace of a great lady. Purposely, she was modeling herself upon the gestures and mannerisms of her heroine, Nita Van Sloan. This little girl was Elaine Robillard. Not so long ago, a dreadful blight had descended upon the City in the shape of one who called himself the Living Pharaoh. Wentworth and Nita had fought this Living Pharaoh through three months of cruel, merciless warfare. In the end they had conquered; but one of the casualties was little Elaine Robillard, who had been left an orphan. Now, Nita Van Sloan had adopted the child. It was a gesture indicative to Nita's steadfast love of Wentworth. For, since he had dedicated his life to a constant battle against crime, there could be no marital happiness for either of them. Nita found her natural urge for motherhood partially satisfied by the adoption of Elaine.

There were three other men in the room. They were Wentworth's personal servants. One, a huge, bearded Sikh, was garbed in the traditional costume of the high-caste Hindu, with a ceremonial turban wound about his head. His long beard was carefully trimmed, and a jewel-hilted dagger rested in a sheath at his belt. The other two were Jenkyns, his butler, and Jackson, his chauffeur.

All three of these men were as devoted to Richard Wentworth as it is possible for one human being to be to another. Jenkyns had served Wentworth's father before him. Jackson had been under Major Wentworth's command in France, and the ties that lay between them were far greater than those of master and servant. As for Ram Singh, the Sikh came from a long line of warriors, and his fierce pride was a thing he would defend with his life. Yet he found it not inconsistent to be in the service of Richard

16

Wentworth, whom he respected as a warrior greater than himself.

Jenkyns had just finished pouring the liqueur, and was resting with the decanter. Ram Singh and Jackson had entered the room a moment before, and were standing at the door.

Ex-Commissioner Kirkpatrick was about to raise his glass, when Wentworth stopped him. "Just a moment, Kirk. I have an announcement to make. But first—" he arose, pushing his chair back, and faced his three servants. His voice assumed the curt ring of command. "Jenkyns! Jackson! Ram Singh!"

The three loyal servants drew themselves up to attention. Wentworth went on: "Jenkyns, you will pour three more liqueurs, and set three more chairs at the table. Then, you three will seat yourselves."

The old butler looked slightly dismayed. Jackson was shocked. And Ram Singh spread his hands, palms upward, in a gesture of negation. "Nay, *sahib,* we are but servants," he protested. "A servant does not sit at the same board with his master!"

Wentworth's eyes were glowing, and his voice throbbed with emotion. "You three are far more than servants. We have all gone through so much together, that there can be no question of master and servant between us. Seat yourselves."

"But, sir," Jenkyns exclaimed, "it's against all precedent—"

"We can listen to you standing up, Major," Jackson said.

"And it will be more seemly," Ram Singh added, "in deference to your distinguished company." He

17

bowed slightly toward Commissioner Stanley Kirkpatrick.

Richard Wentworth's eyes regarded the three affectionately. A smile hovered at his lips, but he quickly suppressed it. Sternly he rapped: "An end to this discussion. You will seat yourselves. It is an order!"

Ram Singh glanced at the other two servants, then shrugged his shoulders helplessly. "If it is an order, *sahib,* that is different. An order is an order."

Reluctantly, Jenkyns set three more places, and poured some of the golden brown liqueur into three additional glasses. Then, as if celebrating a special rite, the three took their places at the table—Ram Singh and Jackson on the side at which Nita sat, and Jenkyns next to little, golden-haired Elaine Robillard. They sat stiffly, ill at ease.

Elaine clapped her hands gleefully. "Fine! Now we are all like a great big family. Jenkyns is nice, and so is Jackson. But I like Ram Singh best. He lets me pull his beard!"

They all smiled, and then Richard Wentworth got to his feet. He looked around the table slowly.

Elaine Robillard knew him only as Richard Wentworth, a wealthy gentleman who had been incredibly good to her. Nita Van Sloan, Jackson, Jenkyns and Ram Singh knew that he was also the *Spider*. They had fought with him, risked their lives, with and for him, a hundred times. They were completely in his confidence, and they knew that on the occasions when Richard Wentworth disappeared unaccountably from his usual haunts, somewhere the *Spider* was working alone against crime.

18

Stanley Kirkpatrick was the only one who did not know definitely that he was the *Spider*. As Commissioner of Police, Kirkpatrick had waged a relentless war against that scourge of the underworld. He more than suspected his true identity, and when he was Commissioner he had as much as told Wentworth that if he ever got the goods on the *Spider* he would prosecute him without mercy; for the *Spider's* unorthodox method of dealing with criminals had placed him outside the pale of the law. But on many an occasion the two blazing guns of that mysterious and dreaded character had cut short the cruel and vicious lives of underworld nabobs whom the red tape of the law had been unable to reach.

Now Richard Wentworth saw that the faces of all these people were fixed upon him questioningly. They were wondering what important announcement he was about to make, and for which he had set the stage so carefully. He spoke to them in a low voice which barely carried beyond the bounds of the table.

"My friends," he said, "we have all of us lived through some very perilous and some very exciting times. In our association we have learned to love and respect one another. You, Kirk, were a brave and efficient police commissioner. No one can blame you if you resigned at last, because you are richly entitled to the rest that you are going to enjoy. In the war with the man who called himself the Living Pharaoh, we were all close to death. By a miracle we triumphed, and now the city is rid of the menace of that supercriminal.

"I, too, want a rest. I feel that the time has come when I can retire from the work that I have been

19

doing. The underworld is quiet, except for a few occasional crimes. Ram Singh, Jackson, Jenkyns, I am releasing you three from service. I have established a trust fund for all of you, which will give you an income amply sufficient to live in comfort for the rest of your lives.''

There was a stunned silence around the table. It was broken at last by Jackson.

"But, sir, you can't let us go,'' he burst out. "It's not the money we want. You know we'd never be happy if we weren't working for you—''

Wentworth raised a hand to silence him. He glanced down at Nita Van Sloan, and she nodded, lowering her eyes. Wentworth smiled and addressed the gathering once more. "The reason I am releasing you three from service will become apparent when I make the next announcement. Nita and I are going to be married. We are going to take Elaine with us on a cruise around the world!''

Slowly, Wentworth sat down, and placed a hand over Nita's slim one. Little Elaine cried out joyously: "Hurrah! Hurrah! We'll see all those beautiful countries that they tell about in the geography book!''

Jenkyns furtively brushed the back of his hand across his eyes. Jackson was grinning broadly. And Ram Singh said in his deep booming voice: "*Inshallah!* It is a good thing. There are no two in the world who would make a better match. We three servants will resign ourselves to live alone.''

Stanley Kirkpatrick arose from his seat. His voice was a bit unsteady. "You two have richly deserved this. I trust that you will lead a full and happy life.''

He raised his liqueur glass, and his eyes rested on Nita. "I drink to a most brave and beautiful lady!"

They all raised their glasses and drank the toast. Then Wentworth leaned over and kissed Nita lightly on the lips.

Ram Singh said with a sly look in his eyes: "And the *Spider*, Master? What of the *Spider?* Does he, too, retire?"

They all tensed, watching Wentworth. His face suddenly became hard. He said harshly: "The *Spider*, my friends, is dead! Let him remain the myth and the legend that he always has been. Let us forget that there ever was such a person as the *Spider*."

Kirkpatrick sighed. "Let's drink one more toast," he said. "Let's drink to the hope that the *Spider* will never walk again!"

Just then, the buzzer in the foyer rang, announcing a caller. They looked at each other questioningly. Nita Van Sloan grew pale. She put an impulsive hand on Wentworth's sleeve.

"Dick! Don't answer it! I have a strange feeling. Something tells me it's—"

Abruptly, her voice dropped. "Dick, I knew it was too good to be true." The words came from her lips as if she were uttering a dire prophecy. "I'm afraid—the *Spider*—*will*—walk again!"

The buzzer sounded once more, and Jenkyns half rose from his seat, glancing at Wentworth for instructions. Dick nodded, and the old servant made his way around the table, left the room in the direction of the foyer. The others sat silent. They were all impressed by the sudden feeling of foreboding which had assailed Nita. They knew very well from past experience that those premonitions of hers usually bore fruit.

In a moment, Jenkyns returned, and announced: "Mayor Larrabie calling to see Mr. Wentworth—"

He was interrupted by the abrupt entrance of a short, stocky, florid-faced man. This was Mayor Phillips Larrabie, who had been elected only recently on a reform ticket following the sweeping revulsion of the city at the long list of crimes which the previous administration had countenanced. Larrabie had sworn, upon taking office, to rid the city of crime, and to drive every member of the underworld out of the Metropolitan District. But so far he had been unable to find a commissioner to take the job of directing the Police Department in its work.

Now Larrabie advanced quickly into the room, walking with short, jerky steps. He glanced around the room, nodded in satisfaction when he saw Kirkpatrick, then hurried over to Wentworth and grasped his hand. He spoke in the quick, sharp accent of a busy man who always knew what he wanted and went after it as directly as he could.

"You must excuse me for breaking in on you this way, Wentworth. I assure you that only a grave emergency would have induced me to do so."

Wentworth smiled tolerantly and pressed the Mayor's hand. "You're always welcome here, Larrabie. I want you to meet Miss Van Sloan, my fiancée, little Elaine Robillard, Ram Singh, Jackson, and Jenkyns. You know Stanley Kirkpatrick, of course. These are all old friends of mine, and I'm sure they will all join me in asking you to have a drink with

22

us, especially as Miss Van Sloan and I are soon to be married, and make a trip around the world."

"No, no," Larrabie said quickly. "Nothing would please me more than to drink with you, but you must excuse me. I've come here on an extremely serious matter." His gaze met squarely that of the ex-commissioner across the length of the table. "Stanley Kirkpatrick, I would like to talk to you privately. No doubt, these good people will excuse us—"

Kirkpatrick stretched a hand across toward him. "Sit down, Larrabie. I have no secrets from anyone in this room. You must feel free to talk before them."

Larrabie bit his lip in vexation, then shrugged and took the seat which Jenkyns had provided for him.

"All right!" he snapped. "I called your home, and they told me you were here so I came directly, without telephoning. I'll tell you what I want in a nutshell." He leaned over the table, and there was a queer gleam in his eye. "Stanley Kirkpatrick, I want to appoint you Police Commissioner of New York City. And I want you to accept!"

Kirkpatrick's face set sternly. "No, Larrabie. I won't do it. I've been through enough, and I'm going to take a rest. There are plenty of men in New York who will be glad to take the job. You don't need me."

"But I *do* need you, Kirkpatrick. I need you badly. I'm going to give you an idea of how badly I need you." Larrabie kicked back his chair and rose. He placed both hands on the table and leaned over to emphasize his words. "Six days ago I appointed Patrick Sargent police commissioner. He died of poi-

23

son. Four days ago I appointed Harlan Foote to the post of commissioner. Foote became insane.''

Kirkpatrick nodded. ''We all know that. They were unfortunate occurrences—''

Larrabie smiled twistedly. ''You think they were accidents? Let me tell you this. Today I appointed Howard Appleton to the commissionership. *At eleven forty-two o'clock tonight, Howard Appleton was shot to death on the steps of his own home!''*

Larrabie waited while the full force of that announcement struck home to those around the table. Silently, Richard Wentworth and Nita Van Sloan exchanged understanding glances. This was the thing that Nita had feared when the doorbell sounded. When catastrophe struck three times like this in quick succession it could be no accident. There was something deeply sinister underlying the sudden madness of one, and the death of two newly appointed police commissioners.

Larrabie nodded, reading their thoughts. ''You get the idea. There is something more than appears on the surface here. There've been a few isolated holdups in the city during the last week, crimes that might be attributed to occasional gangsters. But *I* think that they are directed from a single source— the same source that is eliminating each new commissioner as fast as I appoint him.

''There've been rumors in the underworld about a hooded master—a dictator of the underworld, a man who intends to force me or trick me into eventually appointing a police commissioner whom he can handle. I'm going to fool this dictator. I'm going to appoint Stanley Kirkpatrick as commissioner.''

Nita Van Sloan exclaimed: "You want to put Kirk in danger? If three men have already been killed, what is there to prevent Mr. Kirkpatrick from meeting the same fate?''

Larrabie sighed. "Yes, I'm putting Kirk on the spot. But I think I'm outsmarting this dictator by doing it this way. Do you know why?''

Kirkpatrick looked uneasily across the table at Wentworth and Nita, but said nothing.

Larrabie went on impetuously: "You see, I know that while Kirkpatrick was in charge of the Police Department, a certain very notorious character was very active in aiding him against the underworld.''

He spoke slowly now, as if wishing to impress every word he said upon his hearers. And as he spoke, he allowed his gaze to travel around the table and to rest significantly upon Wentworth.

"That notorious character was the *Spider*. I feel that if Kirkpatrick becomes commissioner, the *Spider* will take an interest in the situation. And, my friends, I think the situation is serious enough to warrant such intervention. As an officer of the law, as the chief executive of this city, I cannot openly enlist the services of the *Spider*. But I *can* appoint the *Spider's* best friend as commissioner!''

Kirkpatrick wiped perspiration from his forehead. "What makes you think that the *Spider* is my friend? Do you—er—know who the *Spider* is?''

Larrabie smiled twistedly. "I have a good idea—'' once more his gaze returned to Wentworth—"but I wouldn't want to make a statement unsupported by fact. I will say, however, that if the *Spider* is looking for excitement, he will find it in this city, *without taking any trip around the world.*"

Wentworth stiffened. Larrabie, like some few others, guessed that he was the *Spider*. Wentworth was not worried by that so much as by the sudden challenge that had been laid at his door by Larrabie.

And in the eyes of Nita Van Sloan there was a sudden dawning fear. When Richard Wentworth looked like that, he wasn't thinking of love, or of trips around the world, or of peaceful and complacent happiness; he was thinking of battle, of swift adventure and of sudden death. And Nita's heart throbbed in fierce revolt beneath her breast. Now, on the threshold of happiness, she was to be denied it. Why, *why* did this thing have to come up just at this moment? Couldn't Larrabie have waited until tomorrow? By that time they would have been on the high seas.

Kirkpatrick was talking now, low-voiced, moody. "So you want me on the job, Larrabie, in order to enlist the support of the *Spider?* You hope that the *Spider* will exert himself to protect me, and in event that I'm killed, you think that the *Spider* will avenge me by going after this dictator of yours?"

Larrabie struck the table with his fist. "By God, Kirkpatrick, I'll protect you plenty. I'm not going to have the same thing happen to you that happened to the other three. If you accept, you're coming downtown with me, and I'll give you a bodyguard of the best men the Department has. Not only that, but I'll give you a free hand. Regardless of whether the *Spi-*

der comes into this or not, you are the only man who can cope with the present situation.

"Kirkpatrick, it's your duty to accept the job. The city needs you. *What do you say?*"

Stanley Kirkpatrick hesitated. It was very evident that a struggle was going on within him. He had been through a good deal in the days of the hectic fight against the Living Pharaoh. Unjustly accused of murder, he had been deprived of his position and incarcerated in jail. Only by Wentworth's clever strategy was he finally cleared of that charge. Disillusioned and weary, he had been glad to find rest in retirement. Now he was being virtually forced back into public life.

He drummed nervously with his fingertips on the table. Larrabie saw his hesitation, and urged: "I've given you all the facts, Kirkpatrick. You know what you are going to face. They will try to get you, the way they got Sargent and Foote and Appleton. If I thought you were a coward, I would never have asked you in the first place, and I wouldn't have put the cards on the table the way I did."

Suddenly Kirkpatrick raised his eyes. He spoke in a low, decisive voice. "I'll take the job, Larrabie!"

The Mayor sighed in relief. "Good! I knew you wouldn't fail me. Come on. We'll go down to headquarters right now, and I will install you. And I'll see that you're damn well guarded!"

Slowly Kirkpatrick arose and walked around the table. Nita and Richard Wentworth also arose, and he shook hands with Nita, then with Wentworth. Kirkpatrick said significantly: "I don't want this to stop you, Dick, from taking that cruise around the

27

world. I don't think it's as serious as Larrabie makes out.''

Wentworth said nothing. But Nita and Kirkpatrick both knew that Wentworth would not leave for any world cruise while his friend was entering upon a period of danger.

Larrabie and Kirkpatrick drank one toast with the others to the success of the new commissioner, and then the two of them left. When the door closed Nita said, with a catch in her voice: "Dick, does it mean—''

He looked at her somberly. "I'm afraid so, darling. Would you want me to leave now?''

She sighed. "I suppose not. I suppose I couldn't love you the way I do if you were the kind of man to leave your friend when he needs you. But it all seems so unfair!''

Dick Wentworth said nothing. He looked preoccupied. He pressed Nita's arm, said abstractedly: "This set-up doesn't look right to me. Excuse me, Nita.''

He left her side swiftly, and hurried toward a corner of the room where a queer-looking mirror stood on a low table. This mirror was part of a complicated periscope arrangement by which Wentworth could see everything that went on down in the street below, as well as around both corners of the building. The periscope mirrors were arranged in a false drain pipe in such a way that it was almost impossible for the tenants of the building to notice them. From the penthouse windows there was a clear view of the Hudson River and of the Jersey shore on the other side.

But Wentworth paid no attention to that now. He gazed into the periscope, and his face tautened. He said reflectively: "That's funny. I've never seen a hearse with portholes before."

Suddenly he jerked away from the periscope, his eyes blazing with excitement.

"Ram Singh! Jenkyns!" he exclaimed. "Your high-powered rifles, quick! There's a hearse slowly moving toward the doorway of this building from the corner. Stop it if you can!"

Himself he raced across the room, while Nita and Elaine Robillard watched him, wide-eyed. In the foyer he slipped open a drawer of the telephone table and snatched out two blued-steel Colt automatics, then launched himself out through the front door into the hall. Fortunately, there were two self-service elevators serving the penthouse. Wentworth had been careful to see that he had the additional elevator in case of emergency. The indicator of one of the two elevators showed that it was just passing the second floor on its way to the lobby. The second elevator was at the penthouse floor, and Wentworth swung into it, jabbed hard at the ground-floor button.

As the door swung shut, he caught a last glimpse of Ram Singh and Jackson, through the open door of the apartment. They were racing toward the terrace of the penthouse, carrying their long rifles, with which they were crack shots. Then the cage began to slide downward.

Wentworth's body was taut as it reached the ground floor. He had slipped off the safety catches on both automatics, and now he swung open the door, leaped out into the lobby, both guns thrust out straight ahead of him. At the doorway he saw

Kirkpatrick and Larrabie in the act of stepping out onto the sidewalk. And just at that instant the dark bulk of the undertaker's hearse which he had glimpsed from up above came pulling slowly in front of the entrance.

Wentworth opened his mouth to shout a warning, but his cry was drowned by the sudden sharp staccato barking of machine-guns.

The elevators were at a slight angle from the doorway, and Wentworth himself escaped that blast of lead. Ahead of him, he saw Larrabie suddenly stiffen, then quickly heave against Kirkpatrick, and send the Commissioner sprawling on the floor to one side of the doorway. Larrabie himself was left in the entrance, and his body caught the full blast of that machine-gun barrage.

Like a tortured thing the body of the Mayor seemed to dance in live agony as wave after wave of hot lead slammed into him. Wentworth uttered a hoarse cry and raised his automatics, sent twin streaks of blue flame searing in the direction of the hearse. His slugs rebounded harmlessly from shatterproof glass. He saw four open portholes from which four machine-guns dealt lead. He also saw a man in the driver's seat crouching over the wheel, and beside him another man whose face and head were covered by a black hood.

Wentworth swerved his guns from the useless fusillade against the bullet-proof glass, and aimed for the driver. He had only one shot left in each automatic, and he fired each in quick succession. The driver's head seemed to disintegrate under the two powerfully-propelled slugs. The hearse swerved, careened, and the machine-gun fire suddenly ceased.

Larrabie was on the tiled floor now, writhing feebly, a spark of life still in his eyes.

Kirkpatrick was picking himself up from the floor where Larrabie had thrust him. The Commissioner was crawling toward the entrance on all fours. Being in evening dress, he had come unarmed, and had no gun.

Wentworth's guns were useless, for he had fired the last shot. But he leaped over the body of the still-quivering Larrabie, and raced out into the open in time to see the truck, out of control, swerve and smash head-on into the lamp-post thirty feet beyond the doorway.

From the driver's seat the figure of a man suddenly errupted. It was the man who wore the hood. He leaped to the ground and ran, zig-zag, diagonally across the street into the safety of the shadows of Riverside Park, on the opposite side. In a moment he had disappeared down the steep slope of the cliff.

The four men who had operated the machine-guns within the hearse leaped out of it and dashed after the hooded man. They had left their machine-guns in order the better to escape. But now they were pulling revolvers out of their shoulder holsters.

Wentworth disregarded the danger of those revolvers, and raced after the four fleeing men. One of them turned, snarling, and levelled a gun at him. But the man never had an opportunity to fire. For at that moment a rain of lead spattered onto the sidewalk on all sides of him as well as around the other three gunmen. Ram Singh and Jenkyns were firing swiftly, with deadly precision, from the penthouse overhead.

The two thugs nearest to Wentworth fell, riddled with bullets. The other two ran a few more paces, reached the edge of the cliff above the railroad tracks, and then toppled over into space as more slugs from the rifles of the two men on the roof pounded into them.

Wentworth smiled tightly, but there was a bit of disappointment in that smile. Ram Singh and Jenkyns had surely saved his life, but the hooded man who must have been the leader of the gang had escaped. He shrugged, left the bodies of the dead gunmen in the middle of the street and hurried around to the front of the hearse.

The radiator was entirely smashed in, and clouds of hot steam were pouring from it. The dead man behind the wheel was unrecognizable, for both of Wentworth's bullets had gone through his head, tearing away most of his face. Richard Wentworth reached in grimly and turned off the ignition, in order to prevent the hearse from catching fire. Then he turned and strode back into the building. His eyes were bleak and hard as he knelt beside the dying Mayor Larrabie. On the other side of him knelt Kirkpatrick. The Commissioner's hands were trembling, and there was sweat on his forehead.

"My God!" Kirkpatrick exclaimed. "He gave up his life to save me. If he hadn't pushed me out of the way, I'd have got it too!"

Wentworth nodded. "Yes, I saw it. It was a brave thing to do. Larrabie—was a man!"

Abruptly he knelt lower, as he saw the Mayor's eyes flickering, and his lips moving feebly. A mumble was coming from Larrabie's mouth now, mingled with the gurgling of blood in his larynx. The tiled floor was being stained a deep crimson by his life's blood. But there was an uncanny perseverance, a stubborn courage that kept the man alive until he had spoken what he wanted to say. Now his lips were forming a message that he was trying desperately to get across. Wentworth caught these words:

"I—saved Kirk's life—because—he's needed— more than I . . . and I—promised him protection. . . ." A wry smile pinched at Larrabie's pallid lips. "I— made—good. Now he must fight for me—must fight the Dictator. . . . I wish—to God—the *Spider*— would help him too. . . ."

A police whistle was sounding outside, and Wentworth motioned to Kirkpatrick, who arose and went to the doorway to meet the uniformed men who had come running. The elevator indicator showed that one of the cages was at the fifth floor on its way down. For a moment or two Wentworth would be alone with the dying Mayor. He bent low, and said clearly, strongly, "Larrabie! Can you hear me?"

The spunky Mayor's eyelids flickered. *"If the Spider would only help!"*

Wentworth suddenly said through clenched teeth: "Larrabie, the *Spider* will help. You have my word for it. The *Spider* will avenge you!"

A sudden access of energy seemed to surge through the Mayor's body. "You—promise it? How do I know—"

The exertion was too much for him. He dropped

back to the floor from which he had pulled himself up, and lay panting.

Wentworth said softly: "This is how you can know it, Larrabie." From his pocket he extracted a platinum cigarette lighter. Swiftly he unscrewed the back of it, exposing a small seal. He pressed the seal upon a drop of the blood that spattered the floor, and said: *"Look!"*

There, perfectly etched in the smear of blood, was a miniature replica of a spider—the seal of the man who was known and feared throughout the underworld.

Larrabie's eyes widened. He had seen that seal upon the foreheads of many dead men during the past years. He knew that whenever the *Spider* "executed" a dangerous underworld character he left that seal of his handiwork upon the man's forehead. And he knew now that Richard Wentworth was the *Spider*.

A slow, happy smile spread upon his pain-wracked features. For a moment it seemed as if he suffered no agony whatsoever. His eyes brightened, and he spoke clearly. "Now I can die. Now I know I have not died in vain. Remember, *Spider*, you—have promised—to avenge me."

Larrabie's eyes closed as if he were weary, and a tremendous spasm racked his body. A gurgle sounded in his throat, and he stiffened, his eyes opening wide, staring upward emptily. He was dead.

CHAPTER THREE

The *Spider* Walks Again

Police were pushing in from the street past Kirkpatrick; Ram Singh and Jackson were coming
out of the door of the self-service elevator.
Wentworth arose swiftly, and scraped his foot over
the spot of blood where he had imprinted the seal of
the *Spider*.

His eye alighted on the corner of a paper of some
sort that was protruding from the inner pocket of
Larrabie's dress suit. He bent and drew it out.

A hand grasped his shoulder.

A plainclothes detective, who had just come in,
seized him by the arm and whirled him around.
"Say, you, what do you think you're doing?"

The sight of the dead body of the Mayor had
caused the police to see red; and now they were
gruffly herding everyone into a corner of the lobby.
The plainclothes detective raised a clenched fist to
strike Wentworth. "You give me that paper—"

Kirkpatrick interrupted. "It's all right, Dennison," he said mildly. "Mr. Wentworth is—"

Dennison swung on him, snarling. "Never you mind, Mr. Kirkpatrick. We ain't taking orders from you. You're not the commissioner any more. This is a case of murder, and I'm going to act—"

He was interrupted by the soft voice of Richard Wentworth, who had unfolded the document taken from Larrabie's coat. "You will excuse me, Detective Dennison, but you are mistaken in your facts. You *are* taking orders from Commissioner Kirkpatrick whether you like it or not. Here is a certified document, signed and attested at the City Hall, which Mayor Larrabie must have executed before coming here. It is an order appointing Stanley Kirkpatrick commissioner of police. That means, my friend, that you will take orders from Commissioner Kirkpatrick until Mayor Larrabie's successor appoints another commissioner!"

Dennison turned back to Wentworth, his mouth agape. Dick held up the paper so that the detective could read it.

Kirkpatrick said in an awed voice: "Larrabie knew I'd never be able to refuse him. He had the appointment all drawn up!"

Dennison saluted awkwardly. "Sorry, Commissioner. I hope you will overlook what I said before. I never knew—"

"That's all right, Dennison. Now suppose you get around and organize this thing, and leave Mr. Wentworth alone."

Kirkpatrick, now that he was commissioner, swung with smooth ease and efficiency into the discharge

36

of his duties. He gave crisp orders, and in a moment it seemed that he had never been out of the Police Department.

While he was directing the handling of the body and the setting up of police lines outside to keep the crowds of curious away, Wentworth drew Ram Singh and Jackson out of the building to the sidewalk. He frowned at them. "What happened to you two?" he asked. "You had the rifles—"

Ram Singh lowered his eyes. "Master, only one escaped us—the one with the hood. Of the others, two lie dead here in the street, and the other two have fallen over the side of the cliff. But the man in the hood escaped, because we shot at those others first. We wished to protect you."

Before Wentworth could speak, Nita Van Sloan came hurrying out of the building. She had thrown a cloak over her shoulders, and Wentworth's heart skipped a beat as the full force of her beauty struck him, flushed as she was with excitement and the scent of danger. Her eyes were wide, and she came up to Wentworth, put both hands on his chest. "Dick! You're all right?"

He nodded grimly. "I'm all right, darling. But Larrabie got it. It was only by a miracle that Kirk is still alive. Larrabie sacrificed his own life to save Kirk."

Nita said: "What now, Dick? Our plans—they're all wrecked?"

Soberly, he inclined his head. "I'm afraid so, darling. This looks like war. It seems that everything Larrabie said is true. And I've sworn to avenge him."

Nita faced him bravely. "All right, then. We'll work together—"

She stopped, and her face grew pale. He was shaking his head, smiling grimly.

"No, Nita, we won't work together. I—I've been a fool, letting you risk your life all those other times. Darling, you're too precious to me. If anything happened to you, I—I don't think I could go on. And I've no right to let Ram Singh and Jackson take such terrible risks. From now on—" his voice became hard, with a decisive finality—"from now on, the *Spider* walks alone."

Nita bowed her head. She recognized that tone. There would be no use arguing the matter with Wentworth now. But Ram Singh and Jackson both broke into voluble protestations at once.

Wentworth frowned, and ejaculated sharply: "Ram Singh! Jackson! I have made up my mind. There is no use arguing. I will not expose my friends to any further risks. I'm leaving now. You won't hear from me until this is over."

He grasped Ram Singh's hand, pressed it warmly, then shook Jackson's hand. "I will expect you both to take good care of Nita. I want nothing to happen to her."

He turned from them, and drew Nita Van Sloan into his arms. Bravely, she smiled up at him as he held her warm, throbbing body close against him. For a moment the whole world dissolved away from these two as they stood there. Wentworth's lips meet Nita's in a long kiss, and she clung to him, her small hands gripping hard at his shoulders as if to keep

38

him from leaving her. At last he tore his lips away from hers.

"Dick! Dick, dear! Must you do it this way? Can't you let me fight by your side—"

"No, darling. I want to know that you'll be safe and alive when I come back. Good-bye, darling. Tell Kirkpatrick to go ahead full blast with every facility of the Department against this Dictator. Tell him that the *Spider* will be working too!"

And Wentworth twisted out of Nita's arms, raised a hand to Ram Singh and Jackson, and hurried quickly up the street.

The three of them gazed after his broad back for a long moment. And then Nita Van Sloan suddenly came out of the daze in which his abrupt departure had left her. Her voice throbbed with urgency. "Ram Singh! Jackson! Go after him. Follow him everywhere. I am afraid for him. I know—he goes into great danger."

Ram Singh's eyes gleamed with eagerness, and Jackson smiled broadly. "You want us to stay on his trail all the time?"

"Yes, yes. I shall be in no danger. But I have a feeling—that this Dictator is stronger than Dick imagines. Stay with him, you two. Never leave him out of your sight. But don't let him know you're following him."

Ram Singh and Jackson needed no second urging. Jackson saluted stiffly, Ram Singh salaamed, and then they both slipped away into the night after the fast disappearing figure of Richard Wentworth.

For a long time after they had gone Nita Van Sloan stood there in the street, regardless of the bustling police and the newspaper reporters, of the crowds of curious who had gathered around the building. Her little hands were clenched hard at her side, and she blinked her eyes to keep back the suspicion of tears that welled within them. Then, abruptly, raising her chin, she turned back and reentered the building. . . .

In a room in the basement of police headquarters on Center Street in New York City, curly-headed young Frank Dunning sat in a chair under a powerful light that nearly blinded him. The room was bare of furniture except for a single table and chair at which sat a police stenographer. Grouped about Dunning's chair were three plainclothes detectives, together with Sergeant Thayer and Inspector Strong, the Head of the Homicide Squad.

"You've got to talk!" Thayer was saying. "By God, you'll stay here all night and all day tomorrow if you don't talk. I tell you, Dunning, you'll wish you'd never been born if you don't come across with the dope!"

Dunning raised haggard eyes to the sergeant. His hair was ruffled, and there was a bloody crack across his lips. He had the look of a desperate, cornered animal.

"I swear to God, Sergeant, I didn't kill Mr. Appleton. I tell you, I don't know a thing about that gun. I don't know how it got in the car—"

Thayer's rasping laughter cut across Dunning's frantic protestations of innocence. "You can't get away with that stuff, Dunning. Brock, the butler, says you asked Appleton for a raise last week, and you were sore as hell when you didn't get it. He

40

says you told him you'd like to knock Appleton's block off. Did you say that, or didn't you?''

"It wasn't anything like that," the young chauffeur wailed. "I just said it was a shame he wouldn't give a fellow a raise. I'd been with him six months, and he was only paying me twenty-two dollars—"

"You didn't feel like that when you got the job," Thayer interrupted. "Your uncle, Argyle Dunning, the President of the Board of Aldermen, got you that job with Appleton, didn't he?"

"That's true. My uncle got me the job, and I was grateful. I never said I'd knock Mr. Appleton's block off. Brock is lying." He looked up beseechingly. "Won't one of you please get in touch with my uncle? He'll help me—"

"Nix. Argyle Dunning isn't going to know anything about where you're being held, until you're arraigned in court tomorrow. We're not letting him send any high-priced lawyers in here to drag you out."

Inspector Strong, who had been watching from a few feet away, now stepped forward. He spoke in the soothing voice of a father confessor.

"Why don't you confess, my boy? I'm sure it will go easier with you if you do. You won't have a leg to stand on when you go on trial for murder, if you don't come clean with us. Those two detectives, Sorenson and Masters, claim they saw you fire the gun. The bullet in Appleton's body was checked by the Ballistics Bureau, and there's no doubt at all that it was fired from that gun you had in the car. Not only that, but Hugh Varner and Comptroller Pelton both testify they saw you hiding the gun in the battery

41

compartment. It's an air-tight case, Dunning. You'd do well to come clean.''

Frank's voice rose in an hysterical shriek. ''I won't confess! I tell you, I won't confess. I won't admit doing something I never had a hand in. Sorenson and Masters are lying. Varner and Pelton were mistaken. I never shot Appleton, and I never put that gun in the car.''

Strong exchanged significant glances with Sergeant Thayer. Then the Inspector said flatly: ''All right, Thayer. If that's the way he feels about it, go to work on him!''

Sergeant Thayer grinned smugly. ''Okay, Inspector. We'll give him the works—from soup to nuts. Before we are through with him, he'll be begging to talk!''

''I needn't tell you,'' Strong cautioned, ''to be careful. Don't leave any marks that will show in court tomorrow.''

Thayer nodded. ''The boys know their business, Inspector. Leave everything to us.''

Dunning plunged up from his seat. ''Damn you, leave me alone! I'm innocent—''

Thayer's fist crashed full into his face, sending him smashing back into the seat, sobbing in frantic helplessness. Thayer nodded to the three plain-clothesmen. ''Go to work, boys.''

Inspector Strong started for the door, but stopped when he heard a discreet tap, and a uniformed attendant entered with a slip of paper. The man's holster at his side was empty of its revolver, and his face bore a flushed, excited, half-terrified expression.

Inspector Strong rapped out, frowning: ''What's the matter, Griggs?''

The man exclaimed: "Gawd, Inspector! The *Spider* was just here!"

"The *Spider!* He was here—and he got away?"

"Y-yes, sir. He suddenly appeared out of nowhere in the Charge Room, and he pulled a gun on us and made us all line up against the wall. Then he stuck a piece of paper in the typewriter and typed a message. It's for you. He backed out of the room and got away before we could do a thing. He took all our guns with him."

Inspector Strong grated: "You're a fine bunch of guys. Letting one man get away with a thing like that! So the *Spider* is back, is he? Let's see that note!"

He snatched the slip of paper from Griggs. At the top appeared the imprint of the *Spider's* seal. Below it were written the following terse lines:

> You are wasting your time with Dunning. Masters and Sorenson are lying. Varner and Pelton are either lying or mistaken. Dunning is innocent. I know that you are putting him through the third degree without the knowledge of Commissioner Kirkpatrick. You are doing this either through stupidity or malice. If it is stupidity, take warning and cease now. If it is through malice, you will have to answer to the *Spider*. Here is a tip for you: concentrate on Sorenson and Masters rather than on Dunning!

There was no signature on the note, but it needed none. The imprint of the *Spider's* seal at the top was sufficient to identify it.

Strong swore softly under his breath, and read the

grim message aloud to Sergeant Thayer. The two of them glanced around to make sure they were not overheard, then moved over to a corner and whispered between themselves.

Finally Thayer shrugged and said: "Kirkpatrick phoned that he wouldn't be back to headquarters for another hour. We have an hour to work on this kid. To hell with the *Spider!* If we can break Dunning down and make him confess, it will practically close the case."

Inspector Strong nodded. "Go ahead. If Kirkpatrick comes and finds out about it, you can refer him to me. I'll take the blame. *I* know how to handle that baby!"

Thayer nodded, and turned back toward Dunning, grinning evilly. Inspector Strong went out, and issued swift orders to the Broadcast Room to notify all radio cars to be on the lookout for the *Spider*.

"He's gone too far, invading police headquarters like this. Give out a statement," he ordered Griggs, "for publication in the newspapers. Say that the *Spider* raided headquarters and wounded one of our men. We'll get the public turned against that guy. There won't be anybody in the city will have any sympathy for him when we catch him and shoot him down!"

Inspector Strong hurried into his office, closed and locked the door, then picked up his own private telephone which was not connected through the headquarters switchboard. He dialed a number; then, when his connection was made, he said cautiously: "Hello, this is Number 27 talking. I have a report to make. . . ."

*   *   *

In a richly furnished room in a tall building over-looking the Public Library of New York City a telephone bell tinkled musically. The walls of this room were covered with rich hangings which screened even the doorway. The furniture was expensive and richly upholstered, and the rug was thick and luxurious.

At one wall, directly opposite the window which looked out across the library, was a broad desk of carved mahogany, into which had been worked the figures of tawny-maned lions. On the hanging behind the desk, which was a drape of purest cloth of gold, was emblazoned an heraldic design. It consisted of the figure of a lion seated upon a golden crown. The lion's fore paws were outstretched, and in one paw it held a sword while in the other it held a miter.

The chair behind the desk was suggestive of a throne. It was massive, with a high back upon which the emblem of the lion was repeated.

A man sat in this chair. He was impeccably garbed, dressed in evening clothes, but his hands were gloved, and his head was covered by a hood. The soft, indirect lighting of the room left the eyes behind the slit in the hood in deep shadow.

Opposite him sat a woman beautiful in a dark, exotic way. Black hair was coiled in a deep mass at the back of her head and over her ears, from which hung long emerald earrings. The white skin of her throat and bosom was daringly revealed by an extremely low-cut, brilliant red gown. Long, dark-lashed eyes gazed steadily at the hooded man. Small red lips formed a flash of crimson in an otherwise white face.

She did not move as the telephone rang, but the man behind the desk broke off in the act of speaking to her, made a gesture of impatience, and picked up the 'phone. His voice was harsh, impatient, as he spoke into the instrument: "Yes?"

Over the wire came the voice of Inspector Strong: "This is Number Twenty-seven talking. I have a report to make."

"You may speak, Twenty-seven," said the hooded man.

Inspector Strong's voice came over the 'phone once more. It no longer had the ring of authority with which the Inspector spoke when at headquarters. "We have Dunning downstairs, but we haven't been able to make him talk yet. The *Spider* just visited headquarters—"

"*What?*" The hooded man's gloved hand tightened on the instrument. "Repeat that!"

"I said, sir, the *Spider* just visited us at headquarters. He left me a note."

"Read it to me!"

Quickly, Strong obeyed.

The hooded man spoke harshly into the 'phone: "You are a fool, Number Twenty-seven. You have allowed yourself to be hoodwinked. Did I not instruct you that you were to have Dunning's signed confession in court tomorrow *at all costs!*"

"But, sir, I did my best. I threatened, and I cajoled. He's stubborn. But Thayer and the boys will break him down—"

"You fool! They won't break him down any more. Did you read that note from the *Spider* aloud in Dunning's presence?"

"I did."

"Don't you see, you idiot, that the *Spider* wanted you to do just that? He knew you were down there with Dunning. He did it that way to make it spectacular, so you would be taken by surprise and read the note right there. It contains nothing that he couldn't have told you by calling you on the telephone. His purpose was to give Dunning enough courage to resist, to withstand the third degree. And he succeeded. Now Dunning knows the *Spider* is behind him. Dunning also knows that as soon as Kirkpatrick learns he is being held there, he will be released from the third degree. That is all the *Spider* wanted to accomplish!"

Inspector Strong's voice came over the 'phone now, much weaker, much less sure of himself. "I— I'm sorry, sir. I didn't think of that. It took me by surprise—"

"Of course it did. I am displeased with you, Number Twenty-seven. Do you know what it means when I am displeased with one of my numbers?"

"No, no, sir! I beg you, be merciful. I'll do better next time. I'll do anything you say. Give me another chance—"

"I seldom give another chance. In this case I will be lenient. Let Thayer and the others do what they can. And in the meantime use every means at your disposal to capture the *Spider*. Hold yourself in readiness for further orders."

The hooded man carefully replaced the 'phone in its cradle. For a long time there was utter silence in the dimly lit room, while he seemed to be meditating. The dark-haired, white-skinned woman opposite him said nothing, but watched through veiled eyes. There was a slight hint of a smile upon her carmine lips as minutes ticked into minutes while the hooded man was lost in meditation.

At last he spoke. "My dear Olga, I have made a serious mistake."

She raised her eyebrows in mock surprise. "What! Is it possible that the clever, unscrupulous, infallible Count Calypsa has actually made a mistake—"

She stopped, choking back the rest of her words. The hooded man was leaning forward in his seat, with hands clenched in anger.

"Stop!" he thundered. "I have forbidden you ever to mention that name." His voice dropped suddenly, became sulky, threatening. "I think, my dear Olga, that you presume too much upon our past acquaintance. One of these days you will go too far—and there will be no turning back for you."

Olga smiled tauntingly at him across the desk. "I know, dear Count. One of these days I will die, just as so many others who have displeased you have already died. But for the present I think I am safe—because you still need me. When my usefulness to the Dictator is over, I shall be prepared for death."

The hooded man's hands slowly unclenched on the desk. He lost his tenseness. "Let us hope for your sake, dearest Olga, that you will remain useful to me for a long time."

"Believe me," she said earnestly, "I shall try very hard to do so. But what about this mistake you speak of. It is in connection with the *Spider?*"

"Yes. My mistake was in underestimating him as

an adversary. I knew that in this operation I would doubtless have the *Spider* to contend with. But I thought I had planned well and carefully, so as to eliminate that danger. Now I find I must destroy the *Spider* before going on with my other plans. You, Olga, are going to be the principal means of trapping him for me.''

She moved her chair a little closer to the desk. ''That will be interesting,'' she murmured. ''Tell me more.''

The voice of the hooded man came in muffled tones through his gruesome-appearing headgear. ''We know, but the police do not know, that young Frank Dunning, the chauffeur, is secretly engaged to Evelyn Appleton, the daughter of the man he is accused of murdering. We are going to make use of that secret connection to bring the *Spider* into our little net.

''Leave me now, Olga, and return in an hour. I will have full instructions for you. You can spend that hour in imagining the things that would be done to you if you should be so indiscreet as to mention anywhere else the name which you spoke a few minutes ago in this room.''

Looking at that expressionless black mask which covered the face of the man behind the desk, the woman Olga shuddered. ''I—I'll never repeat that name again—even to myself.''

The man whom she had addressed as Count Calypsa watched her without speaking as she arose and crossed the room to the wall at the left. She pulled aside the hanging, revealing a dark panelled wall. She stood there waiting, and the hooded man pressed a button on his desk. Soundlessly a section of the wall slid away, revealing a passageway.

She spoke again, nervously: "Thank you. I will be back in an hour." She stepped through the opening, and the panel slid back once more, leaving the hooded man alone in the room.

He did not remove his mask. Instead he pressed another button on his desk and the call-o-phone box at his side became illuminated. A voice from the box said: "At your service, sir."

The Dictator's unemotional orders flowed from the slit in his hood with cold efficiency.

"My plans have not been going through as smoothly as they should. At Riverside Drive, where I directed operations personally, I was almost shot. The machine-gunners in the hearse were bunglers. They fired a full minute too soon. Number Ninety-two, who furnished those men, must be punished. You will assign Numbers Thirty-six, Thirty-seven and Thirty-eight to that task."

"Your order is noted, sir," the voice came through the call-o-phone box.

The hooded man went on: "Commissioner Kirkpatrick is still alive. He must be eliminated at once. You will assign Numbers Fifty, Fifty-one, Fifty-two and Eighty-three to that task."

The voice from the call-o-phone repeated: "Order noted, sir."

"Further, there is now no doubt in my mind that Richard Wentworth is the *Spider*. He, too, must be eliminated. He has disappeared from his Riverside Drive residence. He has probably assumed the disguise, and I am now at a disadvantage as I cannot

50

put my finger on him. I want him located with the least possible waste of time. You will assign as many men as may be necessary to the task of locating the *Spider*—even up to a hundred."

"Order noted, sir. The *Spider* to be located at all costs."

"Operation Number Thirteen, which is planned for tomorrow evening at eight-thirty, must be carried out on schedule."

"But, sir, that is the Grand Central Station operation. According to your plans, it will be necessary to control the movements of the police for the successful completion of that operation. If Kirkpatrick remains as commissioner, that will be impossible—"

"That will be taken care of, Number One, before tomorrow night. If your men succeed in eliminating Kirkpatrick, I am thoroughly certain that my own man in the Police Department will be appointed commissioner. But see that you do not fail, or it shall be necessary for me to find another Number One man."

"I will do my best, sir. Do you wish Kirkpatrick killed or—"

"No, I think that since the failure of the Riverside Drive attempt, we will change our method here. The same treatments that we used for Harlan Foote should be employed now."

"Very good, sir. Any further orders?"

"The girl, Evelyn Appleton, the daughter of Howard Appleton, is to be found and put under surveillance at all times, I shall want to arrange a meeting between her and Olga Laminoff sometime during the night."

"Noted, sir."

"Also, the woman, Nita Van Sloan, and the girl, Elaine Robillard, must be placed in custody. If our plans for trapping the *Spider* should fail tonight, we will exert pressure upon him through those two. That is all for the present. Sign off."

There was a click, and the light in the call-o-phone box became extinguished. For a long time the hooded man sat in the tall, throne-like chair under the emblem of the lion, and he did not move. Then, arising from his chair, he went to the door in the opposite wall from that through which Olga Laminoff had passed. He pressed his thumbs against two different spots in the wall under the hangings, and another sliding door opened soundlessly. He passed through this, and suddenly the light in the room went out, leaving it in utter darkness.

CHAPTER FOUR

A Job With Five-Star

A poorly-dressed man shuffled along Broadway, apparently without any definite destination. He wore no overcoat, though the weather was quite cold. His trousers were baggy, and his jacket collar was turned up as a meager protection against the inclement weather.

To the casual observer he might have been a working man come over to Broadway from some squalid residential district to see the bright lights; or he might have been an habitual hanger-on of the Great White Way who was down on his luck. In any case, there was not enough about him to attract a second glance from anyone.

However, a really careful observer might have been impressed by the breadth of this man's shoulders, by the narrow waist-line, and by the gleam of keen alertness in his eyes, which was veiled by his general appearance of casualness.

In addition, a close observer might have noticed the two almost imperceptible bulges under this man's armpits.

This shabby man stopped for a moment before one of the many run-down office buildings which offered space to the numerous questionable enterprises that seek to do business along Broadway. His eye rested on one of the brass plates in the directory of occupants. That plate read:

FIVE-STAR DETECTIVE AGENCY
Confidential Investigations Everywhere
Room 511

The shabby man paused before the building for only a moment, then entered. He took the elevator up to the fifth floor, and walked down the corridor until he came to Room 511. At this hour of the evening most of the occupants of the building had gone home. But a number of theatrical agencies were still open, and one or two lights showed on the floor in addition to that in the office of the Five-Star Detective Agency.

The shabby man pushed open the door, and blinked at the flood of light in the main office of the detective agency. Half a dozen girls were busy at desks, transcribing reports. A switchboard operator was busily answering the phone. Behind the general office there was a corridor from which opened the doors of four inner offices. Apparently the Five-Star Detective Agency was a prosperous, busy concern—so busy that it kept going into all hours of the night.

The shabby man blinked as he approached the

switchboard operator, and he asked her: "Can I see the boss, please?"

The girl looked at him quizzically. "Have you an appointment?"

"No. I'm looking for a job."

She hesitated, looked him over carefully, then shrugged and plugged the wire into her switchboard, rang one of the inner offices. She conveyed the message, listened a moment, then with an upward glance said to the visitor: "What's your name?"

"Smith."

The girl raised her eyebrows and repeated the name into the telephone. She listened a moment, then said: "The boss wants to know who sent you."

"Nobody sent me. But I heard around the street that you were hiring extra help."

"I'm sorry, mister, but there are no jobs open. You came to the wrong place."

Mr. Smith suddenly showed a little aggressiveness. He leaned over the switchboard: "Look here, miss, you better let me talk to your boss. I want a job, see, and I'm going to stay here till I talk to him."

The girl said: "Oh, yeah." Surreptitiously her finger touched a buzzer at the side of the switchboard. Almost at once a tall, burly man came out from an office at the side, not in the corridor with the private offices.

The visitor had a glimpse for a moment of the room from which the burly man had come. It was filled with smoke, and he could see that there were at least a dozen men seated in the room.

* * *

The burly man came up to the switchboard, glared at the visitor, and said to the switchboard operator: "Whatsamatter, Mamie?"

The girl jerked her thumb at Mr. Smith. "It's this guy, Mr. Sorenson. He wants a job, and he won't take no for an answer. Says he will stay here whether we like it or not."

At the name of Sorenson, the shabby man's face seemed to tighten just a trifle. Keen eyes studied the big fellow carefully. Sorenson came up close to the visitor, growled: "Tough guy, huh? You gonna get out of here peaceable, or will you get thrown out?"

Mr. Smith suddenly shed his slouching attitude. He straightened, and amazingly it appeared that he was as tall as, if not taller than, Sorenson. The slouch had disappeared from his back, and his voice assumed a hardness that had not been there before. "Listen, you," he rapped, "I came here for a job, and I'm going to talk to the big boss. It will take more than you to throw me out."

Sorenson grinned wickedly. "Just askin' for it, ain't you?" One big hand went into his hip pocket and came out with a leather-thonged blackjack. His other hand reached out to grip the shabby man's coat lapels.

But Mr. Smith suddenly revealed a deadly speed. His left hand caught Sorenson's wrist, and twisted it savagely. Sorenson gasped, and dropped the blackjack. In the same instant, Mr. Smith's right fist pistoned in a short jab that caught Sorenson square in the abdomen and doubled him up, sending him crashing back into the wall.

Sorenson's face purpled with rage as he gasped,

trying to catch his breath. Mr. Smith straightened his coat and smiled slightly. "Sorry, Mr. Sorenson, but you asked for it."

The girls in the office had suddenly stopped the clattering of their typewriters, and gasps of surprise went up from all of them. The switchboard operator was frantically pushing the buzzer alongside her switchboard. The door of the room from which Sorenson had come now opened once more, and men began piling out in answer to the switchboard operator's summons.

Sorenson picked himself up from the floor, cursing, and his hand went for the gun in his shoulder holster. He shouted to the other men who had come rushing into the room: "Hold everything, guys. I'll take this monkey!"

Several of the other men were already drawing guns. But Mr. Smith was in no way overawed by this display of belligerency. Instead, his two hands moved with such lightning speed that it was almost impossible for the eye to follow him. They crossed over his chest, then swung back in almost one continuous motion. In each fist there was a snub-nosed, blue-barrelled automatic. Sorenson and the other men froze under the threat of those two deadly guns.

Mr. Smith said mildly: "You'll have to excuse me, gentlemen. I don't like this business of gunplay. But I got to talk to your boss."

Sorenson's hand slowly came away empty from his shoulder holster. His eyes were wide with unbelief. "Gawd!" he muttered. "I never seen a draw like that. Say, you ain't no ordinary punk!"

Mr. Smith smiled. "That's what I've been trying to tell you, Mr. Sorenson. It's—"

He stopped as one of the doors from an inner office opened and a tall man stepped into the outer office. This man, in his late fifties, carried himself with an air of authority. He was Martin Kreamer, the head of the Five-Star Detective Agency.

Kreamer frowned, demanded shortly: "What's going on here?"

Sorenson had already picked himself up from the floor, and he motioned for the other men to retire into the back room. They backed out, throwing respectful glances toward Kreamer.

Sorenson said: "This man says his name is Smith, Mr. Kreamer. He came here looking for a job, and when he got tough I tried to throw him out. But he's got the goods. I never saw a draw as fast as his. Maybe you could use him."

Mr. Smith smiled, and deftly replaced the two automatics in his shoulder holster. "I heard you were hiring men, Mr. Kreamer, so I came up. All I want is a chance to make good."

Martin Kreamer studied him carefully for a moment, then nodded to Sorenson. "All right. I'll talk to him. Come inside."

Mr. Smith eagerly followed Martin Kreamer across the outer office into the inner room. Sorenson did not accompany them.

Once in the private office, Kreamer motioned to a chair and seated himself behind his desk. He lit a cigar without offering one to his visitor, then puffed it slowly, letting his shrewd eyes study every characteristic of his visitor's face and attitude.

Mr. Smith's face was not an extraordinary one. The nose was a little wide, the teeth slightly stained and discolored. The forehead was low, topped by very black hair parted in the center. The eyebrows were very thick, and there were lines around Mr. Smith's mouth. He was apparently somewhere in his late forties.

Of course, Martin Kreamer could not know as he inspected his visitor that the wide nose was caused by two very cleverly constructed platinum plates which had been inserted in the nostrils; that the discolored teeth were really artistic caps carefully mounted upon the man's natural teeth; that the hair had been painstakingly dyed black from the roots out, and that the thick, bushy eyebrows had been artificially superimposed upon Mr. Smith's natural eyebrows.

Stripped of all those disguising touches, the face of Mr. Smith would have become the face of Richard Wentworth, alias the *Spider*.

But if Martin Kreamer noticed anything unnatural about his visitor's appearance, he gave no sign of it. Instead, after a suitable interval of inspection, he said: "So you want a job?"

Mr. Smith nodded eagerly. "Give me a chance, Mr. Kreamer. I'm a fast man with my fists, and I guess I'm even faster with a gun. I need dough badly, and I'll do anything."

Kreamer said noncommitally: "We're not in the habit of hiring strangers who walk in on us like this. We generally investigate our men carefully. We like to know whom we have working for us. You'll have to tell me more about yourself."

"All right. The name is Jake Smith. I come from Cleveland. I might as well come clean with you. The cops are looking for me."

"What for?"

Smith grinned. "There was a jewelry store that got held up there ten days ago. Maybe you read about it in the papers. The proprietor thought he was a wise guy, and reached for a gun. He got a slug between the eyes."

Martin Kreamer frowned. "You have the nerve to walk in here and tell me that you're wanted for murder? How do you know I won't turn you in to the police?"

Jake Smith did not appear too much disturbed. "I didn't say I had committed murder. I only said there was a jewelry store held up. And besides, I've been hearing that you're taking on a lot of the boys that's on the lam from other cities."

"Where did you hear that?" Kreamer asked crisply.

Smith shrugged. "Oh, here and there. I've been in town a couple of days, and I get around. How about the job?"

Kreamer was looking at him speculatively. "Let's see that draw of yours again—"

"Sure," said Smith. And before the word was out of his mouth his hands had crossed over his chest, and the two automatics were pointing unwaveringly at the detective agency proprietor's chest. Smith smiled tightly.

Kreamer jerked back, startled at the suddenness

60

with which those guns had appeared. The long ash fell from the end of his cigar. "God! Sorenson was right."

Satisfied, Jake Smith holstered his guns once more. "Glad you like it, Mr. Kreamer. Can you use me?"

"I might," Kreamer said reflectively, "be able to use you, at that. I think you're the one man who could meet a certain person that interests us. In a gun fight. You know who I mean?"

Smith shook his head.

"I mean—the *Spider*."

Smith's eyes narrowed. "You tangling with the *Spider!*"

Kreamer's eyes were fixed steadily on his visitor. "Would you take a job that would mean your coming up against the *Spider* in a gun fight?"

"Why not? I never yet met a guy who was faster with a gun than me. This *Spider* might not be what he's cracked up to be."

Kreamer nodded. "All right. But you'll have to be passed on by somebody besides me. That somebody will check up on you every which way. He'll find out all about your past. If you shape up okay, the job is yours. You'll be paid a hundred dollars a week."

Smith's eyes were gleaming. "Why, that's what I call gold! And only a few minutes ago I almost got chucked out of the office!"

Kreamer leaned forward in his chair. "But there's something else for you to bear in mind. When this party that I speak of checks up on you, if it turns out that you're a phoney, *you'll wish to God you had never walked into this office!"*

"I'll take my chances," Smith said flatly.

Kreamer nodded. "Wait a minute while I get the okay on you."

He picked up the phone, and dialed a number. While he was doing this, Smith leaned back in his chair, and closed his eyes as if he were relaxing. In reality, his mind was sharply alert, and his ears were listening carefully. Each time that Kreamer released the dial indicator, Smith was counting the number of clicks which it took to return to the normal position. To the average ear those dial clicks seemed to merge into one another into one long scraping sound. But to the keen senses of the man who sat in that chair, there was a distinct number of clicks. Mentally, he tabulated them one after the other: *two, four, three, nine, two, ten, ten.*

Wentworth's alert mind stored that series of figures in his memory. *Two, four, three, nine, two, ten, ten.* He would be able to call those numbers up in his mind when he needed them again. By referring to a telephone dial, he would be able to tell exactly what number Kreamer had just dialed.

Now, he opened his eyes again, seemed to watch lazily, without any special interest, as Kreamer talked with his mouth close to the hush-a-phone attachment on the telephone. It was impossible for him to hear what Kreamer was saying. But his blood was racing with excitement. He had spent a whole day ambling around Broadway, going from one underworld retreat to another, having a drink here,

62

another there, mingling in conversations wherever possible. And he had picked up a very meager amount of information.

But among that information was the hint that Martin Kreamer, the head of the Five-Star Detective Agency, was the Number One man for the mysterious Dictator. And here, by an incredible stroke of good fortune combined with the skillful playing of the cards as they had fallen, he was sitting in Kreamer's office while the latter was actually arranging to give him a job in the Dictator's organization.

He knew very well that he was by no means to consider himself an accepted member of that organization. He knew very well that there would be some sort of test as a very careful examination of the story he had told. But he had laid the ground carefully. Unless this mysterious Dictator were a man of a much greater degree of intelligence than Wentworth credited him with, he should stand a good chance of getting away with his imposture. He wished that he could listen in on that conversation. The hush-a-phone rendered that impossible, but it would have been very enlightening to him had he been able to hear.

For Kreamer was saying: "This is Number One, sir. I've got a man here who gives the name of Smith. His story sounds a little queer, but he's the fastest man with a pair of guns I've ever seen. I thought maybe we could use him in a pinch if it came to a question of burning down the *Spider*. I don't think even the *Spider* could be faster than he is."

From the other end of the phone came the voice

of the hooded Dictator: "You must be careful, Number One. Do not forget the possibility that this man may even be the *Spider* himself, in disguise. Have you thought of that?"

Kreamer restrained a visible start. "I haven't thought of it, sir. But now that you mention it—he's uncannily swift with those guns of his. I imagine that's the way the *Spider* would be—"

The Dictator chuckled evilly. "Wouldn't it be funny if the *Spider* walked in on us that way? But I don't think even he would have the gall to try it. Have you got his fingerprints?"

"Yes, sir. I let him open the door of my office when we came in. His prints are on the knob outside, and my men have probably taken them off already. I'll have a report in a short time."

"Good. We'll give this man a chance. If he proves to be bona fide, we can make good use of him. As a first assignment, send him over to the Casey Grogan Dance Hall. There's a bouncer's job vacant there, and I want one of our own men stationed in that place, to make reports of everything that happens. In the meantime, you will check his fingerprints, and I will conduct other investigations about him. Tell him not to take no for an answer, but to make Grogan give him the job by whatever means he can."

Kreamer laughed shortly. "With this guy's guts, I'm sure he'll get the job. Any further orders, sir?"

"No. Report to me as soon as you have found Evelyn Appleton. Sign off now."

* * *

Kreamer hung up, and smiled at Smith. "Well, you're hired. Now this first assignment is going to be a sort of test. You know where Casey Grogan's Dance Hall is located on Fifty-fourth Street?"

"I think I know that place. You want it shot up?"

"No, no. There's a job as bouncer open over there. You're to go and get that job. Sell yourself to Casey Grogan. Get him to give you the job, and then keep your eyes and ears open. You'll report back here to me whatever happens that might be of interest."

"Such as what?"

Kreamer shrugged. "Oh, you can keep your eye out for any strange characters, or anything like that. After you've been there a day or so I'll give you definite instructions as to what to watch for."

Smith nodded. "I get it. This is just a test. If my—er—references turn out to be okay, then I get a better assignment. Is that it?"

Kreamer smiled twistedly. "That's the idea. Now get going."

Mr. Smith got up, and as Kreamer did not offer to shake hands, the visitor quietly left the office. In the outside room, Sorenson was waiting for him. Mr. Smith said: "I'm sorry about that jab in the stomach I gave you, Mr. Sorenson."

"Never mind that," the big man growled. "I've been socked harder than that in my life. Did you get the job?"

Smith nodded. "I'm on trial."

"Well," Sorenson told him, "lemme give you a tip. Don't you ever try to pull nothing on Mr.

Kreamer or on anyone else in this outfit. It's dangerous."

"Thanks," Mr. Smith said dryly. "I'll remember that."

With narrowed eyes, Sorenson watched him leave the office. The big man shook his head. "I don't like that guy," he said to the switchboard operator. "He's too damn smooth!"

Martin Kreamer came out from the inner office. "Sorenson!" he called. "Did you check on his fingerprints?"

"I took off the knob with his print, and stuck another one on the door. Masters is in the next room now, developing the print."

Just then the door of the operatives' room opened, and Masters came in. This was the man who had been Sorenson's partner at the time of the young Dunning's arrest.

Masters' face wore a puzzled frown. He was holding the door-knob which Sorenson had removed from Kreamer's door. It was an old trick, which the Five-Star Agency had often used in the past. All of their doors were equipped with highly-sensitized, quickly removable door-knobs, for the purpose of recording the fingerprints of any visitors. In this way many callers who never suspected it had their fingerprints on file in the offices of the Five-Star Detective Agency.

Now, however, something seemed to have gone wrong. Masters was fingering the knob in a puzzled way, and he looked at Sorenson, then asked: "Did this guy wear gloves?"

Sorenson shook his head. "No. I'm sure he didn't. Why?"

Masters still looked puzzled. "Well, he couldn't have touched this doorknob, because there ain't a single fingerprint on it!"

"Impossible!" Martin Kreamer exclaimed. "I was very careful not to touch that knob when I went out, and when we came back in the office I stood aside and let Smith open the door. *I distinctly saw him touch that door-knob, and he did not wear gloves!*"

"Then," Masters exclaimed, "there's something phony here. This door-knob is as clean as a whistle!"

Kreamer barked: "Let me have that knob!" He took it from Masters, examined it carefully, then sniffed at it. His eyes narrowed. His lips pursed into a noiseless whistle. "Smell that!" He thrust the knob into Sorenson's hand.

Sorenson sniffed at it, too, said: "It's got a funny smell—like ether—"

Kreamer swore softly. "Ether is right, Sorenson. That man Smith is deeper than he looks. You know what you smelled on that? That's collodion. He had his fingertips coated with collodion, and they left no print!" Kreamer's voice dropped, and he said very low to Sorenson and Masters: "I think this man Smith is more than he appears to be. You two boys had better get out after him and keep tabs on what he does. Understand?"

"We understand, boss," Sorenson said softly.

"He's going over to Casey Grogan's," Kreamer went on. "Pick him up from there."

"Right," Sorenson said.

The two detectives turned and swiftly went out after the mysterious Mr. Smith.

Kreamer stood in the center of the office, frowning, lost in thought for a moment. Then he hurried back into his private office, and dialed a number. As soon as he had his connection, he said: "This is Number One again, sir. This man Smith, sir—I'm afraid there's something phoney in that set-up. . . ."

CHAPTER FIVE

Doom on the Wire

When Richard Wentworth, alias the *Spider*, alias Jake Smith, reached the street from the offices of the Five-Star Detective Agency, Broadway was growing more crowded by the minute. A steady stream of New Yorkers was jostling into the subway kiosk at the corner. Other hundreds were already moving in closely packed throngs up and down Broadway, on their way to dine and dance. Times Square seemed to be a seething mass of hurrying humanity. Barkers for picture shows and burlesque theaters shouted their raucous messages in an endeavor to tempt the passersby to patronize their respective houses.

Wentworth's thoughts were bitter as he scanned all these thousands of people, hurrying home, or to leisurely dinners, heedless of the sinister undercurrents of crime which were threatening to drag men down to their death.

What if these people were suddenly to be informed that a sinister dictator of the underworld was welding all the criminal elements of the city into a vast organization that would soon strike at their own homes, at their own lives, at their own wives and children? Somewhere in the city this dictator was sitting at this very moment, possibly reviewing his accomplishments of the last few days—the murder of Patrick Sargent, the madness of Harlan Foote, the slaying of Howard Appleton and Phillips Larrabie. Perhaps he was chuckling at the thought of young Frank Dunning in the clutches of the law, accused of the murder of his employer. Perhaps this dictator was planning the next great step in his campaign for power. What would that step be?

Wentworth tried to put himself in the place of this mysterious master of the underworld. Where would he logically strike next? Larrabie had guessed that Wentworth was the *Spider;* would it not therefore be logical that this dictator should also have guessed the same thing? Would he attempt to strike at Wentworth through those whom Wentworth loved—Nita or Elaine Robillard? Or would he attempt to follow up his efforts to eliminate Kirkpatrick?

Wentworth moved north on Broadway toward Casey Grogan's Dance Hall. He tried to isolate in his mind a name that might identify the Dictator. For this dictator must be some one well known in the city—some one with many connections, enabling him to operate in this fashion. He must be someone who was ruthless, clever, cruel, and powerful enough to command the obedience of an unscrupulous man like Martin Kreamer.

Hugh Varner, the banking attorney, and Stephen Pelton, the City Comptroller, had both given false testimony which tended to incriminate young Frank Dunning. That false testimony might be the result of honest mistakes in observation on their part; yet, on the other hand, it might have been deliberately done. In the latter case, both Varner and Pelton must come under suspicion. Both wielded great influence, both were clever men, and they were both ambitious. It would not be difficult to imagine either Varner or Pelton as aspiring to attain the power which a dictator of the underworld could command.

Inspector Strong, Wentworth was certain, was not of a calibre to be the guiding force behind this movement. Wentworth knew that Strong had been appointed Inspector of Homicide from the outside, over the heads of dozens of other deserving officers. Kirkpatrick would never keep him. And if Strong was a tool of the Dictator, then it would become imperative for the Dictator to remove Kirkpatrick. Wentworth felt that his friend, the commissioner, was in imminent danger. But Kirkpatrick was warned, and would see to it that he was well guarded.

The *Spider* stopped at Fifty-fourth Street and bought an evening newspaper, scanned the headlines. The main story of the day, spread across the whole front page, gave him food for thought:

ARGYLE DUNNING BECOMES MAYOR

At a special ceremony this afternoon, Argyle Dunning, President of the Board of Aldermen, was sworn in before Chief Justice Murray as Mayor of this city to succeed Phillips Larrabie, who was assassinated last night. Mayor Dunning announced he would appoint a new police commissioner, but there is some question as to whether his authority permits him to revoke Mayor Larrabie's appointment of Commissioner Kirkpatrick.

Argyle Dunning's nephew, Frank Dunning, is still being held in the Tombs pending trial on the charge of murdering his employer, Howard Appleton. Mayor Dunning announced that young Frank Dunning, his nephew, would receive no special consideration as the nephew of the Mayor. The chauffeur will have to stand trial as if he were an average citizen. . . .

Wentworth folded the paper and stuffed it in his pocket, then continued east on Fifty-fourth Street toward the tall Neon sign in the middle of the block which read:

CASEY GROGAN'S DANCE HALL

He walked slowly, because his mind was struggling with a problem—the problem of just where Argyle Dunning stood in the situation. As President of the Board of Aldermen, Argyle Dunning was the person to benefit most directly by the death of Phillips Larrabie, for he automatically became mayor.

On the other hand, it was unreasonable to suppose that a man would deliberately frame his own nephew for murder. And since it was logical to assume that the same hand was behind the murders of both Larrabie and Appleton, one would have to believe that if Argyle Dunning was responsible for Larrabie's death, he was also responsible for having placed his nephew in jail as the accused murderer of Howard Appleton.

Whoever this Dictator was, he had been clever enough to so confuse the situation, to so befuddle the issues, that it would be almost impossible to point the finger of suspicion at any one man as the result of a logical course of reasoning. For that, Wentworth's respect for this unknown Dictator increased tremendously.

The *Spider* still remembered that series of numbers he had memorized in Kreamer's office. He repeated them now as he walked: *two, four, three, nine, two, ten, ten.* He did not delude himself into the belief that by merely checking these numbers back on the dial phone he could trace the mysterious Dictator whom Kreamer served. That would be expecting too much stupidity from a man who had shown himself so clever thus far. There would be some blind connection there along the line—some break in the back trail to the Dictator; for the unknown ruler of the underworld would not make it that easy for his Number One man to search him out. Nevertheless, it would afford an avenue of investigation if all else failed.

Wentworth had arrived in front of Casey Grogan's Dance Hall now, and he abruptly put all speculation behind him. Once more he was Jake Smith, the fugitive killer, trying to make good on an assignment given him by the Dictator's Number One man. His keen eyes glanced up and down the street, sizing it up out of force of habit.

He saw a taxicab pull up across the street, and momentarily the faces of the two men within it were illuminated by a street lamp. Then the taxi moved on a few feet before stopping, and the faces were thrown in darkness again. But that moment had been sufficient. Wentworth recognized Sorenson and Masters. He smiled to himself.

That door-knob trick back at the Five-Star's offices had not been lost on him. Kreamer was very clever—clever enough to have caught the scent of collodion on that door-knob. His suspicions had been aroused, and he had sent Sorenson and Masters to check up. Well, he would give them no grounds for suspicion. The fact that he had used collodion on his fingertips would not of itself damn him in the eyes of the Dictator's organization; rather, it should recommend him to the Dictator as one worthy of promotion in the organization.

Wentworth gave no sign that he had recognized the two men in the cab. He walked under the wide, brilliantly illuminated marquee of the dance hall, stepped past the doorman and the hat-check girl without surrendering his hat, and went up the flight of stairs which led to the dance hall.

This was a cheap, old, run-down building. It had at one time been used as a manufacturers' showroom and warehouse; but the neighborhood had deteriorated, and this building had long been unoccupied. Some six months ago Casey Grogan, an ex-prize-fighter had leased the building and renovated two

74

floors at great expense. He had hired two bands, put in a bar, and set about a hundred girls to work as dancing partners. Men in search of fun could come here and buy a strip of tickets at ten cents each. These tickets entitled him to dance with one of the "hostesses" at the rate of one ticket per dance.

The income of the place was greatly increased by the bar, as each hostess received a commission on the amount of money her customer spent on drinks. The upper of the two floors was devoted to what Grogan called private dance studios, where one could learn to dance at moderate cost, under the instruction of attractive young women. All in all, Casey made a good living out of the dance hall, though it did not run into a fortune.

There was a good deal of speculation as to where he got the money to equip the dance hall with. He had not been widely known in the boxing world prior to his venture into this business. He had appeared in a few preliminary bouts in the Middle West, and then had graduated to the semi-final class, but he had never really reached the top. Some said that he had made his money by running arms into South America, while others said that he had won it at the race track. Wherever it came from, he was now running a semi-legitimate business which, though frowned on by reformers, was tolerated by the police. Wentworth wondered as to the cause of the Dictator's interest in knowing what was going on in a place of this type.

When he reached the top of the stairs he did not enter the dance hall proper, but passed by the two ticket booths where one bought dance tickets, and made his way through the bar, which was fairly well crowded. At the rear of the bar were two doors. One was marked "Office of the Manager," and the other was marked "Office of Mr. Grogan."

Wentworth knocked at this latter door, and a gruff voice from inside called out: "Come on in. What are you waiting for?"

Wentworth smiled, pushed open the door and entered. Casey Grogan was sitting at a battered old desk facing the door. He was a well-built man with a long head and lively, intelligent eyes. His face was that of a battered prizefighter. His nose was twisted, giving evidence of having been broken in at least two places. His left ear was bunched and gnarled, and his lips were thick. There was a scar over his right eye, and another over his temple. He looked up as Wentworth closed the door behind him, then frowned.

"I thought you was Krauss, my manager. What the hell do you want?"

In spite of the gruffness of his tone, there was a lively, boyish curiosity in the way he spoke, and in the look on his face.

Wentworth smiled and said: "I hear you got a job open, Mr. Grogan. A job as bouncer. I'd like to get it."

"What's your name?"

"Jake Smith. I'm from Cleveland. I could handle the job for you swell, Mr. Grogan. I'm handy with my dukes, and I can take care of any trouble."

"H'm," said Grogan, musingly. He looked Jake Smith up and down appraisingly. "You look like a good hefty guy. Who told you about the job?"

"Martin Kreamer, over at the Five-Star Agency—"

"Is that so!" Grogan roared. "So Kreamer told you about it, did he? Well, you scram to hell out of here and go back and tell that skunk of a Kreamer I won't have nothin' to do with any of his crew!" Grogan pulled open a drawer of his desk and snatched out a revolver. "I know all about Kreamer. Now you get to hell out of here before I shoot you full of holes—"

He stopped, open-mouthed, the revolver still half out of the drawer. He was staring straight into the twin black holes of Wentworth's two automatics, which had appeared miraculously as if by some unexplainable legerdemain.

"Hold everything, Mr. Grogan!" Wentworth said. "You got me all wrong. I came to this town looking for a job, and I ribbed Kreamer first because I heard he was hiring a lot of men. I don't know him from a hole in the wall. He sent me here. Now if you got anything against Kreamer, don't hold it against me. I need a job bad, and you got one open. Why can't we get together?"

Slowly, as if fascinated by those two unwavering gun muzzles, Grogan replaced the revolver in the drawer. Then he sighed deeply, and leaned back in his chair. He wiped a trace of perspiration from his forehead.

"L-listen," he gasped, "did you really pull those guns outta your pocket? I never even seen your hands move."

The spurious Mr. Jake Smith smiled and holstered

the automatics. "I guess I'm pretty fast with a roscoe," he said modestly.

"I guess you are," Grogan said earnestly. He got up and came around the desk. Wentworth noted that his body was amazingly supple, and he walked with the grace of one who was accustomed to handling himself fast in the ring. Grogan said: "If you're as fast with your dukes as you are with a gun, the job is yours. Let's try you out. Put 'em up."

He squared off, and Jake Smith grinned, put up his fists. Grogan said: "Don't pull your punches. This ain't foolin'. When I try a guy out, I try him out—what I mean."

Grogan feinted with his left, came in hard with a right. Jake Smith moved his head barely an inch, and Grogan's huge right fist whistled harmlessly through the air. Wentworth had studied boxing under greater masters than Grogan would ever know; and though Grogan was a professional, Wentworth knew at once that he could take the man's measure.

He allowed the boxer to try for another swift knock-out, dodged that one, then stepped in, his right and left pistoning with the timed precision of a powerful machine. His fists sank into Grogan's stomach mercilessly in quick alternate blows that gave the man no chance to defend himself.

Grogan backed away, covering up feebly. He sidestepped, attempted to land a blow below Wentworth's belt. But Wentworth saw it coming, watched him, and sent a left to the side of his jaw that rocked Grogan's head. Grogan jumped backward and yelled: "Hey! That's enough!"

Wentworth dropped his hands and stepped back,

smiling. Grogan leaned against the wall for a minute, shook his head to clear it, then exclaimed: "Whew! You got what it takes, guy. The job is yours." Grogan grinned. "If I could fight like you can fight, guy, I'd still be in the ring—instead of running a joint like this!"

He went back to his chair behind the desk. "I pay thirty-five a week. Any drinks you have at the bar you got to pay for out of your own pocket. Your job is just to hang around in case of emergency. You dance with the girls, just like a regular customer, and you float around the place and in and out from the bar.

"There's a buzzer in the hall and one on the dance floor and one in the bar. One ring means trouble in the barroom, two rings mean trouble on the dance floor, three rings mean trouble upstairs in the dance studio.

"Wherever there's trouble, that's where you earn your dough. It's your job to grab those trouble-makers and take 'em apart and see what makes 'em tick, and then kick 'em out on their ear. You got to treat 'em rough, so they won't want to come back. Get the idea?"

"I get it," Jake Smith said. "When do I start?"

"You can start tonight if you're ready. It's early. You come to work about half past eight, and you stay on the job till three-thirty when we close."

Grogan was looking him over closely. "I wonder what a guy like you wants with a cheap job like this." Suddenly his eyes narrowed in suspicion. "Listen, if you showed Kreamer what you showed

79

me, that guy would put you on at a hundred a week. How come he didn't give you a job?''

"I had a scrap with a guy named Sorenson in there," Wentworth told him non-committally. "I smacked him around a little, and I guess Sorenson is sore at me."

Wentworth had told him nothing but the truth.

Grogan's eyes lit up with amusement. "So you mussed up Sorenson, huh? You should have broke that big baboon's neck. If you ever see him or his sidekick Masters in here, you pick them up by the seat of their pants and chuck them out. Understand?''

"I understand."

Grogan nodded. "Okay. You be back here by eight-thirty. And be ready to work."

Jake Smith said: "Thanks, Grogan. I'll be here."

He left Grogan in the office, and made his way out past the dance floor. There were a few men in the barroom, but only half a dozen couples on the dance floor. Places of this type did not begin to do any amount of business until the very late hours of the night.

As he had gone through the barroom, Wentworth had glanced around keenly to see if Sorenson or Masters had come in after him. He saw neither of them, but he also failed to see the face of the man who was talking to the head bartender.

This man had followed Wentworth all the way down Broadway to the building where the office of the Five-Star Detective Agency was located; and he had then followed him back to Casey Grogan's Dance Hall, Now, as Wentworth disappeared, the

80

man raised his head. Had Wentworth looked back he would have recognized his chauffeur, Jackson!

Jackson had come in after Wentworth, and when Wentworth had gone into Grogan's private office, the chauffeur had lounged over toward the door and leaned nonchalantly against the door. The sound of voices had come to him through the office door, and he understood that Wentworth was getting a job here. While he had been listening, he also noted that there was only one bartender on duty. So when he was sure that Wentworth was getting the job, Jackson had approached the bartender and asked him if he needed help. It was while Jackson was talking to the bartender that Wentworth had passed through.

Now, the bartender was saying: "We can use a good man here. We're a little short-handed. Put on an apron and let's see if you can mix them."

Jackson had often assisted Jenkyns in mixing drinks at Wentworth's home. There was nothing in the way of fancy concoctions that he could not make. So he gladly took off his coat, put on the apron that the bartender gave him, and stepped behind the bar. At that moment, Krauss, the manager of the place, came in from the dance hall. The bartender called him over, and introduced Jackson.

Krauss was a short, stubby man, with an entirely bald head. He watched carefully while Jackson made in quick succession a side car, a Bacardi, a Tom Collins and an old-fashioned.

The bartender watched with grudging approval. "Say," he exclaimed, "that's fast, clean work. Where'd you pick it up?"

"Here and there," grinned Jackson. To Krauss he said, "How about it?"

Krauss nodded. "You're pretty good. Have you got your union card with you?"

"I have it at home," Jackson lied. "You want me to go back and get it now, or will tomorrow be all right?"

"That's all right," Krauss told him. "You can bring it tomorrow. Start right in now." He explained that the other bartender had not had a day off all week, and that he could go off now since Jackson was capable of taking charge.

Jackson said: "Just give me a chance to make a telephone call, and I'll go to work. I want to tell the wife I won't be home."

"You can use the phone right here," Krauss told him, pointing to the instrument behind the bar.

Jackson thanked him, and picked up the phone. Krauss left, and went into the office of Casey Grogan. "I've just hired a bartender," he told Grogan. "He's making a telephone call. You want to kind of check on him?"

Grogan nodded, picked up the phone and threw in a switch which connected him with the extension upon which Jackson was talking. He caught Jackson's voice in the middle of a sentence:

"I've got a job here, Miss Nita, and I'll be able to keep an eye on the boss. He—"

Nita's voice came back sharply on the phone: "Be careful, Jackson. Someone may be listening in!"

"All right, Miss. I'll call you again when I go off duty."

Krauss had been holding his ear close to the

receiver so that he could hear as well as Grogan. Now as they caught the click of Jackson's phone being hung up, Grogan and Krauss exchanged glances.

"That's damn interesting!" Grogan said softly.

"*Very* interesting," Krauss said. "I thought that guy was too good for an ordinary bartender. What do you think we ought to do with him?"

Grogan was thoughtful. "He'll keep for awhile. He's a spy of some kind, and we've got to find out what it's all about. Trace that call he made if you can, and then we'll go to work on him after we close."

He got up from behind his desk. "I'm going out now. You can handle everything here. I'll be back around eleven o'clock. Don't let that guy go away."

He got his hat and coat and left through a rear entrance in the office.

Krauss was thoughtful as he came out into the barroom again. He stood there for awhile, watching Jackson deftly serve the customers at the bar. There was a strange gleam in the eyes of the dance hall manager. He strolled into the dance floor, and checked in a number of the girls who were reporting for work. He looked in once more to make sure that Jackson was still on the job, then went downstairs into the lobby and entered one of the telephone booths there. He inserted a coin in the machine, and dialed a number.

When he got his connection he said:

"This is Number Sixty-nine talking. I got a report to make. There's a guy came here and got a job as bartender just now. Right after that he called up a dame named Miss Nita. This guy is too good to be an ordinary bartender. There's something phoney about him. You want I should do anything about it, sir?"

The voice of the man at the other end was the disguised voice of the hooded Dictator. "What does this man look like?"

"He's a guy about thirty-five, sir. He's dark-haired and well built. About five feet seven, and he weighs about one-sixty."

"Well, that can't be the *Spider*."

Krauss' voice sounded a bit startled. "The *Spider*! Say, boss, are you after that guy?"

"Never mind what I'm after!" the Dictator rapped out. "I don't like people who ask me questions. Do you understand?"

"Oh, sure, boss, I didn't mean a thing. I just wanted to help. I wouldn't think of askin'—"

"All right. Remember it in the future. Now about this man—does Grogan suspect he's not what he pretends to be?"

"Yes, sir. Grogan listened in with me on the telephone conversation. I couldn't help it."

"All right. Pay no further attention to this man. I will have the matter looked into myself. I am sending a lady named Olga Laminoff to investigate him. You will assist her in any way you can."

"All right, sir. I'll take care of her."

"Very well. Sign off now. If there are any further developments before Olga Laminoff arrives, call me again."

Krauss hung up and went upstairs again. He was very well satisfied with himself. He looked into the barroom again, and grinned as he saw Jackson at work.

"You poor sap," he whispered. "If you knew what was coming your way tonight, you'd jump outta the window."

CHAPTER SIX

Calling the *Spider!*

When the *Spider* left Casey Grogan, he
moved swiftly, for he had much to accomplish in the two hours before he was
scheduled to return. First he stepped into a drug
store, entered a telephone booth, and wrote down on
a slip of paper the series of seven numbers he had
memorized from Kreamer's office. Two, four, three,
nine, two, ten, ten.

Two clicks of the dial meant that the second circle
had been signaled. That would be A, B, or C. Four
clicks on the dial meant that the fourth circle had
been signalled. That would be G, H, or I. Three
clicks meant that the third circle had been signaled
again. Since the third circle represented a number
and not a letter, the only thing that could stand for
would be 3.

He therefore had an exchange which began with
A, B, or C, and whose second letter was G, H, or

I, with a number 3 following. The only exchange that could be was Chester 3. From there on it was easy. The nine, two, ten, ten represented 9200 on the dial. He had his number—Chester 3, 9200.

Swiftly he inserted a coin in the coin box, and asked for the telephone business office. The telephone company made it a rule never to give the name of a subscriber at any particular number. But Wentworth knew how to get it.

"This," he said, "is Special Agent Lawrence of the United States Treasury Department, Badge Number Eighty-three. It is vitally important that I have at once the name and address of the subscriber to Chester three-nine-two-zero-zero."

He was wired through to the Night Investigation Department, and once more gave the name of Special Agent Lawrence, Badge 83. As Richard Wentworth he knew Lawrence well, and knew also that Lawrence would not object to his use of the name and badge number. In less than three minutes he had the name and address of the subscriber.

And his eyes narrowed calculatingly as he jotted it down. It was—

Hugh Varner, Electrical Building, Forty-second Street.

Wentworth had not expected to find it so easy. That Hugh Varner, the clever attorney for a large banking syndicate, should be the Dictator was not beyond the bounds of possibility; but that he should have been so careless as to permit his Number One man to know who he was, indicated he was so sure of his power that he didn't mind his identity being discovered.

But it didn't jibe with the hooded figure that Wentworth had seen in the murder hearse. The discovery that the telephone was listed under Varner's name made the problem more difficult rather than more simple. Wentworth wished now that he had not cut himself off from his friends. Formerly he had been able to command the services of Ram Singh and of Jackson as well as of Nita. He could have sent one of them to investigate that telephone. Now he must plan all his activities with a view of doing everything himself.

He decided with a shrug that he should not follow up the clue of the telephone number at present. Leaving the telephone booth, he stopped at the soda counter for a sandwich and a cup of coffee. He had not eaten since early in the morning. Though he could have gone for another similar period without food, he seized this opportunity to fortify himself while reminded of the necessity. Wentworth's mind, when he was working on a case, operated with such concentrated efficiency that all his physical wants were forgotten.

While he was eating the sandwich the radio behind the counter was blaring forth the program of a popular comedian. That program ended, and a new broadcast followed. Wentworth tensed as the news announcer spoke:

"Tonight, my friends, events here in the city overshadow national and international news. The city seems to be in the grip of the most daring and ruthless criminal organization which it has ever known. One after another, three commissioners of police appointed by Mayor Larrabie have met with death or with madness. Mayor Larrabie himself has been killed. Argyle Dunning, the new Mayor, appears to be entirely helpless to cope with the situation.

"Commissioner Kirkpatrick, the last man appointed by Mayor Larrabie, seemed to be doing a good job, but Mayor Dunning has asked him to resign. Kirkpatrick has refused, and there now exists the peculiar situation of a police department with two commissioners. The police are demoralized, and in no position to cope with the criminal elements who are running amuck."

The announcer's voice halted for a moment, and then came again over the radio, tinged with excitement.

"*Flash!* Late bulletin! The Pandora Theatre on Broadway has just been held up by a gang of armed men using sub-machine guns and tear-gas bombs. The entire receipts of last night and this afternoon totalling eighteen thousand dollars were taken. The gangsters fired three bursts from sub-machine guns into the crowd of patrons who had rushed into the lobby in a panic. They then used the tear-gas guns to affect their escape. Thirty people were killed and nine seriously wounded. For some reason there were no police radio cars in the vicinity to give chase, and the bandits escaped without interference! That is all we know now. As soon as further bulletins arrive we will broadcast them."

Wentworth finished his sandwich quickly. The announcer went on: "It becomes more and more apparent that there is a giant intellect at the head of the criminal underworld once more. The rumors of a Dictator of the underworld are becoming substanti-

89

ated. Never before has a criminal band engineered a hold-up in the heart of Times Square in such a blood-thirsty manner, and escaped—

"*Flash!* Police, when questioned as to why there were no radio cars available, stated that orders had come in from Mayor Dunning to concentrate all radio cars in Manhattan around the Brooklyn Bridge sector, as he explained he had received information that a hold-up would take place there. So far that move seems to have accomplished nothing except to facilitate the escape of the Pandora Theatre hold-up men.

"Commissioner Kirkpatrick protested vigorously, but Mayor Dunning informed him that he was no longer commissioner. A very difficult legal problem has arisen. When is a commissioner not a commissioner? Mayor Dunning has taken over control of the police department himself, and has demanded Commissioner Kirkpatrick's resignation. But since Kirkpatrick has refused to resign, he remains technically the head of the department. The hunt for the criminals is being hampered by the fact that contradictory orders are being issued by Kirkpatrick and by Dunning. It would seem that the Dictator of the underworld has been successful in entirely disrupting our police force. The city is now at his mercy."

There was more to the announcement, but Wentworth did not wait to hear the rest of it. He paid for his sandwich and went out. Down at the middle of the block he could see the large Neon sign of Casey Grogan's Dance Hall. He looked carefully for Sorenson and Masters, but could not see them.

A man was standing in a doorway across the

street, and Wentworth's eyes narrowed. If he were being followed, he wanted to know it.

He started around the corner up Broadway, and stopped to buy a newspaper. The Pandora Theatre robbery had not yet reached the street, but this edition of the paper contained the story of how the *Spider* had invaded Police Headquarters and left a warning note for Inspector Strong. There was an editorial in the first column demanding that Mayor Argyle Dunning retain Kirkpatrick as commissioner.

"Kirkpatrick," said the editorial, "has experience, as well as the respect of every honest policeman in the department. If anyone can cope with this new menace that has arisen to bleed the city, it is Commissioner Stanley Kirkpatrick. In the interest of justice and good government we demand that Mayor Dunning retain Kirkpatrick in his position!"

Wentworth skipped the rest of the editorial, and let his eyes stray to a box item at the top of the page. He had not noticed it before, because he had had the paper folded over to the first column. Now, the heading struck his eye with the force of a blow:

EVELYN APPLETON APPEALS TO THE *SPIDER!*

The daughter of Howard Appleton, who was murdered yesterday, believes that Frank Dunning is innocent of her father's killing. She disclosed to reporters for this paper that she has been secretly engaged to Frank Dunning for three weeks. All day she has been striving frantically to obtain help for her fiancé. She visited the City Hall this afternoon in an effort to see

Mayor Argyle Dunning, her fiancé's uncle. Mayor Dunning refused to see her. Back at the Tombs where she visited Frank Dunning, she issued the following appeal to a man of whom we have all heard but whom nobody knows:

"I wish to thank the *Spider* for his faith in Frank. I appreciate the risk that he took in sending the note to Inspector Strong. If the *Spider* is still interested in helping Frank Dunning to clear himself, I beg that he will get in touch with me in some way. I shall be here at the Tombs all night. No one can make me go home. I shall stay here until Frank is released. *Spider,* I beg you—do something to help Frank, or they will railroad him to the chair. I have important information to give you if you can get in touch with me. I will go anywhere, or do anything you tell me. For God's sake, help us."

Wentworth's eyes were warm as he read that urgent appeal from a girl in love. He knew how she felt, how frantic, desperate she must be. If he himself were in the same position he knew that Nita would feel that way too—with perhaps the difference that Nita would not be as helpless as Evelyn Appleton was. Swiftly, Wentworth's mind went over the possibilities. Evelyn Appleton had said in her appeal that she had information of importance to impart to him if he could get in touch with her. But why had she chosen to remain at the Tombs? She must know that it would be difficult for him to contact her there. For a moment he wondered if this might not be some trap of the Dictator's. Why should Evelyn Appleton have chosen to appeal to him instead of going to Kirkpatrick whom everyone knew to be honest and efficient?

Wentworth decided to take the chance.

But he could not go as Jake Smith. He would have to change his identity. For that purpose it would be necessary for him to go to his present headquarters on Sixty-sixth Street. He had a furnished room there under the name of John Worth.

He had had this room for many years, holding it always under this name, keeping it stocked with change of clothes and material for changing his appearance. It was an evidence of his foresight, and it enabled him now to operate without the necessity of getting in touch with his home or with Nita or the others.

But first it would be necessary to make sure that he was not being shadowed.

He walked north on Broadway, and stopped in the middle of the block before an automobile showroom. He looked in through the window at the glittering display of cars just received from the factory.

After a moment or two, he threw a glance backward, and saw the figure of a man turning the corner. He could not see the man's face, but he recognized a tall, well-knit figure. It was the same man. The trailer was careful to keep his face away from the electric light, but Wentworth could note that it was clean-shaven. There was something familiar about this trailer's manner of walking, but the momentary glimpse of the swarthy face, almost black-skinned, gave Wentworth no identification.

The *Spider* frowned thoughtfully. Somewhere, at some time, he had met that man, he was sure. He turned and walked slowly up the street, and when he reached the corner he crossed to the east side of Broadway. The man who was following him was clever enough not to cross after him, but continued on up Broadway, keeping close to the building line and away from the street lamp.

Wentworth walked easy on Sixty-sixth Street, without looking back. He was puzzled by this shadow. If the man had been placed on his trail by Kreamer, he must at all costs not appear to notice him. It was possible that Sorenson and Masters had left this fellow to trail him. He must give the man the slip in such fashion as not to arouse his shadow's suspicions. He kept on walking without looking back, and at Fifth Avenue he leaped aboard a south-bound bus which was just starting with the changing lights.

Climbing to the top, he saw his follower boarding the bus behind.

At Sixty-second Street he ran down the steps of the bus, leaped off, and walked quickly west once more. He saw the second bus pass without stopping, and the man who was trailing him did not get off. Wentworth nodded to himself in satisfaction, and hailed a taxicab, drove to the corner of Sixty-sixth Street and Broadway. He glanced back frequently to make sure that he was not being followed now. He had given his shadower the slip. The man had not expected him to leave the bus so soon. He paid off the taxi, and walked west on Sixty-sixth Street, stopping to tie his shoelace and steal a glance backward. No shadow in sight. He quickly turned into the brownstone-front house where he had his furnished room. He let himself in with his key, mounted the flight of steps to the second floor, and entered his room.

He made sure that the door was locked and the shade down, then drew out his suitcase of make-up material and quickly altered his face, rendering it a little older and more dignified in expression. He had now become, to all outward appearances, a dignified businessman of about forty-five. He discarded his shabby suit and donned a well-pressed blue serge suit from the closet. He then picked a grey fedora hat, an ivory-nobbed walking-stick, and a briefcase. From a compartment in his valise he extracted a small box containing business cards bearing different names. Out of these cards he selected one with the name of Mark Hawley, Attorney and Counsellor-at-law.

Now he was going to try to see Evelyn Appleton.

Into the briefcase he stuck the cape and hat of the *Spider*. He expected to have use for that outfit before the night was over.

He descended the steps to the ground floor very carefully, and looked out through the ground-glass panel of the front door. A dismayed exclamation broke from his lips as he discerned the figure of a man across the street from the boarding house—the same man who had followed him on the bus. The chap was still careful not to show his face, but Wentworth knew him by the way his coat hung, and by his physique.

Wentworth had been positive that he had given this fellow the slip on Fifth Avenue. He could not guess how the man had managed to pick up his trail again.

Now he boldly stepped out through the front door. His present disguise would be sufficient to carry him past the watcher. No one could connect this dignified, stately-looking businessman with the shabby Jake Smith.

Wentworth walked boldly east to Broadway without looking around. At the corner he hailed a taxicab and told the driver: "Tombs Prison."

As a cab moved down Broadway, Wentworth glanced out the window and was startled to see his trailer boarding another taxicab immediately behind him. The man had pierced his disguise!

Suddenly, Wentworth felt a deep hopelessness within him. If this unknown who was following him was working for the Dictator, then his every step for the last couple of days must be known to the mysterious master of the underworld. And it spoke well for the cleverness of the Dictator's henchmen that this trailer had been able to follow him so persistently, and to pierce his disguise. What then would be his chances of checkmating an antagonist who was so well served?

Grimly, Wentworth faced forward in the cab. He would have to take care of that shadower somehow, before the man could report to headquarters.

For if the Dictator learned that Mark Hawley, the attorney, and Jake Smith, the gunman, were one and the same person, Jake Smith would meet short shrift when he returned to duty at Casey Grogan's Dance Hall. . . .

CHAPTER SEVEN

The Trap at the Tombs

As Wentworth's cab passed Fourteenth Street, he saw ahead of him, on the west side of the street, the undertaking establishment of Nicholas Wishard. Wishard had been the head of a large bootleg ring during Prohibition days. With the going of Prohibition, Wishard had sought another business and had purchased this undertaking establishment. But his reputation had not changed. He was known in the underworld as one who could be relied upon to supply weapons and getaway cars to criminals. The undertaking business was merely a front for his other activities.

In sudden inspiration, Wentworth snapped his fingers. That hearse, which had figured in the killing of Mayor Larrabie—the police had not yet been able to identify it, for the motor number and serial numbers had been eradicated, and the license plates were stolen. What if Wishard had supplied that hearse?

As they passed the undertaking establishment, Wentworth saw that there was a light in the place, far in the rear where the office was located. He also noted that a sedan with four men was parked at the curb. His single glimpse of the tense faces of those four men told him that they were not parked there for any idle purpose; for two of them were Sorenson and Masters.

Quickly he tapped on the glass separating him from the driver, and ordered the man to pull in to the curb. He got out, told the cabby to wait.

He noted that the cab with his shadower had passed them, and had also pulled in at the curb farther down the block. He shrugged. Let his trailer follow him now. He didn't care. This was too hot a lead to ignore.

He started back toward the Wishard establishment, and just at that moment he saw that the light in the undertaking parlor was put out. The tall, stoop-shouldered figure of Nicholas Wishard appeared, and the man turned his back to the street as he shut and locked the door.

At the same time, the doors of the sedan at the curb were thrown open, and Masters, Sorenson and the other two men stepped out, each of them holding a revolver.

Richard Wentworth was less than thirty feet away, and he distinctly heard Sorenson call out to Wishard: "Sorry, Wishard, this is by order of the big boss!"

Wishard whirled about, saw them for the first time, and screamed: "Don't! Don't shoot!"

Masters, standing next to Sorenson, mocked him: "Can't take it, huh?"

"Wait!" Wishard yelled. "I can square everything with the Dictator. It wasn't my fault those guys flopped—"

He stopped talking, and his voice fairly rose into a scream of terror as the four guns were raised to a level with his chest.

Wentworth was running now, and he had dropped his briefcase and cane. His hands crossed over his chest, came out with the two automatics, and the guns spurted twin jets of flame in the direction of the four men.

Masters dropped with the first shot, as did another of the four. Sorenson and the fourth man fired at Wishard three times quickly, and Wishard fell to the ground, screaming, his voice cutting shrilly above the deep-toned reverberations of the gunfire. Wentworth cursed, fired again, and Sorenson's companion fell. Sorenson himself dropped to one knee, aimed at Wentworth.

And Wentworth in that instant heard gunfire behind him!

He knew that the man who had trailed him must be shooting. But strangely, the shadower was not firing at him, for the bullets whined past well to his right, and thudded into the body of Sorenson before the big detective could shoot. Sorenson was hurled backward to the sidewalk, dead almost before he dropped.

Wentworth, puzzled, swung around and almost collided with the trailer who had just killed Sorenson. The two stood stock still, staring at each other. Wentworth slowly lowered his two automatics. A slow smile appeared on his face.

"Well!" he exclaimed, "Was it you all the time, Ram Singh?"

The man who stood there now, the man who had trailed him all the way from Casey Grogan's Dance Hall, was none other than Ram Singh—without his beard.

Ram Singh lowered his head. "It was I, Master. Jackson and I have been trying to watch over you since you left. It was the *memsahib's* order. I—I even made myself unworthy of my race by shaving off my beard the better to follow you."

Wentworth pressed Ram Singh's hand hard. "It was against my orders, but I appreciate it, Ram Singh. Come now, quickly, before a crowd gathers."

He ran swiftly toward the doorway of the undertaking establishment. Sorenson, Masters and the other two gunmen were dead. But Wishard still breathed feebly.

Wentworth raised his head. "Wishard! Why did these men shoot you? Why did the Dictator order you killed?"

Wishard was bleeding through the nose. "I'm dying," he murmured. "I—I was Number Ninety-two in the Dictator's organization. He—he thought I had laid a trap for him. Damn him, he kills everybody who fails!"

Wentworth bent closer. "You're dying, Wishard. The Dictator ordered you killed. You hate him. Tell me who he is and I'll get him for you."

"God help me," Wishard groaned, "I don't know—who he is. But—" A horrible laugh mingled with the bloody gurgling from his throat—"I'll even up with him. I know something. He's planning—a

100

big operation of the gang—at Grand Central Station—*tonight at twelve*. Whoever you are—be there—with plenty of help. Get the Dic—"

His voice died to a whisper, and the last words faded into nothingness.

"What sort of operation is he planning?" Wentworth demanded.

Wishard mumbled: "Hold-up tonight at—"

Suddenly Wishard's jaw fell open, slackly, and his eyes glazed. He became limp in Wentworth's arms.

The *Spider* lowered his head to the ground, stood up. A crowd had gathered, but was keeping its distance. Somewhere a policeman was blowing his whistle. The traffic cop from the corner at Fourteenth Street was running toward them. Ram Singh was standing beside Wentworth, gun in hand, keeping the crowd at its distance.

Wentworth said urgently: "Come quickly, Ram Singh. We must not be held here. We have work to do!"

He led the Sikh away from the crowd, away from the approaching policeman. The bluecoat shouted: "Hey, you! Stop! Stop, or I'll shoot!"

Wentworth and Ram Singh paid no attention to the policeman's shout. They leaped into Wentworth's cab and the *Spider* thrust his gun against the back of the driver's head. "Drive quickly. Get away from here!"

The cold muzzle of the gun was sufficient urging for the cabby. He threw the car into gear, and sped away, down Broadway. Ram Singh had picked up Wentworth's briefcase and cane as they ran, and he put them on the seat.

101

Behind them another cab was swiftly giving chase, with the patrolman on the running board. Ram Singh grinned, knocked out the glass of the rear window with the butt of his revolver, then aimed a shot at the front wheel of the pursuing taxi. The tire exploded with a loud bang, and the cab swerved, almost mounted the sidewalk before the driver fought it back into control. By that time Wentworth's cab had gained almost a full block.

At the next corner Wentworth made his driver turn right, then left, then right again. At Seventh Avenue and Tenth Street they got out and ordered the driver to keep going down the one-way street. They hailed another cab, got into it, and drove for ten blocks, then changed cabs once more. By the time they had got down to Sutter Street they had thrown off all pursuit.

Wentworth laughed harshly. "We're doing almost as well as the Dictator's gangsters, Ram Singh." He looked at the Sikh's unfamiliar, clean-shaven face, and smiled. "You must be very deeply devoted to me, Ram Singh, to have cut off your beard for my sake."

Ram Singh lowered his eyes. "I could not help it, *sahib*. The *memsahib* Nita would have given me no peace if I had stopped following you. And you would surely have noticed me with the beard."

"And what of Miss Van Sloan?"

Ram Singh put out a hand impressively: "I beg you, *Sahib,* do not be angry with me. I disobeyed you only because—"

"Yes, yes, I know," Wentworth told him. "Because you love me so." He sighed. "Maybe if you loved me less you would obey me more. I am afraid that Nita is in danger. This Dictator knows almost everything that there is to be known. He seems to have spies everywhere. He will know, of course, my connection with Nita. And with only Jackson to defend her—"

Ram Singh broke in awkwardly: "*Sahib,* there is something more I must tell you. Jackson—he, too, is not with Nita. He, too, follows you."

Wentworth's eyes suddenly flared with anger. "What! You mean to say that you have left Nita without protection?"

Ram Singh spread out both hands in a gesture of hopelessness. "What could we do, Master? She ordered it. She insisted on it. Nothing would please her but that we keep you under observation day and night."

"Ram Singh," Wentworth said solemnly, "if anything happens to Nita, I shall hold you personally responsible. And I give you warning, that the next time an order of mine is disobeyed, it will be the last order I shall ever give you!"

The faithful Sikh looked so crestfallen that Wentworth suddenly put a hand on his knee. "All right, Ram Singh, I forgive you this time. We will call Nita at the first opportunity and make sure she is safe. Where is Jackson?"

He followed you into Casey Grogan's Dance Hall, *sahib.* He remained there. I do not know where he is."

Wentworth was worried. He hoped that Jackson would do nothing indiscreet in Grogan's place. Now

103

he thrust all that from him. The cab was approaching the Tombs.

He had to see Evelyn Appleton, and he had to do it quickly. Also, he must find some way to discover further information about the Dictator's plans for the operation at Grand Central Station which Wishard had mentioned. *Tonight at midnight,* Wishard had said. He glanced at his watch. It was almost seven-thirty. He was due back at Casey Grogan's in an hour. But that would have to wait. This other thing that Wishard had mentioned—he must be free to work on it tonight, not hampered by a job in a dance hall.

They got out of the cab two blocks from the Tombs and walked down. Wentworth was taking a chance—a double chance—in coming here now. First, the appeal of Evelyn Appleton might be a trap in itself; second, there would no doubt be an alarm out for a person of his description as being the one who had fled from the scene of Wishard's murder at Fourteenth Street. But the *Spider* was taking big chances tonight.

He left Ram Singh at the corner, and approached the Tombs alone. His eyes narrowed as he scanned the street. There seemed to be a good deal of activity on Center Street tonight. Four of five cars were parked at intervals along the curb. He passed three groups of men who seemed to be conversing idly among themselves, but who bore a furtive and tense expression. They looked him over carefully as he passed them.

There were no policemen in sight. Wentworth wondered if Argyle Dunning had removed the police from this section as he had done from the neighborhood of the Pandora Theatre earlier in the evening. There could be only one explanation for this unusual gathering around the gloomy old prison at this hour of the night—the Dictator had set his trap for the *Spider*.

Wentworth changed his plans instantly to suit the conditions. He passed by the entrance of the Tombs and did not turn in. Glancing in casually, he noted that the door was open so that he could see into the small waiting room. He got a glimpse of a young woman and of three or four men inside. That young woman would be Evelyn Appleton, he had no doubt. The quick glance he got at her face showed him that she seemed to be under a great strain of some sort.

The door of the prison had been opened to permit another woman to leave. This other woman was older than Evelyn Appleton, dark and svelt. Wentworth's heart skipped a beat. He recognized her. Probing back into the recesses of his memory, he fished that older woman's name out of a dim and murky past. She would be Olga Laminoff.

He remembered her well. Olga Laminoff, the international adventuress. She and a certain Count Calypsa had been arrested and tried in France many years agone, as the guiding geniuses of a huge mass murder plot. Calypsa and the Laminoff woman had been sentenced to Devil's Island for life; but they had escaped when the prison ship which was bearing them to their banishment was wrecked off the Azores. They had not been heard from for many years, and the police had marked them down as dead,

105

thinking they had perished in that wreck. At times rumors penetrated the underworld that Count Calypsa was operating now here, now there. And crimes of fiendish ingenuity in widely-scattered places over the globe had borne all the earmarks of the Count's cunning hand.

Now this woman was coming out of the Tombs!

By no sign did Wentworth betray the fact that he recognized her, or even noticed her. He continued to walk slowly past the prison. Olga Laminoff came out and started in the opposite direction. Wentworth's pulse was racing. He wanted to follow that woman.

Her presence here indicated that she was connected in some way with the campaign of the Dictator. If that were the case, then the Dictator must be Count Calypsa.

That would be reason enough for the Dictator's hood. Count Calypsa's face appeared on the wanted list of every police department in the world. If he was seen he would be immediately apprehended.

But it was impossible that the Dictator should forever remain behind his hood. There must be times when he came out into the open. There must be times when he mingled as an ordinary man with other men and women. He must have some other personality— some other identity under which he posed. Could he be any one of the men whose names had so far been connected with this case—men who occupied a high position in the city's life?

Wentworth recalled that Hugh Varner had come to New York not so many years ago from Australia. He had come with excellent recommendations, had brought with him a certificate indicating that he had been a barrister in New South Wales. He had taken the necessary examination, and had been admitted to the New York Bar, then had simply developed such powerful financial connections that he had become attorney to the largest banking syndicate in the East. Could it be that Hugh Varner was Count Calypsa?

In these days of facial surgery, the Count might have done away with the true Hugh Varner in Australia, might have had his features changed, and come here posing as the attorney. But a man as clever as the Count would not have left such an easy trail to himself by giving his telephone number to Martin Kreamer.

This woman, Olga Laminoff, might give him the answer. But he dared not turn around and follow her now. There were too many men here in the street, and they were very obviously watching him. They would know that the *Spider* would come to meet Evelyn Appleton. They would know that he would devise some means of entering the Tombs. And they would know that he would come in disguise. So they suspected every man who approached the Tombs. If he were to turn to follow Olga Laminoff now, it would be as if he shouted at the top of his lungs to these men: ''I am the *Spider!*''

He must, perforce, let her go. But there was just the chance that Ram Singh would recognize her. Ram Singh was around the corner which she must pass as she walked north. Ram Singh had been with Wentworth in those days when they had known Calypsa and the Laminoff woman. Would Ram Singh recognize her?

He let the Laminoff woman walk her way, and

107

continued past the entrance of the Tombs, crossed the street and walked down along the broad facade of the Criminal Courts Building, which was connected with the Tombs by the grim, notorious old Bridge of Sighs over which thousands of prisoners had marched after being convicted.

Wentworth glanced behind once, and saw Olga Laminoff get into a car at the far corner. He also saw that three of the watching men had detached themselves from one of the groups, and were coming down after him. Even if they did not suspect him as yet of being the *Spider,* they were doing their job thoroughly; they no doubt were investigating everyone who appeared on that street at this time. The *Spider* would have to work fast if he were to meet Evelyn Appleton in the Tombs under the very eyes of these men.

Not daring to hasten his stride, he turned the corner and went swiftly to the side entrance of the Criminal Courts Building. This entrance, he knew, would be open all night to permit the entrance and the egress of the porters and the cleaning women. For a moment he was out of sight of the three men who had started after him, and he slipped quickly in through this entrance, made his way upstairs. He was unobserved as he made his way swiftly through the deserted corridors into the empty detention room, and out to the hall that led into the Bridge of Sighs.

He crossed the Bridge of Sighs, looking down from the barred windows into the street below. He saw the waiting cars, and the waiting gunmen, then passed swiftly to the other end of the bridge where

108

there was a gate barring further progress into the Tombs. A uniformed attendant stood on the other side of the gate and rose suspiciously as Wentworth approached.

The attendant exclaimed: "Say, what are you doing here—"

Wentworth gave him no further chance to finish. He wasted no time on the man. His cane came up, and the end of it jabbed viciously, unexpectedly through the bars into the pit of the man's stomach. The attendant uttered a low, choked cry, and doubled up in agony, clutching at his stomach.

Wentworth said: "I'm sorry, friend, but this is absolutely necessary." He reversed the cane, stuck it through the bars, and brought it down lightly on the side of the man's head behind the left ear. The man groaned, crumpled on the floor. Wentworth had struck him just hard enough to render him unconscious.

Now the *Spider* reached in through the bar, and with the edge of his cane he pushed the lever which released the lock on the gate. He pushed the gate open and stepped through. He was in the Tombs!

No one had heard the sound of the attendant's challenge, or of the blow which Wentworth had struck him. Now Wentworth worked swiftly, slipping off his own coat and putting on the uniform jacket of the attendant. He took the attendant's cap, left his briefcase and cane lying beside the man's body, and hurried through the corridor to the stairs leading down into the reception room. He walked in boldly, and threw a quick glance around the room.

Evelyn Appleton was backed against the wall, and two of the three men who were in the room with her, were facing her savagely. One of them was saying: "When this here *Spider* comes, you'll act natural, understand? You give him any kind of warning, and we'll burn you down first!"

All three of the men had guns in their fists. The outer door was now closed, and a man in a keeper's uniform was standing beside it. The keeper was watching the proceedings dispassionately. The thought flashed across Wentworth's mind that this Dictator must indeed be powerful—for he apparently had the personnel of the prison under his control. The keepers were permitting his gunmen to set their traps within the very walls of the Tombs.

Evelyn Appleton shrank from the menacing guns of the gunmen. She was about to speak, when one of them turned and noticed Wentworth. "What do you want?" he growled. "Didn't the Warden get orders to keep everybody out of this reception room while we were here?"

"I'm sorry," Wentworth said, "but the Warden just got a phone call from your boss. He wants to talk to Miss Appleton on the wire. He says you men better stay down here in case something breaks. I'll take her up."

There was no suspicion in the gunman's voice as he said: "All right. Take her upstairs and bring her down again. The *Spider* is liable to be here any minute."

Evelyn Appleton was glad of any excuse to get away from those men. She hurried to Wentworth's side, and just then the keeper at the door said: "Say, how come I don't know you? I've never seen you around here before."

"I'm the relief man," Wentworth began. "I just came on tonight—"

The keeper shook his head. "That can't be. I checked in everybody on the job when they came to work tonight. You weren't here."

The gunmen in the room suddenly tensed. One of them stepped forward, eyes narrowed, raising his gun. He sneered: "So, you're—"

He never finished. Wentworth had left the four top buttons of his tunic open, and now his hands darted in and out from his shoulder holsters, while at the same time he leaped sideways, thrusting Evelyn Appleton out of the way. The gunman's revolver blasted, but Wentworth was not there.

The *Spider's* guns began to bark in quick staccato succession as he sprayed the room with lead. For the space of a minute the small chamber was filled with the acrid smell of cordite and with the screams of men who were shot. Wentworth was firing from the floor now, and each shot was placed with deadly accuracy.

One of the gunmen, who had started to rush toward him, died with a bullet between the eyes, and his body fell across Wentworth. Wentworth fired from behind the dead man's body, hit the last of the gunmen, just as the uniformed keeper at the door managed to get his gun out from its holster.

The keeper levelled the weapon at Wentworth, and the *Spider's* last shot caught him in the shoulder, sending him spinning around. The man dropped the gun, shrieked with pain. He crawled along the floor, trying to pick up his gun in his left hand, but Wentworth stepped in and struck him across the temple

111

with the butt of his automatic. The man dropped like a log.

Swiftly Wentworth stooped beside the dead man, and drew the platinum cigarette lighter from his pocket, implanted the seal of the *Spider* upon the foreheads of the dead men. He laughed harshly. "A little memento for the Dictator—from the *Spider!*"

He arose and seized Evelyn Appleton by the arm. She was pale, horrified at the sight of the sudden slaughter. But he gave her no breathing space.

"Come on, Miss Appleton," he urged her crisply. "We've got to get out of here!"

She followed him out of the reception room, asking: "W-who are you? W-what do you want?"

He didn't answer, but rushed her up the steps. In the rear of the building they could hear a commotion, the sound of men's shouting voices and running feet. Prisoners in the tiers above began banging on their cell doors, shouting and screaming. Wentworth dashed upstairs, grimly regardless of all of it.

At the Bridge of Sighs gate, the attendant was still lying unconscious. Wentworth stripped off his uniform tunic, put on his coat once more, and snatched up his briefcase and cane. Then, as he inserted new clips in his automatics, he pushed Evelyn Appleton ahead of him across the bridge and down the stairs of the Criminal Courts Building.

In a moment they were outside in the street. The three men who had followed Wentworth down the street were standing outside, apparently wondering how he had disappeared. One of their cars had also pulled up to the curb, apparently following them for support. There was only one man in the car, at the wheel.

When the three saw Wentworth, they uttered a shout, and guns leaped into their hands. Wentworth met their fire with fire. The split-instant of time by which he was faster than they cost those men their lives. His slugs sent them reeling backward, dead almost before they could fire a shot. Each of Wentworth's bullets were catapulted out of his automatics with the deadly accuracy of expert marksmanship, aimed for a vital spot. Two died with bullets between their eyes, the third with a slug right through his heart.

The driver of the sedan had drawn a gun, and he was leaning out of the door to take a shot at Wentworth. Evelyn Appleton screamed a warning, but Wentworth did not need it. His right hand gun moved in a short arc, and a single slug crashed straight into the side of the driver's head. The man slumped over the open window of the door, half in and half out of the car.

Feet were pounding on the sidewalk around the corner, and men were shouting within the Criminal Courts Building and the Tombs Building. Wentworth wasted no time. He wrenched open the door of the sedan, pushed the dead driver out onto the sidewalk, and leaped in behind the wheel. Evelyn Appleton needed no instruction. She jumped in beside him and slammed the door just as Wentworth threw the car into gear and stepped down on the gas.

He raced across town, and swung north on Broadway. Behind him the mad excitement of the chase

113

died away. He drove in silence, fiercely, grimly, until he had lost every vestige of the pursuit.

Evelyn Appleton sat beside him, restless, wide-eyed, marvelling at the skill and dexterity of his sure driving. He cut west, then swung north on Eleventh Avenue. All was quiet here. He glimpsed a police radio car cutting in from Twenty-third Street, and automatically slowed up so as not to attract their suspicion. They passed the police car in safety, and then Evelyn Appleton spoke.

"You—you are the *Spider?*" she asked in a hushed voice.

"I am," he told her. "You wanted to see me?"

She nodded. "I did. But I was hoping against hope that you wouldn't come. Those men were spread out all around the Tombs, and they were waiting for you in the reception room. I never dared to hope that you could escape if you once entered the Tombs. But— you did it. You accomplished the impossible. I—I'm glad I sent for you."

Wentworth glanced sideways at her. She was blonde, pretty, young. Her fresh young eyes looked at him with trusting innocence. "I—I feel safe in your hands, now, *Spider*. I—I almost feel as if everything will be all right. If only Frank were out of jail!"

"We'll get him out, never fear, Miss Appleton," Wentworth said. "You stated to the newspaper reporters that you had important information for me. What is it? Speak quickly. There is much to be done tonight. Your sweetheart is not the only one in danger. The whole city is under the shadow of this Dictator."

114

"Yes, yes," she exclaimed eagerly. "There's a woman—her name is Olga Laminoff. She is the one who originally gave me the idea to appeal to you. She came and said she had been a friend of father's. She suggested that I get in touch with you. And it was she who suggested that I wait for you at the Tombs.

"But I learned that she was lying. She was never a friend of father's. From the conversation of those men in the Tombs I gathered that she is closely linked in some way with the Dictator. And they were talking carelessly near me earlier in the day. They were talking about some great coup that the Dictator expects to pull off tonight at midnight. It's going to be at Grand Central Station. I heard that all police are to be withdrawn from the neighborhood of Grand Central. And there's going to be a monster hold-up there."

Wentworth nodded. "I already know that. But are you sure that they didn't talk about this deliberately so that you would tell me about it?"

Evelyn Appleton gasped. "I never thought of that. I thought I was being so clever in overhearing snatches of their conversation. But now that you mention it, it occurs to me that they talked unnecessarily loudly." Suddenly she put a trembling hand on his arm. "*Spider!* Suppose it's another trap for you? Suppose they deliberately planned it, in case this trap didn't succeed?"

Wentworth laughed harshly. "If it's a trap at midnight, we'll see if we can't spring it the way we sprung the one at the Tombs." He swung east, drove for two blocks and halted the car in the middle of

115

the next block near a small cigar store where there was a telephone.

"What are you going to do?" Evelyn asked.

"I'm going to get in touch with Commissioner Kirkpatrick. If Argyle Dunning has ordered the police away from Grand Central at midnight, we will have a little surprise for the Dictator. I'll get Kirkpatrick to place other police there!"

He left Evelyn Appleton sitting in the car and hurried into the telephone booth.

CHAPTER EIGHT

Reception at Grogan's

Wentworth dropped his nickel in the box, and dialed police headquarters. In a moment he was talking to the operator.

"I wish to speak to Commissioner Kirkpatrick at once," he said crisply.

There was a short laugh at the other end. "Commissioner Kirkpatrick? He ain't commissioner anymore. Inspector Strong has been appointed commissioner by the Mayor. Who wants to talk to him?"

A cold chill went through Wentworth's frame. If Kirkpatrick had been ousted from headquarters, he must find him. But even if he found him, what good would it do? Without the official status of commissioner, Kirkpatrick could do nothing.

"Where is Mr. Kirkpatrick?"

"Didn't you hear it on the radio? Kirkpatrick went nuts suddenly. He's been taken in a straightjacket to a New York Hospital for the Insane, on Seventy-second Street. You'll find him there, if you want him. Ha, ha!'' There was a sharp click as the operator at the other end broke the connection.

Wentworth gasped. The Dictator was moving fast now, cleverly, ruthlessly, eliminating all obstacles swiftly. With Kirkpatrick insane, there could be no question as to whether Argyle Dunning had the authority to appoint another commissioner. And Dunning had apparently done so at once.

With Inspector Strong at the head of the Police Department, and granting that Argyle Dunning acted under instructions from the hooded Dictator, there was nothing to stand in the way of the Dictator's plans. By morning he would have supreme authority in the City of New York. Wentworth didn't know yet whether Ram Singh had stayed at the corner, or had followed Olga Laminoff. In either event, Ram Singh would no doubt come looking for him in Casey Grogan's. He had to go back there to meet Ram Singh and Jackson. His original intention to work alone was gone by the board. Jackson had thrust his head into danger. So had Ram Singh. They would do that whether they were with him or not. And now he needed them, with Kirkpatrick out of the Police Department.

He returned to the car, and slid in under the wheel beside Evelyn Appleton. As they drove uptown, she asked him nervously: ''Is something wrong? You're so silent. Did you get bad news?''

''Very bad news,'' he told her. ''I'm afraid this fight is going to be tougher than we've expected.'' He gave her quick instructions. ''I'm driving up to

118

Casey Grogan's Dance Hall. I want you to go inside alone, and ask for Krauss, the manager. Ask him for a job as a hostess. You're pretty and young, and he'll probably give it to you. I want to keep you out of harm's way for the next three or four hours, and I think you will be as safe there as anywhere. No one will think of looking for Evelyn Appleton among the hostesses in a cheap dance hall.''

Her eyes were shining eagerly. "I'll do whatever you say, *Spider*. I'm leaving my own fate and the fate of Frank in your hands. I—I trust you, *Spider!*''

"Thank you," he said softly. "I hope your trust is not misplaced.''

At Fifty-fourth Street he parked the stolen car two blocks west of Casey Grogan's Dance Hall, and sent Evelyn Appleton ahead to ask for the job. He remained in the car, and using the rear-vision mirror, he altered his features once more to become Jake Smith. His automatics were empty, and he had no more clips for them. He shrugged. He would have to go against the Dictator without guns then.

His disguise completed, he picked up the briefcase, but left the cane in the car.

He walked swiftly across Fifty-fourth Street, keeping a sharp eye out for Ram Singh, in case the Sikh should be looking for him here.

Ram Singh was there. He had been waiting in a doorway directly opposite the dance hall, from whence he could see all who approached. Wentworth paused to speak quickly:

"Ram Singh! There is much to do. I need your help.''

119

The Sikh's face broke into a glad smile. "I am happy, *sahib*, that I can serve you. What is there to do?"

"Kirkpatrick is in the New York Hospital for the Insane, on Seventy-second Street. I am sure that he is being held there by a subterfuge, to permit the Dictator to appoint his own police commissioner. We must get Kirkpatrick out of there. I want you to go to Seventy-second Street now and study the lay of the land. Find out what sort of hospital Kirkpatrick is in, and devise the best means for us to gain admittance to him. Arrange for a car so that we can make a get-away if we succeed in getting him out. I will meet you there within the hour. Hurry."

Ram Singh raised a hand to his forehead, salaamed. "I go, Master."

He turned and went swiftly away.

Wentworth entered the dance hall, carrying the briefcase. A group of a dozen or more people stood at the entrance to the narrow corridor leading to the barroom. Krauss, the manager, faced them.

"It's nothing at all, ladies and gentlemen, nothing to worry about. Just a little argument going on in there, but nobody can go in." The group was boisterous, but did not resent being kept out of the barroom.

Wentworth frowned. He must find out what was going on in there. He swung away from the group, to the corner of the dance hall.

The *Spider* stepped quickly into the smoking room and glanced around to make sure that he was alone. Then he took the cape and hat out of the briefcase and slipped them on. In another moment he had inserted those long, protruding fanglike teeth which

120

made the *Spider* recognizable wherever he went. Then, very carefully, he opened the door leading into the barroom.

His eyes grew bleak and hard at the sight of the tableau which greeted him.

In the center of the room stood the hooded man whom Wentworth had seen in the hearse. Beside him was the woman, Olga Laminoff. Both held guns. Over at the other end of the room, near the bar, Jackson was backed up against the wall, and two stocky, vicious men were beating him methodically. Wentworth could see the flash of brass knuckles on their fists as they struck, cutting Jackson's cheeks to ribbons.

The hooded man was saying coldly: "You had better talk, Jackson. We know who you are. You are Wentworth's chauffeur. Wentworth's girl, Nita Van Sloan, is in our hands. We want you to tell us where to get in touch with the *Spider*. Talk quickly. Where can we find him? You didn't come here by accident. Who sent you?"

The *Spider* was unarmed but he didn't hesitate. Harsh, discordant, terrifying laughter broke from his lips. He leaped to his feet and vaulted on to the bar.

The hooded man and the woman Olga turned startled glances in his direction. The thugs stopped with their fists poised in mid-air.

Olga Laminoff gasped. "It's the *Spider!*"

The little revolver which she held swung around and *spatted* viciously while the hooded man also shifted to fire.

But the *Spider* had already launched himself head-first in a reckless leap directly at those two. So startled and astounded were they that they had shot before aiming. Their slugs went wild, and the *Spider's* solid weight of bone and muscle catapulted into them irresistibly, hurling them to the floor in a twisting, struggling heap.

Olga Laminoff screamed shrilly, and her voice rose above the blaring notes of the dance orchestra in the next room. The two thugs swung around from Jackson, and their hands sped to their shoulder holsters. Wentworth whirled over onto his knees, and his hand swept across the floor, snatched up the small gun that Olga Laminoff had dropped.

His eyes were cold, hard, unemotional as he fired twice at the two thugs. It was a small-calibre revolver, and the shots had to be placed accurately to kill. Wentworth placed both of them dead center through the forehead. The two thugs died on their feet.

Jackson shouted: "Yeah, bo!" and bent and snatched up one of the guns dropped by the thugs. Wentworth swung around in time to see the hooded man racing through the open door of Krauss' office at the other side of the barroom. He raised his gun to fire, but abruptly his arm was clutched by the almost hysterical Olga Laminoff, who sank her teeth into his hand. In that instant he heard the loud explosion of the gun that Jackson had seized.

Jackson cursed. "Missed him!" the chauffeur exclaimed. The door of Krauss' office slammed, and the hooded man disappeared. Wentworth freed his hand from between Olga's teeth, prying her jaws apart, then thrust her away from him savagely and

122

leaped toward the door. The hooded man had locked it from the inside.

Jackson said: "Stand back, sir," and launched himself straight at the door. The wood splintered and gave under the smashing heave of his body, and Jackson went through. Wentworth leaped in over him and stopped, eyes narrowed.

The room was empty. An open window giving on to a fire-escape told its own story. Wentworth leaped through it, climbed out on the fire-escape. He was just in time to see the dark shadowy figure of the hooded man turning the corner of the alley into Fifty-fourth Street.

Wentworth turned back into the room dejectedly. Through the open door he saw the barroom filling with excited people from the dance floor. Krauss was in the lead, a gun in his hand. Jackson had already picked himself up, and Wentworth snapped: "Out this way, Jackson."

They leaped out to the fire-escape, and raced down the emergency ladder along the way that the hooded man had taken. Behind them, shouts came from the milling crowd on the dance floor, and from behind the splintered door Krauss sprang, gun in hand. But Wentworth and Jackson were in the clear. Krauss, standing on the fire-escape, fired down at them. His shot ricohetted from the iron staircase and from the concrete walk below.

Men were yelling: "It's the *Spider!* The *Spider* was here!"

Wentworth raised his pistol, fired up twice at Krauss, and the little man toppled backward through the window.

Then the *Spider* led Jackson quickly out of the alley into Fifty-fourth Street. A police car had just turned the corner from Broadway, and it came to a stop in front of the dance hall. The two policemen leaped out and raced inside. Wentworth nudged Jackson. "Let's go!"

They raced out of the alley, and leaped into the police radio car. Wentworth threw in the clutch, and raced the car away from there.

"It's very nice of the police, sir," Jackson said, smiling, "to provide us with a means of escape."

He was daubing at his cut cheeks and lips with a bloody handkerchief. "Those boys almost had me down with their brass knuckles. You came in the nick of time."

"The Dictator got away," Wentworth said bitterly. "He seems to beat us at every turn."

"At least," Jackson said cheerfully, "we're catching up with him. That was awful close back there."

They left the police squad car at Fifty-eighth Street and Ninth Avenue.

"Where to now, sir?" Jackson asked.

Wentworth led him at a swift walk across Fifty-ninth Street. He had taken off his *Spider* cape and hat, and had rolled it into a small bundle beneath his coat.

"I don't know where to go first," Wentworth said bitterly. "I heard the Dictator tell you that they had Nita. God help us, I don't know where to look for her first. I have no idea where she may be—"

"I'll tell you, sir. I heard that hooded man and the Laminoff woman talking. They said something

124

about having taken her to the printing plant. It seems they're running a printing plant somewhere in the city, where they're turning out a flood of tens and twenties. They expect to overrun the country with them, using New York as their headquarters. Now that they are gaining control of the city, they figure they can use New York as their base of operations.''

"A printing plant? You don't know where it is, do you?''

"No, sir. The woman told the hooded man that she had just come from there. She said she thought she was followed, but she couldn't be sure.''

Wentworth's eyes brightened. "Ram Singh!'' he exclaimed. "Of course! Ram Singh was waiting for me outside there. He must have followed Olga Laminoff from the Tombs. Then he must know where she went before she came to Grogan's Dance Hall. Let's go, Jackson!''

They hailed a taxicab, and Wentworth gave the address of the New York Hospital for the Insane. The driver looked queerly at Jackson's cut-up face, but said nothing.

They got out of the cab at Seventieth Street, and Wentworth gave the driver a ten-dollar bill.

"That's to help you to forget you saw us,'' Wentworth told the man. "In case you should forget about the ten-dollar bill, and feel like talking to anybody, I'll learn about it. I've got your name and address from the card in the taxicab. I'll be able to find you, and it will be too bad for you. Understand?''

The driver grinned. "Don't worry, mister. I ain't looking for trouble. I never even saw you before.''

He drove away, and Wentworth and Jackson

walked swiftly toward the New York Hospital for the Insane. Wentworth glanced at his watch. There was little time left to accomplish what he had in mind. For the time being he must leave Nita in the hands of the Dictator. His objective now was to get Kirkpatrick out of the hospital, and to organize some sort of resistance to the Dictator's plans for the coup at Grand Central Station at midnight.

CHAPTER NINE

Printers . . . and Maniacs

On the edge of the East River, almost under the shadow of the Queensboro Bridge, there stands an old, dilapidated factory building. The building is only three stories high, and across its face, in the old, curlycued characters of a past generation there appears the following name:

HAMLIN'S PRINTING HOUSE
ESTABLISHED 1892

Hamlin's Printing House was a firm which had flourished in the days of the bustle and the one-horse shay. Long ago the building had been abandoned. The building seemed to be deserted. But within its walls was a surprising activity. Though the windows were boarded up, and no sound or light came from within, machines hummed here industriously.

Huge modern printing presses turned out United

States Treasury certificates at appalling speed. Forty men worked in this building, and stacks of the currency were rolled on small hand-trucks down into the basement where they were loaded onto two boats that took them on the first leg of their journey to be distributed throughout the country. In the basement, the huge wheel of a turbine engine had been disconnected from the adjacent machinery.

Half a dozen men worked at this wheel. They had erected a smaller wheel, a sort of controlling mechanism, by which they could turn the larger wheel. They were oiling all the parts of the mechanism now, and testing it to see whether it was running smoothly.

In a corner of this basement, two figures lay on the floor, tightly bound. They were so placed that they could see the men working on the huge wheel, could see where the wheel dipped at its bottom into a tract of water, perhaps two feet deep. The eyes of both of these bound persons were alive with interest, if not with fear.

One of them was Nita Van Sloan. The other was little Elaine Robillard.

Though they were tied hand and foot, they had not been gagged; and little Elaine said in a hushed whisper: "Nita, those are very bad men. They were very rough when they took us away from the house. Why are men so rough?"

Nita's pitying eyes rested for a moment on the little girl. She choked back a sob. The thought of this child in the hands of these men was more than she could bear. For herself she did not care. When the Dictator's men had come for her at the penthouse apartment, she might have escaped had she been alone. She had snatched up a revolver, and would have fired. But Elaine Robillard had come running out of the next room, directly in the line of fire.

And they had both been seized and hustled down in the freight elevator, blindfolded and thrust into a car which had swiftly carried them to this place.

Now as Nita Van Sloan looked at the huge turbine wheel and at the men working on it, she shuddered. She felt as those old French artistocrats must have felt while they watched the guillotine being erected outside the Bastile.

She knew that this wheel was some fiendish method of torture or death which had been devised for her benefit by the Dictator. The Dictator hated Wentworth, hated everything connected with Wentworth. And he was taking this means of venting that hatred.

To Nita, the horrid thing about all this was the utter silence with which those men were working. One might have thought that they were concentrated there upon some complicated structural problem of engineering rather than upon a task of erecting a machine of torture. No one threw a single glance in their direction; it was as if they, as persons, did not exist for those workers.

And looking down upon it all from the lintel of the doorway, which led to the staircase, was the gold-encrusted symbol of the lion crouching upon the crown, with the sword and the mitre in his forepaws. Whoever the artist was that had placed that insignia above the doorway, he was clever, malevolently ingenious. For he had imparted to that king of beasts so malignant an expression that Nita shuddered even to look at the lion.

By this time she had learned enough about the Dictator to know his aims and ambitions. And that lion sitting upon the crown summed up the desires and lust of the master of the underworld; he wanted power. He wanted to rule, to rule ruthlessly and without question. And he was bringing it about by establishing an underworld organization more powerful than any that had yet threatened the civilization of a country.

Elaine was quiet now, watching Nita, taking courage from her. And Nita's brows were furrowed in thought as she tried to imagine who this Dictator could be in the upper world.

That he was one whom everybody saw and knew, there could be no doubt; for otherwise he would never have been able to establish the wide-spread connections that he seemed to have. But who could this person be? With less information than Wentworth possessed at this time, she was even more puzzled.

She knew that Argyle Dunning had demanded the resignation of Kirkpatrick; but she did not yet know that Kirkpatrick had been removed to the Hospital for the Insane. She could not bring herself to imagine that a man like Argyle Dunning would deliberately conspire to seize his own nephew for murder in order to further his interests; yet, noting the fiendish ruthlessness with which the Dictator had operated since the beginning of his campaign, she was forced to admit to herself that he might even be ready to sacrifice a close relative in order to attain his ambition.

                    *   *   *

While Nita Van Sloan was cogitating upon these things in the basement where the wheel was being erected, the hooded man and Olga Laminoff were seated in an office on the floor directly above. Four men, including Martin Kreamer, were facing the Dictator, while Olga sat at the desk at his right. Kreamer was making a report, while the other three men standing with him shifted uncomfortably, their eyes upon the gold-encrusted figure of the lion which was engraved upon the narrow hanging draped behind the Dictator's chair.

The hooded man was sitting quietly at the desk, nothing showing of his face except two lively sparkling eyes behind the slits in the hood.

"We have succeeded in every operation, sir," Kreamer was saying, "except those involving the *Spider*. With the *Spider* we have failed all along the line. That man seems to appear out of nowhere. He got Sorenson and Masters, two of my best operators, when they were knocking off Wishard. Then he sprang the trap we laid for him at the Tombs, and spirited Evelyn Appleton out of our hands. We don't know where she is now."

The hooded man nodded. "Not only that, but he barged right into Casey Grogan's place and snatched his man Jackson right out of our hands. We were just beginning to succeed in breaking Jackson down. He would have talked, would have given us information as to the *Spider's* whereabouts. And just then the *Spider* himself appeared. He hadn't even a gun. But he moved so fast that he almost killed *me*. A

131

half second more and I would never have escaped from the barroom alive.''

Suddenly the hooded man's gloved fist slammed down on the desk viciously. "I tell you, Kreamer, we've got to get the *Spider*. You failed miserably so far. *See to it that you don't fail again!*"

"I—I won't fail again, sir. I think the *Spider* is going to walk right into our trap at Grand Central tonight. I made sure that Evelyn Appleton learned enough to tell him that we are staging an operation at Grand Central tonight. I originally planned to leave him with her for a couple of minutes so that she could tell him that, just the way you instructed me. I couldn't see the reason for it at the time you gave me the instructions, but now I understand. You just wanted to make sure there would be another trap for him in case the one at the Tombs failed.''

Olga Laminoff broke in, her voice vibrant. "I wonder if the *Spider* isn't a super-man. Who would have thought it possible that he could snatch Evelyn Appleton right out of the Tombs, with forty of our men surrounding it—''

The Dictator laughed harshly. "We overlooked the entrance through the Bridge of Sighs. Be sure, my dear Olga, that we will overlook nothing at the Grand Central tonight. Once the *Spider* enters that station, *there will be no way for him to leave alive*. Argyle Dunning has removed all police from the entire Grand Central sector for a radius of ten blocks in every direction. We will be entirely unhampered in the operation. We will secure enough cash to finance us until this newly-printed money can be distributed; and we will get the *Spider*, too.''

132

"But," Olga Laminoff broke in, "why are you preparing all that complicated business downstairs for the Van Sloan woman?"

"For the same reason that I left an opening for a second trap after the Tombs. If by any wild chance the plan at Grand Central Station falls through, we will still have the Van Sloan woman here. And we shall start prying information from her at once. In China, nobody has ever been able to resist the persuasion of the water-wheel. She will talk. She will tell us where Wentworth is holed up."

The Dictator turned to the three other men. "You three are ready to leave at once?"

They nodded.

"Good. All arrangements have been made at the other end. You, Lasher, will take off at once for New Orleans. Franco, you go to Chicago. Bourdon, Montreal for you. The planes are all ready and waiting for you out on Long Island. The counterfeit bills have all been loaded on the planes, and two armed men will accompany each of you.

"See that the people at the other end put nothing over on you. They are to pay in cash—good American currency—for the bills that you deliver to them. You three are all experts, and can tell a counterfeit bill when you see it. Don't let them pay you for counterfeit money with other counterfeit money. Now, go."

The three men bowed, and left the room. The Dictator looked at Kreamer. "All arrangements are made for Grand Central Station?"

"Yes, sir. It's timed to the second, and everybody

has been given his instructions. The thing should go off like clock-work.''

"Very well. You may go."

Kreamer bowed, and followed the other three out of the room. The Dictator and Olga Laminoff were left alone. He rubbed his gloved hand, said in a voice that had suddenly become thick with cruelty:

"Come, my dear Olga. We shall now turn our attention to the beautiful Nita Van Sloan and that brat with her."

He arose, and Olga followed him to the door. She asked, puzzled: "Just what are you going to do to them?"

"Come, my dear Olga. You shall see. It will be far more interesting than if I merely explain it to you."

She followed him downstairs toward the cellar where the wheel was being completed. . . .

The New York Hospital for the Insane was located on Seventy-second Street, with a view of Central Park. It was a small, four-story, immaculately white institution, from its newly sandblasted walls on the outside to its spotlessly clean detention cells on the inside.

At the rear of the ground floor was the observation ward. There were some twenty patients in this ward, of whom half were in straightjackets while the others lay peaceably in their beds without any precautions to prevent their escape.

Two New York City patrolmen were stationed at the door of the ward, while at the other end near the window stood two hard-faced thugs who always kept their hands in the pockets of their coats. These were two of Kreamer's operators, Landers and Mollat. Their sharp, pin-point eyes were fixed upon the third bed from the end, away from the window, where lay Commissioner Stanley Kirkpatrick.

Kirkpatrick was motionless on the bed. He was clad in pajamas, and the upper part of his body was firmly and cruelly encased in a straightjacket. His ankles were handcuffed to the bedpost. He lay with his eyes closed, breathing with great difficulty because of the wicked pressure exerted upon his chest by the straightjacket.

Others of the patients were talking, shouting, laughing hysterically. The din and the noise in the room were almost deafening; yet all these patients cast occasional glances of trepidation not at the two policemen, but at the two thugs at the other end of the room. Those two men had been placed there by Kreamer for the sole purpose of making sure that no efforts would be made to rescue Kirkpatrick.

Dr. Vladimir Ostrevsky, the director of the hospital, entered the ward. Ostrevsky was a short man, with a high, bald-head and big ears. His eyes protruded from his head like the eyes of some predatory pre-historic animal. But his hands were long and thin, and he walked with a birdlike jumpiness that was very irritating.

The New York Hospital for the Insane had been in the founders' hands for many years; about six months before, it had been taken over by new interests. It seemed that the old board of governors had by some means been induced to resign, and give place to a new controlling circle.

This new board boasted some very influential men, among them Argyle Dunning, Hugh Varner, and Stephen Pelton. Dr. Ostrevsky had been appointed director, and he had immediately proceeded to discharge all of the old nurses, internes and doctors, and to acquire a completely new staff.

The doctor minced down the aisle between the two rows of beds, stopping occasionally beside a patient. He would look at the man, with his bald head cocked on one side, mutter something to himself, then turn away and proceed to the next patient.

The din and the noise had suddenly ceased with Dr. Ostrevsky's entrance. The poor, insane patients glanced with terror at those long thin surgeon's hands of his. Apparently they recalled an unpleasant experience which they had undergone at those hands. Had they been questioned, they would have suddenly become silent on the subject. But many of them remembered with horror the small operating room on the top floor of the hospital where they had been taken and tied down to an operating table. Dr. Ostrevsky had manipulated with gleaming knives and saws upon their quivering conscious bodies.

For the good doctor was an experimentalist. And he took this opportunity of testing many of his theories. These poor devils would have obeyed any command from Dr. Ostrevsky rather than be subjected to that experience again.

Now, the bird-like doctor approached the bed of Commissioner Kirkpatrick.

As though he sensed the malignant presence of Ostrevsky, Kirkpatrick opened his eyes. His lips tightened, and he glared up at the little man.

"Damn you!" he shouted hoarsely, "let me out of here. Take this damned straightjacket off!"

Ostrevsky looked down at him with mock sympathy, and clucked gently. "Tut, tut, Mr. Kirkpatrick. You must realize that you are here for your own good. I trust that within a reasonable time I shall be able to cure you of this dreadful malady that afflicts you—"

"Dreadful malady, nothing, you old humbug!" Kirkpatrick shouted. "You know very well I'm not insane—"

Ostrevsky was shaking his head in resignation. "So many of our poor patients insist that they are not crazy. Perhaps you even think that we are the crazy ones—no?"

"Ostrevsky," Kirkpatrick said solemnly, "I promise you that if I ever get out of this straightjacket, I'll throttle you with my own hands."

"That is a threat which I shall remember, Mr. Kirkpatrick. Perhaps—" he bent low and almost whispered the next words "—*you will never come out of that straightjacket!*"

Kirkpatrick's eyes widened at the look of stark evil in the doctor's face.

Ostrevsky went on: "Poor Mr. Harlan Foote was brought here, in a condition like yours. It was so regretful. I had to operate on him, and he died under the knife!"

Kirkpatrick gasped. "You're going to—operate—on me?"

Ostrevsky nodded. "Upon diagnosing your case, Mr. Kirkpatrick, I find that it will be *most* desirable to operate upon you at once. We are going to move you upstairs. The interne is bringing in the wheel-chair now. Prepare yourself, my dear patient, for a very—er—unpleasant ordeal. I do not believe in administering anaesthetics, so you will be entirely conscious during the operation. You will have an opportunity to see how very skillfully I manipulate a scalpel.''

Kirkpatrick heaved tremendously, but could not raise himself from the bed. He yanked violently with his feet against the handcuffs that bound his ankles to the bed, but succeeded only in bruising himself. Several of the other patients who had been watching the scene, but were unable to hear the latter part of the conversation, began to shout and scream once more. They knew what was coming, because they had seen Ostrevsky talk to others.

The noise of their insane shoutings became dreadful, and Ostrevsky swung around, letting his eyes pass from one to the other of the patients; and as he looked at them in turn, each became suddenly silent. They looked away from him, as if fearful that he would decide to operate upon them.

Ostrevsky glanced at the big electric clock over the door. He frowned in impatience.

''What is keeping the interne with the chair, I wonder?'' he asked softly. He shrugged. ''But do not grow impatient, my dear Mr. Kirkpatrick!''

Dr. Ostrevsky did not know that the interne whom he was expecting was at that very moment standing with his back to the wall in the outside corridor, with his hands raised above his head. There was a man on either side of him.

138

The chair stood near by.

The interne didn't know them, but he was quaking at sight of the grim resolve in their eyes. The snub-nosed automatic which Jackson held at his side enforced the commands of the interne's chief captor. While Jackson had him covered, Wentworth motioned to him peremptorily: "Turn around!"

The man turned obediently, and Wentworth twisted his hands behind his back, and reached around to remove the man's belt with which to bind them. At that moment the interne chose to open his mouth to shriek a warning.

Wentworth sensed what he was going to do, and his hand bunched into a hard fist, came up in a vicious blow to the side of the man's jaw. The interne groaned, the shout died in his throat, and he slumped unconscious to the floor.

Jackson grunted: "That's much quicker, sir. He won't bother us for awhile."

Wentworth nodded. From his pocket he took a gun which he had received from Ram Singh when he and Jackson had met the Sikh outside the hospital. Ram Singh was waiting outside.

Wentworth held the gun in his right hand, and wheeled the empty wheel-chair toward the observation ward. He said to Jackson: "Wait out here, and be ready to cover my retreat when I come out."

"Yes, sir," Jackson said, saluting stiffly. He grinned. "Give 'em hell, sir!"

Wentworth wheeled the chair down the corridor, and into the observation room, past the two patrolmen at the door. His quick glance surveyed the room, showed him the two thugs near the window, and Ostrevsky leaning over Kirkpatrick's bed.

The policemen glanced at him suspiciously, seeing his street clothes, but were reassured as they saw the wheel-chair. The two thugs were paying no attention to him, but were watching with gloating eyes the reaction of Kirkpatrick to the vile things Ostrevsky was promising to do to him.

Wentworth reached the bed before Dr. Ostrevsky knew that he was there. The doctor raised his head, saw the wheelchair out of the side of his eyes, and swung around, saying grumpily: "You're late—"

His mouth jerked open, hung slack, as he saw that the regular interne had not brought in the chair. "W-who are you—"

Wentworth gave him no chance to finish. He moved close to the doctor, stuck the gun in his side. "If you don't want your liver blasted out of you, doc, do as I say. Pick up Kirkpatrick, quickly, and put him in that wheel-chair."

The two thugs suddenly became aware that trouble was brewing, and they reached for their guns, just as the patrolmen at the door did likewise. Wentworth raised his voice coldly. "If anyone of you so much as moves, Ostrevsky dies!"

The thugs hesitated, as did the patrolmen. Ostrevsky said, smirking, "I'm sorry, but Kirkpatrick cannot be moved. He is handcuffed to the bed, as you see, and I have not the key."

Wentworth said softly: "I see!"

He seized Ostrevsky's left arm, twisted it hard behind his back, and Ostrevsky gasped from the sudden pain. One of the thugs pulled a gun from his

140

pocket, but Wentworth swung the doctor around in such fashion that he was directly in the line of fire. The thug hesitated. In that instant, Wentworth acted. He swung his automatic away from Ostrevsky's side, placed it close to one of the handcuffs on the bed-post, and fired. The steel was shattered by the heavy slug, and Wentworth immediately moved his gun, fired another shot into the second handcuff.

"Pull, Kirk!" he ordered.

Kirkpatrick yanked hard with both feet, and the handcuffs fell away from the bed-post.

Wentworth now swung around so as to face the ward, with Kirkpatrick behind him. He still held Ostrevsky powerless in front of him, by the arm-lock. "Can you walk, Kirk?" he asked over his shoulder.

"God!" the Commissioner groaned. "I can barely raise myself." The bed creaked under his weight, and the Commissioner tottered to his feet. The long period of inactivity had made him weak. But he managed to totter over to the wheel-chair and slump into it.

One of the thugs now swung his gun around to fire at Kirkpatrick, and Wentworth snapped a shot, shattered the thug's shoulder. Ostrevsky shouted, and twisted away. The two policemen had come rushing forward, and Wentworth sent the doctor spinning dizzily across the room toward the cops, who sprang to save him from falling.

Wentworth leaped into the aisle, seized the wheel-chair and began rushing it toward the door. The policemen raised their guns to fire at him, but Wentworth sent the wheel-chair racing down the aisle directly at them, and one of them was bowled over, while the other barely leaped out of the way.

Behind Wentworth, the two thugs were firing at him, the wounded one having switched his gun to the left hand. Wentworth swung around and snapped two shots at the thugs, aiming deliberately at their hearts. He caught them both dead center, then leaped after the racing wheelchair.

The maniacs in the ward who were not confined by straightjackets were leaping about frenziedly, shouting and screaming at the top of their lungs. Several of them had seized chairs and were leaping out into the aisle to strike at Wentworth. He dodged the blows, menacing them with his revolver, barely managing to keep them at arm's length.

The policeman who had leaped out of the way of the wheel-chair was crouching behind one of the beds, raising his gun to fire at Wentworth. Wentworth crouched, and just then one of the maniacs leaped in on him, raising a chair to smash it down on his head. Wentworth dropped flat to the floor, and the maniac went flying over him. The policeman fired at just that instant, and the slug from the service gun caught the maniac in the leg. The man shrieked and doubled over.

Wentworth got to his feet, and sprinted for the doorway. Kirkpatrick's chair had rolled into the corridor, and now Wentworth seized it again, raced for the front entrance. He passed Jackson, who was coolly kneeling in the corridor, gun in hand and facing toward the observation ward.

"Keep going, sir," Jackson called out cheerfully. "I'll hold them."

*   *   *

The maniacs, with one of the cops in their midst, came piling out of the observation ward. Near the entrance the attendant at the desk got to his feet and came running forward. Wentworth swung the wheelchair with Kirkpatrick in it toward the attendant, and the man leaped out of the way.

At the door, Wentworth wheeled the chair out onto the sidewalk, and over the curb where Ram Singh sat grinning, in a taxicab. Ram Singh leaped out, and helped Wentworth to pile the Commissioner into the cab.

The Sikh said, showing his teeth: "The cab driver did not want to lend me his cab, *sahib*. I had to persuade him with this." He tapped his sheathed knife significantly.

They had Kirkpatrick in the cab now, and Ram Singh ran around to the front and slid in under the wheel. Wentworth held the door open, and Jackson came hurtling out, leaped into the cab. Wentworth shut the door, sprang to the running board and raised his gun to menace the maniacs and the policeman who were crowding out of the doorway of the hospital.

The policeman raised his gun to fire but Ram Singh had already shot the cab out into the middle of the street and was racing around the corner into Fifth Avenue.

Men and women were leaning out of windows, aroused by the blood-curdling screams of the maniacs and the shots of the policemen. Ram Singh paid no attention to them, but drove steadily south on Fifth Avenue. He made no attempt to evade pursuit. The time for avoiding enemies was past. Now they must drive straight through all opposition. So had been Wentworth's orders.

In the rear of the cab, Wentworth and Jackson were busily engaged in removing the straightjacket from Commissioner Kirkpatrick. When they got it off, Kirkpatrick slumped back in the seat and breathed deeply.

"God, what a relief! That straightjacket was almost crushing my ribs!" He looked at Wentworth. "Dick, I don't need to thank you for this. But it was reckless. You shouldn't have done it. With the city in danger, you didn't need to risk your life getting me out of there."

Wentworth grinned at him affectionately. "It wasn't only for your sake I did it, Kirk. I've got a plan in mind, and you've got to help me. If we don't put this over, the city might as well give up and choose the Dictator as its mayor."

"What's the plan?" Kirkpatrick asked swiftly. Already he had forgotten the hours of torture in the straightjacket, and the ominous threat of the operating room in that weird hospital.

Wentworth spoke swiftly: "The Dictator is planning some great coup at Grand Central Station at midnight. Argyle Dunning has appointed Inspector Strong commissioner, and Strong has cleared the whole district of police. There'll be no opposition to the Dictator's men when they strike at Grand Central Station. We have to block them, Kirk. If we checkmate him at Grand Central Station, it will block his plans all along the line. He'll lose the respect of his organization. Do you understand, Kirk? We've got to stop him!''

"But how?" the ex-commissioner asked, puzzled. "I've got no authority. He'll probably have a hundred men at Grand Central. How can we cope with that?"

"You may have no authority," Wentworth said slowly, "but you have the respect of all the honest policemen in the department. I promise, Kirk, that you set up a *sub rosa* headquarters and enlist the aid of all the honest policemen in the city. We will have a private police headquarters in New York—until the Dictator is licked!"

Kirkpatrick whistled. "It's a swell idea, Dick—if it works!"

"It's got to work, Kirk," the *Spider* said through tight lips. *"It's got to work!* We've got to break the Dictator's power, and do it quickly. He kidnapped Nita and Elaine!"

CHAPTER TEN

The Torture Wheel

The city had an air of unquiet and restiveness now—far different than the atmosphere of quiet gayety which Wentworth had noted as he left the office of the Five-Star Detective Agency earlier that evening.

Then, he had seen crowds of people moving through the streets, undisturbed by any thought of crime or personal danger.

Now the populace was fearful, bewildered by the strange series of events that had stunned the city.

They had heard of the strange upheavals at police headquarters, of the peculiar situation by which the nephew of the present Mayor was accused of the murder of a police commissioner; they had heard of the *Spider's* invasion of headquarters, of Wishard's strange and unexplained murder; and they had also heard of a mysterious disturbance at the Tombs. All this, coupled with the daring robbery of the Pandora

Theatre, and the strange rumors that were flooding the city of this new Dictator of the underworld, left them dazed. They saw that great areas in the city had been stripped of police protection, and they began to worry for the safety of their wives and their children. Men gathered in groups on the street corners and discussed the situation in hushed tones. Ordinarily, these citizens went about their business and their pleasure without a thought of the complicated machinery of the law which watched over their safety. Now, when that same complicated machinery was suffering a shifting of great cogs, these men abruptly realized that the city could become a scene of chaos and anarchy overnight.

And this unrest and disturbance was particularly noticeable in the streets of downtown Manhattan. Automobiles and taxicabs flagrantly passed red lights, made left turns against the rules, and violated ordinance after ordinance without reprimand from the police. The uniformed men were fumbling and worried. Ordinarily, the New York Police Force is among the best disciplined and the best-manned law enforcing agencies in the world. But no group of men can be expected to maintain its morale and its spirit when the personnel are aware that its leadership has been impaired.

All these men knew that Inspector Strong was not qualified to be commissioner. They knew some sinister force was spreading its tentacles over the city, and they suspected that that force over-shadowed police headquarters itself. They were fearful to do positive things, for they could expect no backing from their superiors. Therefore, in the course of a few hours the law-enforcing agencies of the city had become entirely disrupted, and the great metropolis was ripe for the organization of the Dictator to step in and take charge.

However, the nearly panic-stricken residents of the city might have taken some slight courage had they seen the three men who circulated in wide-spread sections. Those three men moved about as inconspicuously as possible: Wentworth around the Fourteenth Street section; Ram Singh in upper Manhattan; and Jackson in the downtown area. Wentworth, driving across Fourteenth Street in a Drive-Urself car, consulted a sheet of paper on the seat beside him, and braked to a stop alongside the traffic officer at the corner of Fourteenth Street and Broadway.

The officer had been directing traffic in a listless fashion, not troubling to keep his usually keen eye open for traffic violators. Now, as Wentworth stopped beside him, the officer threw him a quizzical glance. Wentworth smiled, said: "Not giving out many tickets tonight, are you, Officer?"

The man shrugged. "What's the use of giving tickets? There may not even be a judge in the city tomorrow."

"Your name is Blaine, isn't it?" Wentworth asked.

The officer nodded. "That's my name." Then he added suspiciously: "What of it?"

Wentworth was studying him. "You're an honest cop. You don't like the way things are being run today, do you?"

Blaine frowned. "Who the devil might you be?"

Wentworth said softly: "I am a friend of a friend

148

of yours." He lifted the paper that had lain on the seat beside him. "Your name is on this list. You are one of the men whom our mutual friend trusts implicitly on the police force."

"And who might that mutual friend be?" Blaine asked, becoming more and more annoyed.

Wentworth leaned out of the car, whispered a name in the cop's ear.

Blained whistled. "Commissioner Kirk—"

"Don't say the name!" Wentworth snapped. "Enough that you know." He fished in his pocket and produced a letter which he handed to the cop. "Do you know this mutual friend's handwriting if you see it?"

"I do, very well. I still have his signature on the written order promoting me to first grade patrolman. But I saw he was in the insane asylum—"

"Read that!" Wentworth commanded.

Puzzled, Blaine opened the note. It read as follows:

TO ALL MY FRIENDS ON THE
POLICE FORCE:

The bearer of this letter is Richard Wentworth, who has rescued me from unjust and forcible detention in an insane asylum where I was confined in order to prevent me from fighting the person who is known as the Dictator. All authority over the Police Department has been stripped from me. But I know that my good friends on the force are still ready to fight with me. To those who are loyal, I beg that you will

149

do as Richard Wentworth asks—without question. It is for the sake of the city, and for the sake of your own wives and children.

The letter was signed in the familiar bold handwriting of Commissioner Stanley Kirkpatrick.

Blaine looked up, and his eyes met those of Wentworth's squarely. "I'll do anything for Commissioner Kirkpatrick. And I've heard of you, too, Mr. Wentworth. If you're working with Mr. Kirkpatrick, then I'm with both of you. What are your orders?"

Wentworth spoke swiftly. "I want you to round up every one of the men on this list who are in your precinct. Get them on their feet if they're working, or at home if they're off duty. Have them arm themselves as best they can. If they can smuggle any submachine guns out of the station houses, let them do so.

"Then report, in twos and threes, at the foot of Forty-second Street near the East River. At the spot where Forty-second Street goes through the tunnel under First Avenue, you will be safe from observation at this hour of the night.

"Commissioner Kirkpatrick will meet you. He has established *sub rosa* headquarters there—and he's going to organize his own police department in an effort to oust the Dictator!"

"By God!" Blaine exclaimed, "I'm with you, Mr. Wentworth! I'll round up every man on this list. We'll be there."

"Try to make it as soon as possible. There is something important to be done before midnight. I'm making the rounds of the precincts, and lining up the

150

key men whose names Kirkpatrick gave me." He reached out of the car and shook hands solemnly with Blaine. "And may success reward our efforts—for the sake of the city's women and children!"

He drove off quickly, and Blaine waved after him, then deliberately deserted his post, walking swiftly south. In contrast to the lackadaisical attitude before, there was now a sparkle in his eye, and a brave lift to his shoulders. He, like thousands of other honest patrolmen, was glad of an opportunity to risk his life in the service of the city.

In the basement of the old Hamlin Printing House building under the shadow of the Queensborough Bridge, the hooded man and Olga Laminoff stood alongside the huge waterwheel. Facing him, with their hands bound behind them, were Nita Van Sloan and Elaine Robillard. Each of them had her arms gripped tightly by two men who held them upright.

Nita Van Sloan raised her chin, drew herself up, and shook off the hands of her captors. Her brave eyes met squarely the small, glittering black eyes behind the hood of the Dictator. Olga Laminoff watched Nita Van Sloan keenly, sharply, almost jealously, as if she were envious of the younger woman's courage and bravery.

The Dictator was talking in that quick, eagerly cruel voice of his which reminded Nita so much of a predatory eagle's scream.

"You will notice, Miss Van Sloan, that this turbine wheel rests in a pool of water. Observe how it is turned.

"I suggest that you talk first rather than wait until

151

we have you on the wheel. I merely want to know where your friend, Richard Wentworth, is hiding. Manifestly, he must have a room or some other retreat somewhere in the city. You, as his closest friend, must know where it is. That is all I want you to tell me. We will do the rest."

Nita returned his stare bravely. "I do not choose to talk," she said with a wry smile, paraphrasing a statement of an ex-President of the United States.

The Dictator's hooded head nodded. "I thought you would be stubborn." A sigh emanated from the hood. "We are forced to proceed."

Just at that moment, a man appeared on the staircase leading from the upper floor. This man was stocky, fat-jowled, with small, frightened eyes. Nita Van Sloan recognized him at once. He was Argyle Dunning, Frank Dunning's uncle, lately the President of the Board of Aldermen, and now Mayor. That he had been admitted thus without ceremony or introduction could indicate only one thing—that he was high in the councils of the Dictator.

The hooded man turned to Argyle Dunning, spoke impatiently: "You're early, Dunning. I thought I told you to come later."

Argyle Dunning glanced around the room, saw Nita and Elaine, and then his eyes rested on the water-wheel. "W-what is that?" he demanded hoarsely.

The Dictator chuckled. "This is an old Chinese custom which we have transplanted to this country. We are about to try to induce Miss Van Sloan here to give us some information. You may stay. You will be entertained."

"Look here," Dunning exclaimed hysterically,

pushing forward toward the Dictator. "I won't stand for any more of this. You made a tool of me. I never guessed what you intended to do. When you told me you'd make me Mayor, I didn't know you were going to kill Larrabie in order to do it. I thought you'd get me into the city hall by controlling votes in some manner. Instead you committed murder—*murder, you hear!* And then the killing of Howard Appleton—you framed my own nephew for it, and I dare not even see him or his sweetheart, Evelyn, for fear that they will surmise just by looking at me that I have something to do with it. I tell you, Dictator, I won't go on with this—"

"You object to my methods?" the hooded man asked silkily.

"God help me," Argyle Dunning moaned. "I've made a murderer out of myself." His eyes flashed with sudden hate as they rested on Olga Laminoff. "Because I thought I loved you, I have been a fool—and worse. At first you only asked me to do little things, and I yielded to your charms. Then I became more and more enmeshed, until it was too late to back out. Now you've led me all the way down the road of crime. Now you ask me to stand by and watch while you torture an innocent woman—"

The Dictator broke in coldly. "Dunning, you are a valuable man to me. As Mayor, you are the means by which I control the city. But do not assume that you are absolutely necessary to me. Just as I made you Chief Executive of this city, I can unmake you, and place another in your stead. You *must* go on under my orders."

Argyle Dunning drew himself up to his full height.

"There is always the alternative of death, Dictator. My self-respect and my honor are gone. But I can make some sort of amends to society!"

His hand thrust into his jacket pocket, and came out with a small pistol. He covered the Dictator and Olga Laminoff with the gun, and stepped backward, pointing with a shaking finger.

"Release Miss Van Sloan at once, and let her come with me—and the little girl, too!"

The Dictator did not seem particularly frightened by Dunning's pistol. He seemed to hesitate a moment, then his hooded head turned toward Nita and Elaine, and he said airily: "It's too bad that we must lose your company, Miss Van Sloan. Mr. Dunning wants you to go with him."

Just then there was a quick, loud report. Argyle Dunning uttered a short scream, and a black hole appeared in the side of his head just above the temple.

Dunning in his excitement had forgotten the other thugs in the room. They had been in the shadow, near the double doors leading to the pier, and he had made the mistake of not watching them. Now, one of them had fired from his coat pocket.

Dunning's mouth fell open, and his eyes became vacant. For a moment his body teetered on wobbly knees, then he crashed to the floor, lay there inert, unmoving.

The executioner sighed, and moved back to his position at the wheel. The thug who had shot Dunning snickered. But the Dictator growled at him: "You fool! Couldn't you have shot him in the arm instead of killing him? I needed Dunning. Now I

154

have to go to all the trouble of finding myself another mayor to take his place!''

Suddenly, as if seeking some other place to vent his anger, he swung on Nita. ''Now, Miss Van Sloan, we can proceed.''

He motioned peremptorily to two of his men, and they seized her, dragged her toward the wheel.

They swung her up upon the wheel, and in spite of her kicking and struggling, they lashed her tightly to it, on her back, with her head down.

Then they stepped back, and the Dictator approached her. The blood was rushing to Nita's head, and the hooded figure, seen upside down that way, seemed to be dancing before her eyes. She bit her lip, said with an effort at steadiness: ''Perhaps, before I die, you'll tell me who you are. Being only a woman, I hate to die with my curiosity unsatisfied.''

The Dictator chuckled. ''You are a very brave young woman. But your curiosity must remain unsatisfied, as is the curiosity of everybody else. I will tell you, though, that the face behind this hood is the face of a man who is known to many people in this city—yet there is not a single person living in this world who can say that it is the face of the Dictator—not even Olga Laminoff.''

Olga Laminoff stepped forward. ''But I knew you—''

''Yes, indeed, my dear Olga. You knew me in the old days. But my face was not one that could venture with impunity through the streets of any civilized city. Therefore, I have had it changed. It is that changed face which is known to the people of New York. You, my dear Olga, have never seen it.''

Nita Van Sloan spoke desperately, striving for time. "Surely, you can lose nothing by showing your face to me. If I am to die . . ."

The hooded man shook his head. "I regret that it is impossible, Miss Van Sloan. We will now proceed."

Nita shut her eyes as the executioner slowly turned the wheel, and her head approached the water beneath. . . .

CHAPTER ELEVEN

Beneath the Hood

Under the First Avenue ramp at Forty-second Street, a mass of blue-coated men stood closely packed in the darkness, listening to the voice of Commissioner Kirkpatrick as he stood on a soap box, towering commandingly over them.

"You men," he was saying, "are those in the Department whom I know to be honest, trustworthy, and imbued with a spirit of civic pride. You have all seen the Police Department debauched, you have seen the city thrown into chaos by the organization of this Dictator who has appeared to grasp power without opposition."

Kirkpatrick glanced at his watch, "It is close to midnight. We were late in getting together, and now we must hurry. You know what you all are to do. Two hundred men on the Forty-second Street side, a hundred on the Vanderbilt Avenue side, the other three hundred of you to be spread out to cover all the other exits of the station. We must not get there before midnight, or our plans will be given away. We must time our arrival so as to catch all of the Dictator's men within the station—that is, of course, assuming that they will be within the station.

"Now one more word before we start—I have learned authoritatively that the person who is known as the *Spider* is going to try to help us at Grand Central Station. He is there now. I know that the *Spider* has worked outside the law, and is wanted by the law. But in this emergency we must forget that. I ask you, men, not to attack the *Spider* tonight if you see him. And I ask you also, to permit him to leave unmolested if we should be successful."

There was a moment's silence, then Kirkpatrick raised his hand. "Let's go!"

He leaped off the soap box, and started the march across Forty-second Street to Grand Central Station.

At one minute before midnight, the vast expanse of Grand Central Station seemed to be more crowded than usual. Trains were leaving in two and three sections to accommodate the great exodus of residents who were fleeing the impending anarchy which they expected to take possession of the city.

All these people, hurrying with their bags to make late trains, were nervously aware of the fact that there were no police in evidence. Their panic might have been increased tenfold had they noticed the numerous sharp-faced, hard-eyed men who slouched around at many spots in the station, carrying large, awkward bundles under their arms. To the casual eye these men might also have been travellers waiting for their train. But to the eye of Richard Wentworth as he made his way across the station, those men were the shock troops of the Dictator's organization.

His glance, swiftly travelling over the crowd, spied Martin Kreamer standing at the entrance to the waiting room. Behind Martin Kreamer he glimpsed Ram Singh and Jackson, whom he had instructed to wait outside of the main room.

Wentworth saw a dozen or so uniformed men across the station toward the cashier's windows. These were the armed guards from the money wagon which came every night at midnight to remove the day's receipts to the main office of the railroad. These men were marching two by two, each pair carrying a money box.

With a great air of casualness, Wentworth passed several of the lounging men, appearing to pay them no attention. He proceeded to the elevator bank, and took an elevator to the first floor. The tall office building above the Grand Central Station was open all night, but the mezzanine balcony which over-looked the main floor of the station was generally closed after eight o'clock. Wentworth found the hall stair, and descended the half flight to the balcony. The door was locked, but Wentworth withdrew a bunch of keys from his pocket, tried three, and on the last try succeeded in getting the door open. He slipped in quickly, closed the door behind him, and made his way along the darkened balcony toward the railing.

Swiftly, Wentworth removed from under his coat the cape and hat which were so well known to the city as the apparel of the *Spider*. He donned these, and quickly inserted the false teeth, applied the plas-

159

tic material to his face which transformed him into the ugly being that was known as the *Spider*. Now he stepped to the rail and leaned against it, virtually unseen in the darkness up here.

Now his glance focussed on the door of the Chief Cashier's booth, and he saw the armed guards begin to come out, each pair carrying a loaded money-box between them. It was quite apparent that the boxes were much heavier than they had been on the way in, for the shoulders of the guards sagged with their weight. And abruptly a strange tenseness seemed suddenly to have descended upon the whole station.

Wentworth was watching Martin Kreamer. The Five-Star Detective Agency head took a small object from his pocket, placed it to his lips. That object was a whistle. He blew a single blast, and the atmosphere of poised tenseness dissolved into one blinding, deadly action. Wrappers were torn from those awkward-looking packages, and the vicious snouts of sub-machine guns appeared.

Women screamed at sight of the weapons. Wentworth glanced anxiously at the entrances of the station, looking in vain for the appearance of the bluecoats under Kirkpatrick. They were late. He alone, with Ram Singh and Jackson as his only support, must combat this menace.

The armed guards had stopped stock still at sight of those machine guns. And abruptly, without any warning whatsoever, those shifty-eyed thugs began to pull the trips of their machine guns, spraying lead in a deadly hail across the bodies of the guards. Others of the thugs swung their machine guns indiscriminately spouting fire and lead at the innocent

160

bystanders. Men and women screamed, turned and ran in wild panic in every direction. The marching hail of slugs caught many of them in mid-stride, flung them to the floor, riddled in a dozen places.

And into all that chaos of battle and sudden death, there came the twin screams of deadly slugs from the two guns of the *Spider* up in the balcony above. Wentworth had thrown himself into the fray. It was not thus that he had planned. He had merely stationed himself here for the purpose of spotting the hooded Dictator, should he be present. He had counted on the police to be here before the stroke of midnight. For some reason they were late.

From the doorway of the waiting room, Ram Singh and Jackson swung into action in a flank attack on the gunmen. The three of them shot coolly, steadily, methodically, making each shot count. Gunner after gunner among the thugs fell under their accurate marksmanship. But there were too many of them. The sights of machine guns were suddenly raised toward the balcony where the *Spider's* dark shape was discernible in the shadows.

Martin Kreamer, standing near the ticket window, shouted excitedly: "That's the *Spider!* Get the *Spider!*"

Wentworth's magazines were empty. He crouched behind the railing, and his swift fingers slipped new clips into the automatics. Then, raising his head once more, he resumed firing. Those thugs down there were shooting quickly, hurriedly, in their hasty panic. They were anxious—desperately anxious—to get the *Spider* before the *Spider* got them. Ram Singh and Jackson had also reloaded, and one or two of the thugs were swinging their sub-machine guns toward

161

where the two servants stood in the waiting room. Wentworth shot those two before he fired at the ones who were aiming at himself.

Wentworth saw out of the corner of his eye, that Kreamer had run forward toward the balcony, and was now raising his gun, sighting carefully upward. The *Spider* snapped a shot at Kreamer, and the Five-Star Detective Agency head was smashed backward as if a giant hand had thrust against his chest. Now a steady hail of slugs was driving Wentworth back from the railing. He crouched, ran along the balcony for ten or fifteen feet, then raised his head again and began to fire from the new point of vantage. Down below, the thunderous explosions, the acrid smell of cordite and the screams of frightened and dying men and women filled the station, made it a scene of bedlam. These people had been betrayed. The police protection that they had a right to expect was not there.

Above them, one man, a man proscribed by the law, was fighting for them. Down below, two servants of that same man were also fighting for them.

Desperately the *Spider* glanced at the clock. It was three minutes after twelve. Three minutes was a long time for a battle like that to last. Where were the police—

Suddenly he had his answer. Through every entrance there came marching the orderly ranks of blue-coated patrolmen. Commissioner Kirkpatrick strode at the head of those who had come through the Forty-second Street entrance. In the leading ranks of each group of patrolmen were those who were armed with sub-machine guns; and these sprayed the crowd of

162

gunmen grimly, mercilessly. Behind the policemen with the sub-machine guns came uniformed men with revolvers—men who had been awarded medals for marksmanship, who had learned how to shoot in the hardest school in the world—the Police Academy.

And those thugs who had been so brave in cutting down defenseless men and women, lost their nerve before the steady advance of the bluecoated policemen. They fired a few shots, then drew down their guns and raced madly for the opposite entrance of the station.

In a moment the organized attack of these gunmen was changed into a panic-striken rout. The gunmen fled in every direction, stopped at each entrance by the blue wall of uniformed men. And these criminals were suddenly gripped with the white fear of death. They saw no mercy in the grim eyes of the men of the law; nevertheless, they threw down their guns and raised their hands in the air, and begged for mercy.

While the work of segregating the thugs and carrying out the wounded was going on, a dark appariton appeared on the stairway leading from the balcony. Several of the patrolmen saw that fmiliar, caped figure, and their hands streaked once more to their holsters. Then they remembered Commissioner Kirkpatrick's orders, and stood silent, watching the *Spider* cross the floor toward the Commissioner. He reached Kirkpatrick, and the Commissioner glanced around, saw that no one was within earshot of them, and said swiftly: "You've got to cover me, Dick. I told these boys not to molest you, but it would be better if I didn't appear too friendly to you."

"Right, Kirk," Wentworth whispered. Then he raised his voice, spoke so that his tones carried across the whole room; "Commissioner Kirkpatrick, the *Spider* has helped you here. Do not try to detain me."

Kirkpatrick repressed a grin, and said formally: "*Spider,* I am compelled to place you under arrest—".

In a flash, the *Spider's* automatics appeared once more in his hands. "Don't move," he warned everybody, "or I'll shoot the Commissioner!"

It might have been easy for some of the patrolmen in the room to have thrown a quick shot at Wentworth in the hope of killing him before he shot Kirkpatrick. But these men knew that the *Spider* had just helped to fight their battle for them. Perhaps they felt a sneaking admiration for the *Spider*. In any event, no shot was fired. Slowly, the *Spider* marched Kirkpatrick across the station toward the doorway. He caught a glimpse of Ram Singh and Jackson, and jerked his head in their direction. They came swiftly toward them, and when they approached, Wentworth said urgently: "Ram Singh! You followed the Laminoff woman from the Tombs? You saw where she went before going to Grogan's place?"

Ram Singh nodded. "Yes, *sahib*. She went to an old printing house near Fifty-ninth Street. She stayed there only a short time, then went to Grogan's." He had spoken very low, so that none of those in the station heard him.

The eyes of the *Spider* were flashing behind his disguise. "Ram Singh," he said in a loud voice, "if you will go to the old printing house on the East

164

River near Fifty-ninth Street, you will find your master, Richard Wentworth, awaiting you. And you, Kirkpatrick, will have a good chance of catching the Dictator. This is a tip from the *Spider!*"

The eyes of little Elaine Robillard were red from weeping. She was on her knees on the cold basement floor of the Hamlin Printing Concern Building, biting her lips so that the blood came from them. With her hands tied behind her back, it was impossible for her to wipe from her face the tears that coursed freely down her cheeks.

In the center of the room the huge turbine wheel was slowly turning, with Nita Van Sloan tied to it. Nita's head was less than six inches from the water. Her hair, dripping, and hanging from her head, was just touching the water. It was the twentieth time that she had been immersed up to her neck. Each time they had left her in for only a second, then the huge wheel had turned back, dragging her up.

Now, as she was being once more lowered, she was drawing in great, tortured gusts of breath, steeling herself against the next ordeal.

The half dozen of the Dictator's thugs in the room were standing at the far end near the broad open doors which gave egress to the river. Several power boats were tied up here, riding without lights. The crews of those boats, a half dozen in number, had clambered up on the pier which jutted out from the building, and were watching the scene with eager enthusiasm.

Abruptly, with startling suddenness, a single shot sounded from somewhere outside the building.

The Dictator started and raised his hooded head. Almost at once, there were other shots then a veritable fusillade sounded from above. The crackling of machine guns mingled with the duller reverberations of heavy police positives.

The Dictator motioned to his waiting thugs, and started to run toward the staircase. From above there came another sound—the sound of exploding dynamite.

The Dictator cried out: "They've dynamited the doors. We're being attacked!"

The firing upstairs became louder now, as the fighting moved inside the house.

The Dictator backed away from the stairs motioned to his gunmen to go up. They started forward, but recoiled as the figure of a man appeared on the stairs above them.

Nita Van Sloan could not see this man, but little Elaine Robillard saw him. She uttered a glad little cry: "Mr. Wentworth! Come and send these bad men away!"

Wentworth had shed the disguise of the *Spider* and had hurried to join the police here. Now, he came down those stairs like a thunderbolt. In either hand his automatics were blazing death at the gunmen. They retreated swiftly, firing over their shoulders as they ran toward the boats tied up at the pier. Behind Wentworth, Commissioner Kirkpatrick, Ram Singh and Jackson launched themselves down those stairs, guns spitting death, with a stream of bluecoats swarming after them.

The hooded Dictator leaped backward and he put the huge wheel between himself and the attackers. Viciously, he reached over and swung the wheel down so that Nita's head was thrust deep below the water. Then the hooded man dashed for the open doorway leading to the pier.

Now he was in the open, and Wentworth raised his gun, grimly aiming for the man's head.

At that moment little Elaine Robillard screamed: "You wicked man! I hate you!" She stumbled to her feet and threw herself bodily at the Dictator, directly in the line of Wentworth's fire. The *Spider* eased the pressure on the trigger of his gun.

And in that second the Dictator seized Elaine by the arm, ran, dragging her as a shield, toward the pier.

Elaine struggled, kicking at him, and the Dictator swung at her viciously, still running. Elaine's foot caught in the Dictator's legs, and he tripped head-long, letting go of the child.

But as he fell, the hood dropped from his head.

A shout went up from Ram Singh and Jackson. The man's face was revealed in the light. And there, staring at them with intense hate written across his gross features, was the battered, square countenance of—Casey Grogan, the ex-pugilist!

Casey Grogan, the man who had cloaked his bid for power under the disguise of the proprietor of a cheap dance hall!

It was thus that the Dictator had fooled the public. Throwing suspicion in turn upon Argyle Dunning, upon Hugh Varner, upon Stephen Pelton, he had himself trod the streets of the city with immunity, sheltered under the grotesque face of a battered prize-fighter. Count Calypsa had once been a handsome man. He had reversed the usual process of facial surgery—instead of changing his face to a more handsome one, he had changed it to an uglier one. No one would have suspected that a man would deliberately change his face to assume the appearance of a punch-drunk ex-prizefighter.

Now, the Dictator, unmasked, leaped to his feet and raced through the open door to the pier, while the police sent a fusillade of bullets after him.

Richard Wentworth did not fire. Neither did Ram Singh or Jackson. For all three had seen Nita's body tied to the wheel, and they had all rushed to pull her out.

Wentworth untied her and applied first aid. Nita choked and gasped. She had not lost consciousness, for the entire time of her immersion had been less than three-quarters of a minute. In so short a time had the fortunes of the Dictator changed. From the master of the underworld of a great city he had suddenly become a hunted criminal.

The police under Kirkpatrick dashed out on the pier, sent their shots flashing into the night at the motor boat which sped away into the river. It was hopeless to pursue that man. He had escaped.

Kirkpatrick shrugged and turned back into the room. Swiftly he issued orders to his men.

"Down to Headquarters, boys. Place Inspector Strong under arrest as being an accessory to Casey Grogan, alias the Dictator. Take charge of all departments, and wait for my arrival!"

Now he turned to Wentworth, who was supporting Nita. Ram Singh had untied little Elaine Robillard, and had had a good deal of trouble identifying himself without his beard.

Now, Wentworth, with his arm close around Nita's waist, looked sombrely at Kirkpatrick. There was an unspoken question in his eyes.

Kirkpatrick nodded. "Yes, Dick, he got away." The Commissioner's eyes travelled across the floor, over the bodies of dead gunmen, to rest upon the cold, twisted corpse of the beautiful woman, Olga Laminoff. A deep red stain covered her breast. She had been shot in the early minutes of the battle. Whether the bullet which had killed her had been fired from the gun of one of the Dictator's thugs or of one of the police was not yet known. But in death, there was still written upon her face the cold beauty which must have intrigued the ruthless Count Calypsa.

"I wonder," Kirkpatrick said softly, "if we'll ever hear from him again."

Wentworth, clasping Nita close to him, looked across her head at Kirkpatrick and laughed harshly. "I'm afraid we will, Kirk. That man isn't through yet. Did you see the printing presses upstairs? The Dictator must have printed millions of dollars of counterfeit money. That money is probably out now, and will flood the country. He'll have resources—great resources. Yes, Kirk, I'm afraid we're not through with Count Calypsa!"

Nita Van Sloan snuggled closer into Wentworth's arms. "Dick! Then—what about our world cruise?"

He smiled tightly. "It'll have to wait, darling. The city has to be cleaned up. Kirk will need our help. We've got to wipe out the last remnants of the Dicta-

169

tor's organization. We've got to prepare to meet his next blow.''

"What about Hugh Varner?" Kirkpatrick asked. "You told me that you had traced a telephone number to him—"

Wentworth nodded. "It was a blind. Calypsa had ordered a telephone installed in the Electrical Building, in Hugh Varner's name, without Varner's knowledge. Then he had caused the wire to be tapped into his own telephone. When Varner's number was dialed, the telephone in his own office rang, and if the number were traced, it would be credited to Varner."

Little Elaine Robillard tugged at Wentworth's sleeve. "Mr. Wentworth! Take me away from here—from all these dead men. I want to go home!"

With a low cry, Nita reached over and drew the little girl close to her breast. "My little sweetheart," she said softly. "From now on I'm going to make sure that you're never dragged into anything like this. I'll take you away with me—far away from this city!"

"Amen to that!" Richard Wentworth said in a deep-throated voice.

Ram Singh nodded in approval. "It will be better fighting, with all due respect to the *memsahib,* when there are no women to worry about." His white teeth flashed in a smile. "When this evil count returns, we will have a royal welcome for him!"

Nita and Wentworth were looking deeply into each other's eyes. Wentworth knew what it meant for her to go away when there was the prospect of more danger and excitement and thrill. But in his heart he

170

was glad. Because he knew that when Calypsa returned, there would be no mercy in the heart of that man for anyone whom Richard Wentworth loved. . . .

The Mill-Town Massacres

Without any forewarning, the madness struck. One moment the busy steel-mill town of Keystone was a peaceful industrial community . . . the next, it had become a shambles of murder, madness and ruthless midnight slaughter. Horror walked its streets, and terror lurked in every close-locked home. . . . Could the *Spider,* hastening to answer the distressed call of the dismayed inhabitants, prevail against the death which struck from darkness? A stranger in a place of madness, unsupported by friends or allies, Richard Wentworth faces his greatest test—alone!

CHAPTER ONE

The Master of the Madmen

The first sign of trouble in the steel industry came when Big Harry Silvestro went berserk. Big Harry was the foreman of the night shift in the Number Three open hearth shop of the Keystone Iron and Steel Corporation, in the town of Keystone. He had held this job for five years, with never a single day out for sickness. Indeed, a glimpse of his stocky, powerful body, stripped to the waist as he worked, would have made anyone doubt that he could ever be sick.

He was regarded by the superintendent as a plodding, loyal, dependable man. For three years, the unit of which he was foreman had consistently won the intershop pool for the greatest production of ingots.

He had a wife and four children. He did not drink, smoke or chew. His square, almost bovine face topped by close-cropped black hair gave no indication that an original thought had ever entered his brain. But he could work, and he could make his men work. He did not seem to have a nerve in his body, and he never grew angry or flew off the handle. No one ever suspected that Big Harry Silvestro could grow excited or temperamental about anything.

Nevertheless, at two o'clock on Saturday morning, Big Harry went berserk.

It happened while a batch of molten steel was being poured from one of the open hearth furnaces into the huge cylindrical bucket which would conduct the steel by the traveling crane across the shop to deposit it into a row of molds where it would cool into oblong ingots.

Silvestro was directing the operation, when suddenly he doubled over with pain. Both his great hands pressed hard against his abdomen, and a cold sweat broke out on his face and naked torso.

The sizzling molten steel was pouring in a thin stream, glistening silvery, and was spreading heat in every direction. Silvestro groaned and pressed at his stomach, still doubed over. The men of his crew could not go to his assistance because they were handling the hot steel.

But Jack Markos, the little timekeeper, who happened to be passing through the shop at the moment, saw Big Harry's agony and ran to his side, put a hand on the big man's shoulder.

"Harry!" he shouted. "What's the matter with you?"

Big Harry didn't answer. Instead, he straightened with a tremendous effort and turned suddenly red-rimmed eyes at little Jack Markos. Markos looked up at him, and the little man's face went white at the stark madness that he saw in Silvestro's eyes. His jaw fell open, and he took an involuntary step backward, half turned to run.

But he was too late. Big Harry uttered a dreadful cry of mad rage, leaped after Markos, and seized the little man around the waist. Markos screamed, strained ineffectually, as Silvestro lifted him high in the air and hurled his diminutive body straight into the huge bucket of molten steel!

Markos' shrill scream died in a gurgling of agony drowned by the bubbling, sizzling steel. Dense fumes spurted from the bucket, as the steady stream of liquid metal continued to pour into it from the open hearth, to cover what was left of Jack Markos. He had been cremated alive.

A sudden hush descended upon the shop as the men stood in petrified horror. Markos was finished.

Big Harry Silvestro stood panting at the spot from which he had hurled Markos' body. His big chest was heaving and the breath was coming from his throat in great gasps. Saliva dribbled at his mouth, and his eyes were those of a madman. He stood half crouched, and the corded muscles of his stomach rippled with each breath he took. Apparently the pain was gone from his abdomen.

The men turned terrified stares upon him, hardly crediting the dreadful thing they had seen. That Harry Silvestro, their big, placid-tempered boss, should suddenly become a murderer in the twinkle of an eye seemed incredible to them. At first their brains refused to accept the fact.

Then, as they realized that a murderer stood before them, their brows clouded, and they slowly began to advance, encircling Big Harry.

The huge bucket into which the steel was still pouring over Jack Markos' body was forgotten. They had all loved the little timekeeper, and a dull anger began to grow in them.

Big Harry Silvestro watched them close in on him, with eyes that reflected the cunning of madness. He began to back away, and Mike Foley, the operator of the overhead crane, shouted to the men from his booth: "He's mad! Watch out for him!"

Foley seized a huge monkey wrench, leaped from his booth, and ran toward Silvestro.

Big Harry's lips turned back from his teeth in a vicious snarl. The black hair that almost completely covered his chest glistened with perspiration. His tremendously long, gorilla-like arms stretched out toward the nearest of the advancing men, and he hunched forward as if to seize him. Mike Foley was only ten feet away from Silvestro, and he shouted: "Get out of the way! He'll throw you in!"

Big Harry lunged at the nearest man, and his arm twined about the unfortunate fellow's waist. He lifted the man bodily from the floor, then his huge shoulder muscles bulged with the effort of raising the man high above his head, just as he had raised Jack Markos.

Then the other men closed in upon him, and they leaped at Silvestro, smashing at him with their fists, kicking at him with their feet. Mike Foley lunged in through the crowd, holding the monkey wrench high in the air, ready to bring it down on Silvestro's head.

But though these steel workers were powerful men themselves, Big Harry loomed above them all like a giant. Their blows and their kicks seemed to have little effect upon the crazed foreman. The man whom he had lifted into the air was struggling, squirming and shrieking, attempting to claw at his captor, and raking Big Harry's arms with grimy fingernails. Big Harry seemed to feel no pain at all.

The whole shop had stopped work, and all the men were rushing toward the wild scene. Big Harry tried to throw his man toward the seething cauldron of steel, but the workers were packed close about him, shouting and striking.

Suddenly the huge bucket overflowed, and the hot, molten metal began to sizzle on the floor, flowing out in fiery liquid streams along the floor. It was unnoticed by the milling throng around the big foreman. Mike Foley yelled: "Drop that man, Silvestro! I say, drop him!"

Silvestro snarled, and let go of the man, who dropped among his crowding fellows. Big Harry swung around, both huge fists flailing out at his attackers. Men dropped before him, pushed back before his berserk madness. Foley swung the wrench down on Silvestro's head, but he had not been able to get in a good blow in the press around him. The wrench glanced off the back of Big Harry's head.

The foreman staggered for a moment, shook his head to clear it, as a wounded beast might do, then lunged through the crowd. They clung to him, trying to trip him, slugging at him with fists. For a moment it seemed that they would bring him down in spite of his flailing arms.

But the hot molten metal oozing along the floor bit at the feet of some of the men. They shrieked with pain, and leaped out of the way of the flowing rivers of steel. The others turned, startled, and in that moment Big Harry with a shriek of ungovernable rage lunged through the crowd, straight across the shop. Men who barred his way were hurled aside like ten-pins. Silvestro reached the door, lunged out into the darkness of the night.

The shop workers followed him, racing after him into the open, intent on catching the murderer. Mike Foley was in the lead, still brandishing his wrench. But Harry Silvestro ran with such speed that he outdistanced them all. He raced down the wide street between the two long rows of shops, which stretched from Keystone's railroad station straight across to the Keystone River. Behind him the long line of pursuers stretched out, racing to catch him.

Silvestro was not fleeing haphazardly. With all the sudden madness that had abruptly seized him, there seemed to be a sureness in the flight, as if he knew just where he wanted to go. The whole of the mill district was thrown into an uproar by the chase. Men along the street took up the pursuit as they heard the shouts of Foley and the men from the Number Three shop.

They clung to Silvestro's trail through the night, followed him across the railroad sidings, close to the Keystone River, and saw him leap down the embankment toward the mud flats.

These mud flats, the dumping ground of the city, were the homes of hundreds of derelicts who each

180

year converged upon the town of Keystone from the surrounding country. The human flotsam and jetsam gathered in the hovels along the river bank, and when they became sorely pressed for food, would take an occasional odd job in town or in the mills. Many of these men, wanted by the police of other cities, did not leave their mud flat homes at all, hiding until the search for them had cooled. This vicious conglomeration of derelicts and criminals had been tolerated in Keystone for a long time, with Mayor Richard Gaylord generally too busy to plan a concerted drive to clean up the town.

The town itself had been created by the Keystone Steel and Iron Corporation, and had been built up around its huge plant. Richard Gaylord, being one of the directors of the company, had been chosen mayor and had served for five terms, consecutively. In addition to his position with the Keystone Steel and Iron Corporation, Gaylord had extensive interest in the stock market and commuted often between Keystone and New York as well as Chicago, which was near by. Since these derelicts in the mud flats had always been careful not to bring themselves to the attention of the authorities, no campaign had ever been started to drive them out.

Now, however, as Big Harry Silvestro raced toward the mud flats, these inhabitants of the town's underworld gave concrete evidence that they were a potential danger.

Silvestro had crossed the railroad siding which ran along the river, and was racing out toward the hovels on the flats, with the angry mob of workmen from the mills at his heels. Shouts and cries of rage filled

181

the night, and many townsmen across the river in the residential district stopped to stare over, not knowing what was the trouble.

The workmen began to gain on Silvestro, and a lynching appeared imminent, for despite his great strength he could never have defended himself against the several hundred outraged workers in pursuit. But at that crucial moment the hovels along the river's edge spewed forth their grimy, filthy, vicious occupants.

These derelicts and criminals raced out across the flats toward the approaching workmen, as if according to a well-laid plan. They were armed with automatic pistols, and there was a significant silence among them as opposed to the angry shouts from the workmen.

Big Harry Silvestro saw the aid that was coming to him, and stopped running, dropped flat on the ground. Almost at once a sharp command rang out among the criminals. The men raised their automatics, and streams of fiery flame lanced out through the night at the pursuing mill hands. Bullets whined through the air, and men screamed, dropped, mortally wounded.

The criminals continued to send volley after volley into the close-packed ranks of the workmen, and the mill hands were suddenly seized with panic. Cries of fright and terror rose from the press that had advanced with shouts of rage.

Fully thirty of them had fallen to the first volley, and the automatics continued to spit their messages of death. More and more men fell, writhing on the ground, or lying still in death. The mill hands turned

182

to flee in sudden panic, and the criminals, moving up at a second sharp order from among them, continued to fire until their guns were empty.

The cold-blooded slaughter kept up until the surviving mill hands had fled back across the railroad siding, leaving almost a hundred of their number dead or wounded along the mud flats.

To the startled watchers from the residential section across the river the shadowy figures of those murderous criminals appeared like horrid ghouls of the night. And the slaughter that had just taken place seemed incredible, fantastic, like some weird nightmare of the imagination. That such a thing as this could have taken place in the staid mill town of Keystone was beyond their comprehension. They watched, stunned, too amazed to take action.

And over on the mud flats a tall, fair-haired man whose left cheek was disfigured by an ugly scar was issuing further orders to the criminals. At his command, those desperadoes spread out over the flats, walking among the wounded mill hands. Whenever they found one who was only wounded, they would stoop and fire another shot into his brain. They left not a single one of those workmen alive. They moved about leisurely, not seeming to hurry, as if they had no fear of retaliation or capture by the police.

Big Harry Silvestro had arisen from the ground where he had thrown himself and was now standing, watching the slaughter apathetically, with a dazed expression on his bovine countenance.

At last the fair-haired man with the scar uttered another sharp order, and the criminals left off their murderous search. The scarred man turned and made his way north along the river bank, with Silvestro close behind him and the other criminals following. They streamed toward the north end of the city, where a number of low class barrooms catered to the undesirable element in Keystone. The night swallowed them up, and there was no longer any sign of life along the mud flats.

The mill hands began to steal back, kneeling beside their dead comrades. Cries of rage and sorrow filled the night as they discovered friends and relatives among the dead.

A few moments later, almost the entire police force of Keystone came swarming across the Broad Street Bridge. They had been summoned from every portion of the city, by radio. But they were too late. The fair-haired man with the scar, Harry Silvestro, and all those criminals had completely vanished.

The police scoured the city, searching through every corner of the barrooms in the North End section, every room and cellar in the dilapidated tenements and boarding houses. The mill hands helped them with a will. But no trace of the criminals was found.

That night the town of Keystone went into mourning. Throughout the South End section, where the poor but clean homes of the mill workers were located, there was weeping and lamentation. Close to five thousand families lived here in company-owned buildings. In a hundred of those buildings red-eyed women and sobbing children sat beside the biers of loved husbands and fathers who had been massacred that day.

On the other side of the river, in the better class residential section where dwelt the executives and supervisors of the Keystone Steel and Iron Company, there was perplexity and consternation. Over their breakfast tables the following morning this one topic was gravely discussed. It was dreadful that a man like Silvestro should suddenly go mad in this fashion; but it was beyond comprehension that the denizens of the mud flats should suddenly arise, fully armed, as if prepared in advance to protect Big Harry from the consequences of his deed.

Mrs. Silvestro and her four children were brought down to headquarters and questioned and cross-questioned for hours. The big mill foreman's wife had fallen into a state of acute hysteria upon learning what her husband had done. She could not believe that he had thrown Jack Markos into the bucket of molten steel. She screamed again and again: "No, no! Harry no do dat! Harry he like Jack Markos— he like him very much. He no kill Markos. I no believe dat!"

Investigators combed the mills and the homes of the workers, trying to get some clue, some inkling of the sudden malady which had seized Silvestro. It was clear from the stories of the workmen in Number Three shop that Big Harry had apparently been seized by some sort of cramp immediately before he threw Markos into the bucket. This was about all the investigators could get. Beyond that they were met by a stolid silence from the mill hands as well as from their families.

Mayor Richard Gaylord went into conference with Jonathan Spencer, General Manager of all the company plants in Keystone. But the crowning mystery of the whole terrible occurrence remained unsolved. That was the disappearance of the fair-haired man and his followers. There was absolutely no trace of them.

The city was beginning to quiet down a bit the following night, when disaster struck once more. A man in shop Number Four and another in shop Number Six suddenly broke into murderous action during the night shift, just as Silvestro had done the night before.

Kovalko, a furnace man in Number Four shop, drew a knife which he had had concealed in his belt, and slashed three men before he was overpowered. One of the men died, the other two were taken to the Keystone General Hospital across the river for treatment.

Strahl, foreman in Number Six, attempted to hurl one of his men into an open hearth furnace, but was prevented in the nick of time. He put up a furious resistance, when the other men leaped upon him, and, in the course of the fight, someone brought a sledge hammer down on the back of his head, crushing in his skull.

Kovalko, captured alive and taken to the city jail, hanged himself with his necktie before morning.

Now the town was truly aroused. It became evident that Big Harry Silvestro's act had not been an isolated case. Both Kovalko and Strahl apparently had been seized with the same kind of cramp from which Silvestro had suffered.

The next night another man went berserk, and the night after that, two more.

On the fifth night, police guards were placed in every shop, armed with clubs and sawed-off shotguns. On that night all of the men working in open hearth shop Number Three, where Big Harry Silvestro had been foreman, were suddenly seized with the same attack of cramps.

The fifty men began to mill around wildly, their eyes growing red with madness. They shouted, screamed, attacked and clawed at each other, and ripped open the vents which held the molten steel within the open hearth.

The police guards, summoned from all the other shops, subdued these men with their clubs, but had to kill three before they could quell the mad riot. The others were handcuffed and taken to the Keystone General Hospital for observation.

And there Dr. Arvin MacLeod, the Coroner of Keystone County, discovered the terrible truth. He phoned Mayor Gaylord hastily from the Morgue Room in the basement of the hospital, where he had finished the autopsy on the bodies of Kovalko and Strahl.

"Look here, Gaylord!" Dr. MacLeod's voice was fairly quivering with excitement. "It's a disease! The blood of Kovalko and Strahl is tainted with some foreign substance. I can't tell yet what it is. But I injected a drop of blood from each of them into some mice. The mice reacted just as the men did. But whatever it is that they have in the blood, the mice couldn't fight it the way the men did. They died

187

within twenty minutes. I'm afraid it's some sort of epidemic, Gaylord.''

Unfortunately, there were two newspaper reporters in Mayor Gaylord's office when he received the telephone call from Dr. MacLeod. MacLeod's voice, loud and agitated, was plainly audible to the reporters, and they heard every word of what he said. An hour later, every newspaper in the land had issued an extra carrying arresting big black headlines:

EPIDEMIC SWEEPS KEYSTONE!
SPREAD OF MURDER MADNESS
CAUSES STEEL TOWN PANIC!

CHAPTER TWO

Enter—The *Spider!*

Gaylord's daughter, Susan, and her fiance, young Charley Hendrix, were also in Gaylord's office when he received the message from Dr. Arvin MacLeod. Susan Gaylord was a dark-eyed, dark-haired, pretty slip of a girl whose sweetness was heightened by the warm curve of her young lips. Charley Hendrix was young, handsome, boyish. He had starred on the basketball and track teams at Harvard, would have made the football team but for lack of weight. His father was Crawford Hendrix, senior partner of Hendrix, MacIntyre & Hendrix, one of the largest stock brokerage firms of the country, with offices in New York, Chicago and two dozen other cities.

Richard Gaylord carried one of his stock accounts with Hendrix, MacIntyre & Hendrix, and it was through this connection that young Charley Hendrix had met Susan. The two young people had been strongly attracted to each other, and their engagement had followed as a matter of course.

Susan Gaylord and Charley Hendrix heard every word of Dr. MacLeod's report over the telephone, just as the two reporters heard it. Gaylord frowned at the reporters, who scurried from the room to phone in their news story, but he made no attempt to stop them.

While Susan and Charley remained in the room, staring at him with wide eyes, Mayor Gaylord said into the phone: "Good God, MacLeod, do you know what you're saying? Do you mean to tell me that this homicidal madness is going to spread to everybody in Keystone? It'll mean we'll have to shut down our plant—"

"It'll mean more than that, Gaylord," Dr. Mac-Leod's dry voice informed him. "It means that the whole town will have to be quarantined. We don't know the nature of this disease, but it seems to be communicable. It means that you'll have to phone the Governor and ask him to assign state troopers— perhaps militia—to block off the town, and permit not a soul to leave. We're cursed with this plague, whatever it is, and we don't know how far it may spread if we don't bottle it up. Until we isolate the germ of this disease, we can't take a chance on its spreading outside the city."

Gaylord's knuckles grew white as his hand tautened on the receiver. "But, MacLeod, it can't be as serious as all that. Why, it's unheard of; a thing like madness can't be catching—"

"Apparently it is," MacLeod told him dryly. "The twenty-odd men who were brought here from the riot in the Number Three shop last night are all suffering from the same thing. They're the very men who chased Silvestro to the river bank. They saw their own friends and relatives slaughtered by those wharf rats. They're the same ones who saw Jack Markos, the timekeeper, thrown into the vat of molten steel. And yet, they've all succumbed to the same thing themselves. I'm sorry, Gaylord, but as County Coroner it is my duty to demand that you communicate with the Governor at once, and see to it that the town is sealed up!''

Gaylord hung up, and faced his daughter and her fiance, with his shoulders sagging despairingly.

"You—heard?" he asked in a thin voice.

They both nodded. Susan Gaylord exclaimed: "Father! I can't—bring myself to believe that all these things are true. It—it seems like some terrible nightmare; the story of how Markos was thrown into the vat of steel, of how the mill hands were slaughtered on the river bank, and of how Silvestro and those criminals disappeared in the night, together with that man with the scarred face. Oh, father, I'm—afraid!''

Gaylord reached over the desk and patted her hand. Young Charley Hendrix came over and took her in his arms, and she rested her shoulder on his head.

Mayor Gaylord sighed. "I guess MacLeod is right. I'll have to phone the Governor. I'll close all the shops, shut down the plant until this thing is solved!''

That afternoon, two hundred and fifty state troopers were thrown in a wide cordon around the town of Keystone. They were armed with carbines and clubs, and their instructions were that nobody at all was to be permitted to leave the city. Keystone was officially placed under quarantine.

The entire plant of the Keystone Steel & Iron Corporation was shut down. The town was suddenly quiet as the blast furnaces ceased to thrust their flaring flames up into the sky, and the multitudinous noises of the rolling mills and the huge steel presses died into silence. The steel town of Keystone became quiet as the grave by comparison with the cacophony of noise which had overhung it before.

But the disorder did not cease. The mill hands were now stricken by real panic. Word had spread of Dr. MacLeod's findings, and men stared at each other suspiciously while womenfolk stayed within their homes, keeping their children off the streets. Fifty more cases of madness were reported during the day, and in many instances the afflicted men did much damage before they were finally subdued and removed to the hospital ward.

The state troopers did not enter the town, but merely guarded all the exits. The enforcement of law and order was left to the police force, of which Mayor Gaylord was himself the honorary chief. There was no official Chief of Police in Keystone, and Gaylord himself administered the department.

Many of the wealthier families attempted to leave town, but they were halted by the state troopers, turned back. Ugly murmurs began to arise in the mill districts. Agitators were circulating among the workers, urging them to attempt to break through the lines of state police and escape from the danger of being afflicted with that dreadful madness.

Gaylord sent every available policeman out on duty, ordering them to patrol in twos and threes for greater protection, and to quell any disturbances with an iron hand. He didn't want to be compelled to ask the Governor to declare martial law in the town. The Keystone Steel & Iron Corporation regarded this town as its own private property and desired to set no precedents whereby the State Government might step in to supersede them.

It was that evening, in Mayor Gaylord's deserted office in the City Hall Building, that Charley Hendrix finally made the suggestion which was to bring the *Spider* to Keystone.

Gaylord had spent a long day, what with conferences with Jonathan Spencer, the General Manager of the mill, and with long distance telephone calls to New York and other cities, as well as to the Governor of the State. Jonathan Spencer was now in the Mayor's office, at the close of the day, arguing heatedly with Gaylord, while Susan and Charley listened. Spencer had just finished an explosive outburst in protestation against the closing down of the mills.

"See here, Gaylord, do you know how much we stand to lose by closing down? We're working on a thirty-million-dollar order for the new cruisers that the Government is laying down. If we don't get that steel out in time, our contract is forfeited. Don't you realize what that means? I insist on opening the mills at once!"

Gaylord, usually the first to agree to any course of procedure that would be profitable for the Key-

193

stone Steel & Iron Corporation, remained firm this time. His fist came down on the desk with a hard thud.

"No, Spencer. As long as I'm in charge of the administrative branch of this city, those mills won't open. We're not going to risk contaminating the whole population. And we're not going to risk any more riots in the shop. The Government will have to give us an extension of time—"

"They won't give us any extension," Spencer growled. "We'll lose the contract, and it'll go to the Smithtown Steel Company, at the other end of the state. Why, this thing has already done us enough damage. Do you know that our stock has dropped ten points during the day?"

"I'm sorry, Spencer," Gaylord said firmly, "but the price of our stock is not as important as the lives of men and women. The mills remain closed!"

"We'll see about that," Jonathan Spencer roared. "I'm going to wire all the directors to call a special meeting. This is all bosh and bother about epidemics. MacLeod is crazy. This is all a plot of some sort, to close us up so that we lose the contract. Those men have probably been paid to act insane. And you, Gaylord, should be the last to fall for it. My God, man, you own a good block of Keystone yourself. You'll be ruined if the bottom drops out of the stock."

"Never mind about me," Mayor Gaylord snapped. "I'll take care of myself. And I'll also take care of the women and children of this city. You don't seem to realize, Spencer, that we owe a duty to those people. We owe them the duty of keeping them safe and

194

healthy, and of protecting them against things like this. How could you ever sleep nights if you reopened the shop and hundreds of other men died as the result? I don't dispute your statement that there must be some plot afoot; the fact that those criminals from the mud flats were all armed indicates it. And from the reports of that fair-haired man with the scar, I judge that they had good leadership. But that doesn't change the situation. We won't re-open the mills!"

Jonathan Spencer pursed his thin lips, and scowled. "We'll see, Gaylord, we'll see," he murmured softly. And he swung about, stormed out of the room.

Mayor Gaylord watched him leave, then shrugged and looked up at Susan and Charley.

"You two youngsters better run along home," he said. "Stay indoors. There may be more disturbances tonight. I should have sent you out of town before the state police established their cordon around the city. But I was so busy, it slipped my mind."

Charley Hendrix took an eager step forward. "I have a suggestion, Mr. Gaylord. Susan has been telling me about the time, three years ago, when the racketeer from Chicago moved into Keystone and terrorized the city."

"I remember it," Gaylord said shortly. "What has that got to do with this trouble?"

"Nothing at all, sir, except that Susan tells me that at that time the city was saved by a mysterious person whose identity nobody knows—"

"You remember, father," Susan broke in. "It was

195

the *Spider*. He was an awfully ugly-looking man, and he wore a long cape and a wide hat, and I was frightened by him at first. But it was he who finally saved the city.''

Gaylord frowned. ''That's true, Susan. The *Spider* did us a good turn then. But don't forget that the *Spider* worked outside the law. He's a hunted man himself. I don't think that I, as Mayor of Keystone, could ethically call upon him for help.''

Young Charley Hendrix exclaimed impatiently: ''But that's just what we need, Mr. Gaylord. The police seem to be helpless. They can't discover a single clue, they don't know where to start. A man like the *Spider* could go into the underworld and really accomplish things. With the lives of so many inhabitants of this city at stake, you can't let your official position stop you.''

Gaylord frowned thoughtfully. ''No, Charley, I don't think—''

''But you must, sir!'' Charley Hendrix's firm young chin was thrust out at a stubborn angle. ''I insist that you do it. You may do as you like with me, but if you don't send for the *Spider*, I will!''

Mayor Gaylord studied the young man for a long moment. ''You *are* a chip off the old block, aren't you, Charley? Crawford Hendrix would talk just the same way. I believe you'd go ahead with your intentions even though it meant losing Susan, wouldn't you?''

Charley Hendrix hesitated.

Susan exclaimed: ''He's right, dad. And I love him for being like that. When he makes up his mind

196

to a thing, he always goes through with it—just like his father."

Mayor Gaylord threw up his hands in surrender. "All right, you win. But how can we send for the *Spider?* We don't know how to get in touch with him—"

"I think I know how to do that," Charley Hendrix told him. "There have been some disturbances in New York recently, and it is a matter of common knowledge that the city was saved from being thrown into the hands of a vicious criminal, only by the activity of the *Spider.* He apparently acted almost entirely on the side of the law in New York, and it is currently rumored that he is a close friend of Commissioner Kirkpatrick. Suppose you phone Kirkpatrick. Suggest to him that this is a case in which the *Spider* might be interested. And then see what happens."

Gaylord glanced at his wrist-watch. "Eleven thirty," he remarked. "I'd have to try Kirkpatrick at his home."

He picked up the receiver slowly, got long distance, and put through a request for a call with Stanley Kirkpatrick, Commissioner of the New York City Police Department. In less than five minutes he had his connection, and Susan Gaylord and Charley Hendrix listened eagerly while the Mayor explained the situation.

Kirkpatrick's voice over the phone held a serious note. "I've seen about it in the papers, Mayor Gaylord, and you have my earnest sympathy. If there is anything I can do, please feel free to call on me. Have you anything in particular in mind?"

197

"Yes, Kirkpatrick. It has been suggested to me that there is a certain person who is best equipped to handle a situation like this. Perhaps you know of whom I am thinking."

There was a significant pause at the other end. Then: "You mean—"

"I mean the *Spider*."

"Why do you mention the name to me?"

"We need the *Spider* here, Kirkpatrick. If there is any way that we can get in touch with him, beg him to give us his assistance—"

"I'd like to help you, Gaylord, but what makes you think that I have access to the *Spider?*"

"Nothing, nothing," Gaylord said hastily. "But if you should have the opportunity of communicating with him, I wish you would tell him that we need him."

"I'll bear it in mind, Mr. Gaylord," Kirkpatrick replied. "Perhaps the opportunity will arise."

They were fencing with each other, Gaylord eager to emphasize the need for the *Spider,* Kirkpatrick wary of committing himself.

Gaylord said: "The situation is much worse than you can guess, Kirkpatrick. If the *Spider*—"

He broke off as the sudden shattering of glass drowned out his voice. He raised his eyes, and uttered a shout of surprise. A huge fist had smashed through the window in the opposite wall. And now that fist smashed again and again at the jagged pieces of broken glass in the window pane, clearing the opening. Susan uttered a shriek, and Charley Hendrix swung around, amazed.

A terrifying figure appeared in the window, threw

198

one leg over then the other, and vaulted into the room. The man was naked to the waist, with a square, brutish face and a close-cropped shock of black hair. His lips were drawn back from his teeth in a vicious snarl. He stood in a half crouch, glaring at the three.

Gaylord gripped the phone tight, and his lips uttered the words: "Big Harry!"

The man who had broken into the room was Big Harry Silvestro, the fugitive foreman of Number Three open hearth shop.

Silvestro's red-rimmed eyes moved from Gaylord to Charley Hendrix, then settled on Susan Gaylord. He began to advance slowly toward her, his long, prehensile arms reaching out for the shrinking girl. Susan uttered shriek after shriek, and backed away, her eyes fixed on the huge, brutish man in terrified fascination.

Charley Hendrix shouted: "Get away from her, you!" He reached frantically into his back pocket, brought out a small revolver.

But before he could raise it, Big Harry Silvestro uttered a growl of rage, swung around, and smashed a huge fist into Charley's face. Charley Hendrix was sent flying backward, to crumple in a heap in the corner, the revolver dropping from his nerveless fingers. He tried to get up, but slumped back, shaking his head, and groping on the floor for the gun.

Big Harry paid the boy no more attention, nor did he look at Gaylord. But he made straight for Susan, reached out and caught her by the shoulder just as she was turning to flee. Susan kicked, clawed and

199

scratched, but Big Harry only laughed, raising her off her feet as if she had been but a paper doll. He swung her over his shoulder, and turned back toward the window.

Mayor Gaylord sprang up from his desk, raced around to stop him. "My daughter! Susan!" he shouted, and threw himself in Silvestro's path.

Big Harry only laughed again, swung his left arm in a vicious backhanded blow that caught Mayor Gaylord full in the face, sent him staggering backward hopelessly. Big Harry dashed for the window, with Susan's screams ringing in his ears, and with Susan's little nails clawing at his naked back, digging deep furrows in his skin. But Silvestro did not seem to mind, or even to feel those nails. He threw a leg over the window-sill, just as Charley Hendrix succeeded in picking up his revolver.

Charley's nose was bleeding from the blow that Silvestro had landed, but he managed to raise the gun, aiming it carefully. He was afraid of hitting Susan, so he sighted low for Big Harry's legs. As he was about to pull the trigger, Mayor Gaylord scrambled to his feet, shouting with rage, and leaped toward Big Harry, moving directly in the line of fire. As Charley Hendrix held his finger from the trigger, Gaylord leaped at Silvestro.

Big Harry kicked back with his right foot, caught Gaylord in the stomach and sent him crashing back. In a moment he had leaped over the window and disappeared with Susan.

The two men floundered after him, Gaylord sickened by the force of the blow at his stomach, and Charley Hendrix still dazed. They could hear Susan's screams dying into the night, but when they reached the window there was no one in sight. Big Harry Silvestro had disappeared with Susan Gaylord.

On the desk lay the telephone instrument which Gaylord had dropped. He staggered back toward the desk, gasping: "They've got Susan! Charley, they've got Susan!"

He was about to reach for the phone again, when Charley Hendrix exclaimed: "Look at this, sir!"

He was picking up a slip of paper from the floor. Gaylord straightened with an effort, holding his hand at his stomach, and stepped over to read the paper over Charley's shoulder. It was printed crudely in pencil, and it read as follows:

MISTER MAYOR—WE HAVE YOUR DAUGHTER, AND YOU KNOW HOW MUCH A LIFE MEANS TO US. YOU BETTER DO WHAT WE WANT, OR SUSAN TAKES THE RAP. YOU LAY OFF CALLING THE GOVERNOR. NO MARSHALL LAW IN THIS TOWN. ALSO, YOU LAY OFF CALLING FOR HELP FROM OUTSIDE. NO PRIVATE DETECTIVES, NO SPECIAL INVESTIGATORS. YOU'RE TAKING ORDERS FROM US NOW, UNLESS YOU WOULD LIKE TO HAVE YOUR DAUGHTER'S NOSE DELIVERED TO YOU ALL WRAPPED UP IN A NICE BLOODY PIECE OF PAPER. HAVE YOU EVER SEEN A PRETTY GIRL WITH HER NOSE CUT OFF? SHE ISN'T PRETTY ANY MORE.

There was no signature to the note, but a curious, rough drawing was appended at the bottom. It was a picture of a fool's scepter with the curved staff ending in an upright portion that was capped with the face of a clown or jester of the fifteenth century. It was the typical staff which the king's jesters of medieval times had been accustomed to carry; with this different—that the face of the jester was far from a foolish or silly one. The picture had been drawn with great skill and cunning, and the face was replete with evil. The mouth of the clown seemed to have been slit across into the cheeks, and the face was a gargoyle of ugliness.

There was only that fool's bauble to serve as a signature. But it was revolting enough, and even more terrifying because of the fact that no name was signed to the note.

Charley Hendrix turned and looked with dawning terror at the Mayor. "Mr. Gaylord! Only a madman could have written this. We must save Susan!"

Gaylord laughed harshly. "That fool's bauble explained a good deal. The man who wrote it wants to show us that he is dealing with madmen, with fools, with idiots. That Harry Silvestro—he was a quiet, hard-working man. Look at him now!" Weakly, Mayor Gaylord staggered toward the desk. "No detectives, no investigators. That means no *Spider*."

He picked up the phone, said: "Hello, Kirkpatrick. Are you there yet?"

"Yes, yes, man. What's happened? What's been going on there?"

Gaylord hesitated, glanced across at Charley Hendrix. Charley Hendrix leaned over the desk, whis-

202

pered: "For God's sake, tell him never mind. We dare not send for the *Spider* now!"

Gaylord nodded, then forced a laugh. "It was nothing, Kirkpatrick. Say, don't bother about the *Spider*. I've—changed my mind. We don't want him here. You understand?"

"I think I understand," Kirkpatrick's voice came slowly over the phone. "Say nothing more about it, old man. If I can be of help in the future, call me."

Gaylord said: "Thank you," and hung up. His shoulders sagged helplessly as he stared across the desk at Charley Hendrix. "We'll—have to toe the mark, Charley, until we get Susan back."

When Richard Gaylord, the Mayor of Keystone, hung up the telephone in his room, the click of the instrument travelled over a thousand miles of telephone line to the office of Stanley Kirkpatrick, Commissioner of Police of the City of New York. Kirkpatrick hung up his instrument, and stared solemnly across his desk at the faultlessly attired man who sat facing him.

This man had sat silently throughout Kirkpatrick's conversation with Gaylord. His attitude and bearing bespoke poise, culture, and great physical as well as mental powers. Throughout the telephone conversation he had maintained a well-bred air of disinterest while Kirkpatrick was talking to Gaylord. The deep-set keen blue eyes were everywhere except upon Kirkpatrick, and he seemed to have no concern with what the Commissioner was saying.

When Kirkpatrick hung up, the visitor lit a cigarette nonchalantly. Kirkpatrick said: "This will interest you, Dick."

The visitor raised his eyebrows. "Interest me?"

Kirkpatrick grinned sourly. He said with elaborate sarcasm: "I beg your pardon, Mr. Richard Wentworth, sportsman and adventurer. Of course, the well-known Mr. Richard Wentworth wouldn't be interested in ordinary police matters, would he?"

Wentworth returned his smile. "Why not, Kirk? Everything in this exciting life of ours interests me. I heard you mention the *Spider* on the phone—couldn't help hearing it, old chap. Was it something in connection with the *Spider?*"

"It's about that business over at the Keystone Mills, Dick. That was Mayor Gaylord of Keystone on the wire. He called up to ask me to get in touch with the *Spider* for him. He said he wanted the *Spider* to come to Keystone." Kirkpatrick threw his visitor a queer glance. "Peculiar, isn't it, that he should think I could get in touch with the *Spider?*"

Wentworth shrugged indifferently. "Can you?"

"What do you think, Dick?" Kirkpatrick asked softly.

"Well, I don't know," Wentworth told him carefully. "The consensus of opinion seems to be that you have some sort of connection with the *Spider*. I wouldn't be surprised if the *Spider* is a good friend of yours."

"If he is," Kirkpatrick replied, "I'd be doing him a good turn by sending him to Keystone. I think he'd find the excitement that he seems to crave. Mayor Gaylord had just finished asking me to get in touch with the *Spider*, when suddenly there seemed to be

204

some sort of interruption at the other end. He must have dropped the receiver for awhile, and when he came back on the line, his mood had changed entirely. He doesn't want the *Spider* any more. In fact, he asked me to forget all about his request.''

Richard Wentworth seemed to be lost in deep abstraction. "Now that's queer, isn't it, Kirk? I wonder what could have happened to change his mind that fast?''

"I think,'' Kirkpatrick said very slowly, his eyes fixed upon Wentworth, "that the *Spider* would do well to go out to Keystone anyway.''

Wentworth arose from his chair, and picked his hat, cane and gloves off the Commissioner's desk. "No doubt you're right,'' he said casually. Then he added as if it were an afterthought: "Oh, by the way, Kirk. I forgot to mention it before. I am leaving on a little trip today. Probably be away for a week or two. So don't look for me at the club.''

Kirkpatrick restrained a smile. "Rather sudden, isn't it?'' he asked dryly. "Have you decided where you're going?''

"Oh, I thought I'd take a little trip out—er—out west. Just look around the country, so to speak.''

"Out west, eh? Not going in the direction of Keystone, by any chance?''

"Keystone? Oh, yes, that's the town you just mentioned, isn't it? Well, I'll leave Keystone to the *Spider*. Good-bye, Kirk. I'll be seeing you in a couple of weeks.''

He extended his hand, and the Commissioner grasped it warmly. "Good-bye, Dick—and be careful.''

Wentworth hesitated for a moment as if he had

something else to say. Kirkpatrick looked at him quizzically.

"You have something else on your mind, Dick?"

"Er—yes, Kirk. It is about Nita Van Sloan.* She'll be wanting to know where I have gone. Of course, if she should ask you, you don't know, do you?"

Kirkpatrick smiled. "Well, you haven't really told me where you are going, have you?"

Wentworth returned his smile. "You see, Kirk, I'd hate to have anything happen to Nita. When she hears I have left she will, no doubt, be around trying to wheedle out of you some information as to where I can be found. I'd hate to have you making guesses—"

"Such as—Keystone?"

Wentworth's poker face betrayed nothing.

Kirkpatrick laughed good-humoredly, clapped a hand on his visitor's shoulder.

"Don't worry, Dick. I'll do my best to say nothing if she should come here. But you know Nita. It's hard to resist her."

"Well, Kirk, do your best."

Kirkpatrick watched Richard Wentworth's broad back through the doorway. As the door closed behind his visitor, a smile of warm friendship lit the Com-

---

*AUTHOR'S NOTE: Nita Van Sloan, whom Wentworth mentions here, will appear later in the story, where her relation to Wentworth will be more fully explained. To the readers of these chronicles she is no stranger, and those who have met her before will understand Richard Wentworth's love for her.

missioner's face. "The best of luck to you—*Spider!*" he said almost in a whisper.

Between those two men there was a rare friendship—also an unspoken secret. If Commissioner Stanley Kirkpatrick suspected that his friend, Richard Wentworth, was in reality the *Spider,* he never uttered that suspicion. For it would mean that he would have to place his friend under arrest.

As Police Commissioner of the City of New York, he was sworn to uphold the law; and it was a matter of common knowledge that the mysterious being who was known as the *Spider* flagrantly flaunted the law in his unconventional campaign against crime. There had been many instances when the two blazing guns of the *Spider* had laid low a criminal whom the law could never reach. Nevertheless, Kirkpatrick was pledged to bend every energy to arrest and prosecute the *Spider.*

What he would do if he were ever confronted with the definite proof that Richard Wentworth and the *Spider* were one and the same man, Stanley Kirkpatrick dreaded to say. But he was morally certain that the *Spider* would be in Keystone within twenty-four hours. . . .

CHAPTER THREE

"You Bet We'll Fight!"

The south road leading into Keystone was barricaded.

The state police had erected a barbed-wire fence across the highway with a movable portion in the center which could be slid to one side to allow the passage of a single car at a time if necessary. But no cars were being permitted to leave or to enter the town. Troopers were on guard at this gate, as well as at similar points on all other roads leading into the town. Keystone was virtually under quarantine with a cordon of state police thrown all around it.

All shipping on the Keystone River was at a standstill. The sluggish waters of the river, running close alongside the south road, were not barricaded, but a trooper with a sawed-off shotgun stood at the edge of the road where he could command the river. A number of cars were pulled up in the road outside the barricade, and newspaper reporters as well as many curious persons who had come from the neighboring countryside were peering through the gate.

The troopers were constantly on the alert, each carrying a carbine. Several attempts had already been made by the panic-stricken inhabitants to rush the gate and get out of this town in which an epidemic of madness seemed to be spreading. Twice the troopers had been forced to fire over the heads of hysterical mobs. The troopers themselves were careful to keep the townspeople at a respectful distance. They had seen the effect of the epidemic on people who had been stricken, and they had no wish to be caught by the dreadful malady.

At intervals, the sound of shooting and mob fighting had come to them from the heart of the city. They knew that matters were coming to a crisis in Keystone, and they were prepared for trouble.

The crowd in the road outside the barricade parted to make way for a small coupé that approached slowly from the south. The coupé stopped at the barricade, and the driver slid from behind the wheel, just as the sergeant in charge of the state troopers came toward him, frowning.

The man leaving the coupé was tall, athletically built, with broad shoulders and trim waist. He appeared to be in his early fifties, with graying hair at the temples, and subtle lines of weariness around the mouth. If Stanley Kirkpatrick, Police Commissioner of New York, had been here at this moment, not even he would have recognized in this middle-aged, dignified person the Richard Wentworth who had been in his office on the previous day. Careful make-up had removed every characteristic of personality from Wentworth's face. Cunning patches of gray hair at the temples, the judicious use of pigment and facial cream had transformed Wentworth's appearance.

The crowd at the gate watched while the sergeant said gruffly: "You can't come in here. The town is under quarantine. Turn that car around—"

He stopped as Wentworth raised a hand. "I am aware of the fact that Keystone is under quarantine. Nevertheless, I wish to enter." Wentworth extracted a card case from his pocket, and handed the trooper a card. The card, which had been printed only last night, read: *Dr. Elias Benson.*

"I am a diagnostician," said the bogus Dr. Elias Benson. "I have come here to study this disease which is scourging the city. Your Mayor Gaylord has no doubt given you instructions—"

"That's right," the sergeant said. He gave Wentworth a queer look. "It's your funeral, Doc. Go ahead. But I'll say you got plenty of guts, goin' in there."

Wentworth managed to look puzzled. "Guts?"

The sergeant nodded. "They had two diagnosticians here this week. Both of them went mad. They got caught by the disease themselves." He extended a hand. "My name is Murphy. Sergeant Jerome Murphy. I want to shake hands with you, Doctor. You're a braver man than I am. I'd never go in that town of my own free will!"

Wentworth smiled, accepted the trooper's hand. "A physician must never consider such things. How-

210

ever, I appreciate the compliment, Sergeant. And now, if you will open the gate—"

"Sure thing, Doc."

Wentworth got back into the car, and the Sergeant gave the word to his men. The gate was swung open, and Richard Wentworth, alias Dr. Elias Benson, alias the *Spider*, drove through the barricade and down the steep hill into the town of Keystone. He had worked fast since last night. He had created the personality of Dr. Benson, and wired to Keystone in that name, and had secured Gaylord's permission to enter the city for an attempt to diagnose the disease which was spreading like wildfire in Keystone, and driving the inhabitants to homicidal mania.

As he drove down into the heart of the city, he could look to his left across the Keystone River and the mill district. He frowned as he saw that the blast furnaces were all working as usual, and that all the shops seemed to be in full operation. He had heard that Mayor Gaylord had ordered the closing of the entire plant. The move had seemed a wise one, and Wentworth could not understand why the shops were once more reopened.

There were dozens of barges in the river, unloading iron ore, coal, oil and other supplies onto docks close to the railroad siding, on the opposite shore. Here and there a tugboat lay idle in the center of the stream. It was apparent to Wentworth that the mills could not long continue to function, for no new supplies were entering the town. These barges must have come in before the cordon of troopers was laid down.

At each of the small bridges spanning the river, he could see a city policeman on guard. The stores along Main Street were open for business, but the sidewalks were almost entirely deserted. On this side of the river, the inhabitants of the town were keeping close to their homes. Lights were appearing as Wentworth drove along, for night was rapidly descending over the valley.

Richard Wentworth drove down Main Street until he reached the corner of Broad. At his right was the handsome City Hall building, and beyond it, on the opposite side of the street, was the Keystone General Hospital where the victims of this strange disease were being treated. But Wentworth did not go either to the hospital or to the City Hall building. Instead, he turned left on Broad Street and drove over the bridge into the factory section.

The policeman on guard did not stop him. Apparently the man was merely there as a precaution against mob rioters passing over into the residential section.

Once across the bridge, the entire atmosphere of the town changed. Hoarse shouts rose into the night, and here and there Wentworth could see small groups of policemen disbursing crowds of workers with swinging night clubs. Stores were all closed here, and the windows boarded up.

The open hearth shops, where the greatest disorders had occurred, were in full operation. Here he noted barbed-wire fence that had been erected around the entire plant. A detail of private company police stood guard. Other policemen patrolled the streets around the plant, dispersing any groups which attempted to form.

At one corner a little further on, a crowd of workers and their wives stood around a soap box orator whose frenzied words reached Wentworth.

"I tell you, men and women, it's suicide to stay in this town. Every mother's son of you will go mad eventually. There's a plague in this town. They're keeping us here because they want the shops worked. When it comes your turn to go on the next shift, you'll go in those shops, and some of you will be stricken. Why should you go in there and take that chance for the measly pay that the company gives you? Stay out, I tell you. What if the company loses its contract with the Government? What do we care? Should we lay down our lives so that the company can fulfill its contract? I say no!"

Wentworth did not stop, but drove on past the open hearth shops, then made a right turn.

He knew this town almost as well as did the residents. Some years ago he had been here and had done a signal service to the city. The mill workers all knew that the *Spider* had saved them from a serious menace at that time. And though they also knew the *Spider* was outside the law, Wentworth felt he could still command their respect and confidence. He was going to put that feeling of his to the test tonight.

He stopped the coupé before a two-story building which directly faced a vacant lot on the opposite side of the street. Across that lot could be seen the barbed-wire fence around the company plant, as well as the gate at which the police stood guard.

Wentworth's glance travelled across to the building. The ground floor was dark. The second story was brilliantly lit. A plate-glass window extended across its entire width. Light streamed through his window, illuminating the lettering upon the glass, which read as follows:

STEEL WORKERS
INTERNATIONAL UNION

Down below, in the lower left hand corner was the additional wording:

MICHAEL FOLEY, PRES.

Wentworth nodded in satisfaction. He could see men moving about up there in the lighted rooms. He had come at an opportune time. A meeting of the Steel Workers Union was in progress for some reason. Having acquainted himself thoroughly with all the events that had taken place in Keystone since the beginning of this terror, he knew that Mike Foley was the crane operator who had been in the same shop with Harry Silvestro. He knew Foley very well, knew that the man had been thoroughly honest when he had last met him; also that Foley wielded great influence with the field workers not only due to his position as president of the local union, but also because of his personality, and his reputation for integrity.

Men were hurrying through the streets toward the entrance of the union building. Apparently the meeting was either in progress or about to open.

214

Wentworth knelt down on the floor board before the front seat, and took a small, flat leather case from his pocket. He opened this, revealing a mirror in the cupboard. Within the case itslef rested tubes of pigments and facial cream, as well as small aluminum plates for changing the shape of the nose, and other accessories for use in disguise.

Wentworth rested the mirror of the case against the back of the seat, and proceeded to make swift use of the pigment. His nimble fingers moved over his own face with the skill and accuracy of an artist. Slowly the features of Dr. Elias Benson disappeared, giving place to a sallow complexion, discolored teeth, and lined, ugly cheeks. The face that finally peered back out of Wentworth's mirror was a face which was known and feared throughout the underworld of America—the face of that mysterious, as yet unidentified person who was known as the *Spider*.

Satisfied with his work, Wentworth closed the make-up case and replaced it in his pocket. Then he got out of the car, went around to the luggage compartment, and opened it with his key. Within this compartment was a large packing case that almost filled it. The cover of the case was off, and a casual observer would have been startled to see that it was full to the top with blued-steel automatic pistols and with boxes of cartridges.

Wentworth drew from a recess of the compartment, a long cape and a black hat. He locked the luggage compartment once more, threw his own hat in the car, and donned the cape and hat. The tall, athletic figure of Dr. Elias Benson had disappeared.

A twisted, stooping figure crouched in the night alongside the car. This was the figure of the *Spider*. Many criminals had looked at that twisted shape, and had screamed their terror aloud. For where the *Spider* walked his misshapen way, criminals died.

That mysterious figure moved slowly across the street, almost blending with the night. No spot of color showed, not even the white face under that broad-brimmed hat. Black melted with night, and hurrying men were unaware that the *Spider* was passing.

The *Spider* crossed the street, faded into an alley alongside the union building. He moved sure-footedly, soundlessly, toward the rear, and found the narrow side entrance which he knew to be there. The door was locked, but a moment's manipulation with a set of pass-keys opened it, and the *Spider* faded into the corridor within.

He climbed the narrow, rickety stairs to the upper floor. Ordinarily, those stairs creaked and groaned when anyone ascended them. But the *Spider* made no sound. At the top, he found himself on a small landing before a thin, wooden door. The door was unlocked, and he silently twisted the knob, opened it a fraction of an inch.

This was the huge union meeting room. It was illuminated brightly, and the *Spider* could see rows and rows of chairs upon which sat the steel workers. They were facing this small door, which was at the left of the speaker's platform. Peering through the crack, the *Spider* saw the platform, with Mike Foley standing at the speaker's table and addressing the gathering. Behind Foley were seated four other men, apparently also officials of the union. Foley's voice was powerful, and carried ringingly through every corner of the auditorium. It was plainly audible to the man behind the door.

"Men," Foley was saying, "you all know the purpose of this meeting. Certain members of the union have demanded that we call a general strike until the epidemic of madness in this city is wiped out. Our men are dying not only from the epidemic, but they have been massacred in cold blood by a small army of murderers that are holed up somewhere in town. Every day more of our men go mad in the shops. Every day there are new attacks upon us. Only this afternoon that gang of murderers appeared again, and shot down forty men and women on Fleet Street in the South End. We are told that we are being given full police protection; but we are being slaughtered just the same. And we are unarmed, unable to defend ourselves.

"Men, I haven't got the slightest idea of what is happening. I don't know who it is that's driving our men mad, and I don't know who it is that controls this band of thugs that comes out every night to slaughter us. But I do say that we're not going to stand for it any longer!"

Foley's voice was almost drowned by the enthusiastic shouts of the hundreds of men who were packed into the meeting room. "You said it, Foley! We won't stand for it. We want to get out of this town. Close the plant! Stop work!"

These and a hundred other sentiments were expressed vociferously, at the top of their lungs, by the assembled men.

Foley raised his hand for silence, and gradually the shouting died down.

"Men," he went on, "if the five thousand workers in the steel mills of this city were to march out of town, the troopers would never be able to stop us. We have a right to protect ourselves. We have a right to get out of a place like this. We—"

Once more his voice was drowned by the shouts of acclamation. He waited until they were through shouting, then continued to talk.

"Before we take a vote, men, it's only fair that we should listen to the other side of the story. For that reason, I have invited Mr. Jonathan Spencer, the General Manager of the Keystone Steel & Iron Corporation, to come here tonight and speak to you. Let him give you his side of the story. Then we'll take a vote."

The *Spider* crouched silently behind the door while Mike Foley motioned to one of the men seated on the platform behind him. Jonathan Spencer arose. He was attired in a frock coat, and his bow tie was carefully tied. He bowed coldly to Mike Foley, then stepped forward to the speaker's desk, glared out over the heads of the audience.

The men in the room began to heckle him, shouting: "It's old Money-mad himself. He don't care if we die or not. He wants his mills to work. Don't listen to him!"

Other men in the audience cried out: "Give him

218

a chance. Let him talk. We'll hear his side of the story, anyway!''

Spencer stood there, tall and uncompromising, until the noise and the shouting had died down. A slight sneer of contempt twisted his lips out of shape.

''You men are all fools!'' he began. ''Don't you see that there is a conspiracy afoot to put our company out of business? These hoodlums who have been slaughtering you, and this epidemic that is spreading through the city, are all part of a deep-laid plot. Are you going to let yourselves be licked? Are you gong to let yourselves be driven out of a job by a bunch of hoodlums led by a canny criminal? We are quarantined here in the city. As long as you must stay, why not work? I am sharing your risk and your perils. I'm in the plant every day, and I don't ask any man to take a risk that I won't take myself. We're working on a huge contract for the Government—''

He was interrupted by jeering shouts from the audience. ''That's right, it's his contract. His contract is all he cares about. To hell with him. Let's give him the bum's rush!''

Chairs toppled over in the auditorium as the great body of men arose almost with concerted action, and began to rush toward the platform. Spencer had always been disliked as a hard task-master. Now the spleen of the working men was being given a chance to express itself.

Mike Foley shouted: ''Stop! Stand back! Give him a chance—''

Foley's voice was drowned by the excited shouts of the aroused workers. They began clambering up

219

on the platform, and clutching, grimy hands reached for Spencer. The General Manager stepped backward involuntarily, his face blanching at the raw hatred which he saw in the faces of the men who were attacking him. In a moment those men would have their hands on Spencer, and there was no telling what they would do to him in their present state of mind.

Foley tried to stop them, but he was thrust aside as if he had been a child. Men mounted to the platform, while Spencer backed away, reaching for one of the vacant chairs with which to protect himself.

And suddenly a strange, blood-curdling sound echoed through the room—a sound that caused all those men to stand as if petrified. It was the sound of a man's laughter; but such weird hilarity as might have been expressed by some robust god of the pagans upon viewing the antics of the silly little human beings upon this earth. It was laughter that reached into the marrow of men's bones, and froze it.

Involuntarily, all eyes swung toward the little door alongside the platform, from which the strange laughter had come. The door was now swinging wide open, and in the entrance stood the twisted, ugly, caped figure of a man whom many of them recalled having seen once before.

An awed whisper went up from those men in the room. "The *Spider!* It's the *Spider!*"

Slowly, Jonathan Spencer put down the chair which he had raised to defend himself with. Slowly, the rage died in the faces of the steel workers, and they backed quietly down from the platform.

Mike Foley exclaimed under his breath: "Thank God!"

The *Spider's* weird laughter ceased as suddenly as it had begun. And now, as the echoes of his hilarity died away among the rafters, the place grew suddenly quiet—except for the labored, excited breathing of the close-packed mass of men who watched him tautly.

The *Spider's* glowing eyes under the low-turned brim of his hat seemed to be everywhere at once. His cape bellowed out behind him as he leaped lithely up to the platform, and stood half-turned so as to face the audience though he did not expose his back to Spencer, Foley, or any of the other seated men. His voice rang with a note of steely authority.

"Men of Keystone! Many of you remember me. It seems that I have come in time to save you from an act of folly. Jonathan Spencer is right. Everything that has happened here points to a plot against the steel company. By calling a general strike, you are playing into the hands of the plotters. You must not do that. You must fight back."

A man in the audience laughed harshly. "That ain't the *Spider;* that's just one of Spencer's detectives dressed up to look like him. They figure we'll listen to the *Spider*. But they can't put that over on us—"

The man paused, as the *Spider* raised a hand. "I expected you would doubt my identity. I will prove to you who I am!"

He motioned with his hand. "Mike Foley! Come here. Come close to me."

Foley glanced hesitantly at the massed men in the auditorium, then at Jonathan Spencer and the other speakers on the platform. He shrugged, then advanced until he was standing close to the *Spider*. He gazed deep into the glowing eyes of the caped man.

The *Spider's* voice dropped so low that only the union president could hear. "You remember when the *Spider* was here last?"

Foley nodded wordlessly.

"Is there a way that you could identify the *Spider* again?"

Foley gulped. "Yes," he said. "There is a way."

"What is it?"

Foley grinned knowingly. "*You* tell *me*."

The *Spider* nodded, apparently satisfied. "You remember when I shot the two men who were trying to knife you down at the waterfront?"

"I do."

"You remember the mark I placed upon their foreheads?"

"Yes. It was a little seal. Then we both left the building, to escape the fire. Those two bodies were burned, charred to cinders. That mark was never discovered on their foreheads."

"If you saw that mark again would you recall it?"

"I would."

"Then stretch out your hand, palm down," the *Spider* ordered.

Foley complied.

The *Spider's* hands moved so nimbly that it was difficult for any one of those who were watching them closely to see exactly what he did. From his pocket he had extracted a small cigarette lighter. He

222

slipped open the bottom of this, pressed it against the back of Foley's out-stretched hand, then with a motion so swift that it defied the eye, he returned the cigarette lighter to his pocket.

Foley was left there, staring with mouth agape at the small, blood-red replica of a spider which had been imprinted on the back of his hand.

"That—that's the mark of the *Spider!* That's the mark you left on those men's foreheads!"

"Now do you believe?" the *Spider* asked softly.

Foley nodded. "I—believe!"

He swung about, facing the audience of gaping steel workers. "Men!" he shouted. "This is really the *Spider*. I vouch for him."

There was a dull murmur among the men. They believed Foley implicitly. In addition, they had heard the *Spider* advocating a course of action directly contrary to that which Foley had advocated. If Foley identified the *Spider,* then it must be so.

The *Spider* stepped past Foley and addressed the crowd in a strong, authoritative voice. "Foley has identified me. I think you men will admit that the *Spider* is your friend—"

It was apparent that the men in the audience took Foley's word. A subtle change had come over them. There were many places in the United States where the *Spider* would be shot at sight by the law enforcement officers if he were spotted. But in the town of Keystone, the *Spider* was known as a benefactor. Still, there were doubts in the minds of some of them.

The man who had interrupted now broke in again. "You want us to fight, *Spider*. What will we fight with? Gaylord won't even give us weapons. We can't fight those criminals with our bare hands—"

The *Spider* stopped him. "If you had weapons, friend," he asked slowly, "would you fight?"

"Would we! You bet we'd fight! Give us a chance at those guys—"

"Then you shall have weapons!" the *Spider* exclaimed. "Follow me!"

He swung around, took the amazed Jonathan Spencer by the arm, led him off the platform and out through the rear door.

CHAPTER FOUR

Silvestro Fights

The men all stared at one another in puzzlement, then Mike Foley shouted to them: "Let's go! What are we waiting for? The *Spider* is with us!"

With a shout they all trooped out after Mike Foley.

On the way down the stairs, the *Spider* was whispering to Jonathan Spencer. "Those men might have killed you, if I hadn't intervened. You were foolish to try to talk to them."

"But I had to keep the shops going!" Spencer told him fiercely. "The company has millions of dollars at stake. We can't afford to have them go on strike—"

"I don't agree with you," the *Spider* said coldly. "The lives of these men are more important than your company's contract. But at present it suits my purpose to have them continue to work for another day or so. Thus far, I have played into your hands, Spencer. But I give you warning that when I order the men to leave your shop, *you are not to interfere!"*

They were outside now, and Spencer glared at his caped companion. "By God, *Spider,* your tone is too high-handed for me, I'll not close down the shops for any man!"

The *Spider's* hand gripped Spencer's arm so tightly that the General Manager winced. "You'll close them, Spencer—when I give the word. Now leave us. Get back to your office."

Spencer opened his mouth to speak, then seemed to think better of it, and turned away silently, hurried down the street without looking back.

The *Spider* crossed the street swiftly to his coupé, opened the luggage compartment once more, and waited for Foley and the steel workers to gather around him. Then he pointed at the packing case.

"Help yourselves, men," he told them. "There are your weapons!"

With exclamations of joy, Mike Foley and several of the men dragged the packing case out of the car onto the ground, and began to hand out automatics and ammunition.

The *Spider* watched them without a word. Back in New York the previous night, he had looted the warehouse of an exporting firm which was violating the Government Neutrality Act by shipping arms and ammunition to a warring country in Europe. These guns would be put to a far better use tonight than the exporters had originally intended for them.

The men busily loaded their guns, admiring them, commenting about them with the pleasure of children. Mike Foley came up to Wentworth, said: "*Spi-*

226

der, we're taking orders from you. From now on, you're the boss—''

He got no further than that. His voice was lost in the sudden staccato racket of gunfire coming across the empty lot from the direction of the Keystone Steel Company plant. The sound of machine guns and pistol fire rolled through the night with startling abruptness.

The *Spider* was the first to sense what was happening. "The plant is being attacked!" he shouted. "Follow me, men!"

He swung about, and shot off at a long, easy lope across the empty lot. Mike Foley raced at his side, and the steel workers came after them, frantically jamming clips into their new automatics.

As the *Spider* came out into the street on the other side of the empty lot, he got a full view of what was happening at the gate in the barbed-wire fence around the company plant.

That same ugly crew of desperadoes who had terrorized the city, slaughtering unarmed steel workers, were now attacking the guard at the gate. But now, instead of revolvers, they were using sub-machine guns. In the forefront of the criminals the *Spider* saw the huge, ungainly figure of Big Harry Silvestro. The desperadoes were firing with cold deadliness at the guard of patrolmen in front of the gate, which had just been opened to allow a truck to pass through.

Apparently the attack had been planned for just this moment. Half of the police were down, and the other half were returning the fire of the criminals desperately. The air was filled with the staccato barrage of the machine guns, mingled with the deep-

227

throated roaring of heavy thirty-eights and forty-fives. The screams of men echoed above the gunfire.

The *Spider* did not wait to see whether he was being followed by his men. He raced swiftly toward the scene of action, and his two hands crossed in front of his chest, came out each gripping one of his deadly automatics. His two guns began to spit fire while he was still running, and criminals wielding machine guns dropped before his uncannily accurate aim. Behind him Mike Foley began firing, as well as those of the other men who were in range.

The criminals were taken utterly by surprise. They had expected to be opposed only by the handful of guards at the gate, who would be mowed down by the first few blasts of machine-gun fire. Then, apparently, they had expected a clear entrance into the company's plant where they could work as much damage as they pleased.

With the sudden attack of the determined steel workers under the leadership of the *Spider,* they were thrown into confusion. These men were brave when the odds were in their favor. Now the odds were against them, and after half a dozen of them had dropped before the barrage from the *Spider* and his men, they uttered shrieks of terror and turned to flee into the night.

Big Harry Silvestro screamed at them, lashed at them with his fists to halt their panicky flight. But he could not prevail against their fear of bullets. In a moment the street was empty of desperadoes, except for those who had been felled by the new automatics of the steel workers. Big Harry turned,

228

saw the advancing, menacing mass of workers, uttered a mad cry of rage, and leaped across the street, disappeared into an alley. The steel workers had hurried to the assistance of the police, and the *Spider* heard Mike Foley exclaim: "That's Big Harry Silvestro!"

The *Spider* shouted to Foley: "Take charge here. Place a man at the telephone in union headquarters, to await my orders. I'll be back!"

With those parting words, the *Spider* launched himself in pursuit of the fleeing Harry Silvestro. If he could capture Big Harry, there might be an opportunity for him to dig to the bottom of this conspiracy. He did not know whether Big Harry was acting under the influence of the disease which had stricken him, or whether he was a willing tool of the chief of this conspiracy. But whatever he was, he was a tangible lead, a possible avenue leading to the answer to a riddle of these massacres.

The *Spider* swung into the alley down which Silvestro had disappeared, and glimpsed the huge man's ungainly form twisting around a far corner. Wentworth sped after him, pursuing the man in silence. Silvestro glanced behind, saw the flowing cape and the wide hat, and seemed to be stricken with an access of panic. He sprinted forward, swung around another corner; but the *Spider* kept doggedly at his heels, gaining upon him.

If Silvestro hoped to outdistance the *Spider,* he was doomed to disappointment. There were few racers who had ever been able to beat Richard Wentworth at intercollegiate track meets in Wentworth's college days. And throughout the years that followed those college days, Wentworth had kept himself in top form.

Silvestro was heading toward the river front. The pursuit was carrying both men out through the mud flats. Wentworth could easily shoot Silvestro now, but he refrained. He wanted the man alive.

Silvestro reached the railroad siding. But instead of crossing into the dingy mud flats, he doubled back upon his own trail as if he had changed his mind, angling northward. They were in the open now, and Wentworth was gaining on Silvestro.

Big Harry stopped short, swung around suddenly, and raised his hand. He had a gun, and was pointing it directly at the *Spider*. His square, uncouth face was twisted into a hideous mask of rage as he fired three times in quick succession.

Wentworth zigzagged, still running toward Silvestro, with his cape billowing out behind him. In the darkness he was an uncertain mark. All three of Silvestro's slugs tugged at the *Spider's* cape, leaving three ragged holes. But the *Spider* was untouched.

His gun apparently empty, Silvestro uttered a scream of terror as he saw that the *Spider* was still unhurt. He drew back his arm, hurled the empty gun, but it went wide. The *Spider* continued to race toward his quarry. Big Harry, lost in panic, swung around, raced in a straight line across the railroad siding toward the mud flats.

The chase pointed to the group of houses where the desperadoes had lived. The *Spider* made ready to draw his gun if assistance appeared for Silvestro. But there was no sign of life among the dilapidated shacks. They passed half a dozen of them, and then Silvestro ducked into one of them, no more than a one-room shanty with a sloping roof, where a dim light burned.

The *Spider* saw the shanty door slam shut, hurled his body against the door, and sent it crashing inward. Ripping from its rickety hinges, it fell to one side. The *Spider* landed on hands and knees, blinked at the light of a guttering candle, and leaped lithely to his feet, just as Big Harry Silvestro rushed at him with both huge hands flailing.

Wentworth's face twisted into a grim smile. This was what he wanted. He could whip Silvestro into submission in a hand to hand fight; and he felt confident that if Silvestro were whipped, the man would talk.

He blocked Silvestro's blows with little difficulty, circling with superb footwork. Silvestro followed him, frantic with fury, seeking to land a single blow that would knock out his opponent.

But the *Spider* never was there for Silvestro's fist. Always that evasive figure danced out of reach or sidestepped, and each time Silvestro missed, his shadow landed a telling blow against the huge man's face. Each crash of the *Spider's* fist sounded like the dull blow of a sledge-hammer on Silvestro's jaw, nose, or cheek-bone. Soon Big Harry's eyes were discolored, his lips were swollen and bleeding. As he fought, the *Spider* noted out of the corner of his eyes an open trap-door in the far corner of the room. He sensed that Silvestro had been trying to maneuver him toward that open trap door, possibly with the intention of hurling him down into it. He deliberately

231

allowed the man to work him over in that direction, then suddenly changed from defensive to offensive tactics. His two fists worked in and out with the deadly efficiency of piston rods, *smacking* with ruthless thoroughness against Silvestro's naked torso. The big man's abdomen became raw and red from the continuous blows, and he suddenly doubled over, unable to stand it.

The *Spider* stepped back, brought his right fist up in a short, hard uppercut to the side of Silvestro's jaw. It rocked the big man's head far back, sent him staggering just past the open trap door, to crash against the far wall. But with all the weight and power that the *Spider* had put behind that blow, he had failed to knock out Big Harry Silvestro. The bloody, begrimed shop foreman leaned against the wall.

Wentworth said: "Give up, Silvestro. You can't win."

Silvestro scowled, said through bleeding, cracked lips: "Vat you vant?"

"I want you to talk. Who made you like this? Who is the boss of these criminals?"

Silvestro snarled. "I no talk nodings!"

"All right," the *Spider* said regretfully. "I'll have to give you some more of the same."

He stepped in, and Silvestro, unable to back away, put up his fists automatically. Once more the *Spider's* hard blows thudded into Silvestro's stomach, and face. The big man was on the defensive now. He tried to cover up ineffectually. In spite of his great weight, in spite of his massive spread of frame and the rippling muscles of his body, he was no match for the *Spider's* skill. Once more a blow sent him reeling into a corner. He almost slid to the floor, with the whole room dancing before his eyes.

And the big man's hands, groping blindly on the floor, suddenly came in contact with cold metal. It was a crow-bar, left on the floor by some workman. Silvestro's face assumed a guarded look of cunning as he felt the weight of the heavy bar.

The *Spider* was saying: "Well, Silvestro, are you ready to—"

With a yell of bestial rage, Silvestro raised the iron crowbar above his head, gripping it with both hands, and jerked to his feet, leaping across the room at the *Spider*.

"I show you!" he shouted, as he brought the iron bar down in a crashing blow toward the *Spider's* unprotected head.

In a fight, the *Spider* could act faster than the average man could think. He had so developed his mental processes and their coordination with the muscular system that the reaction from a brain impulse took place simultaneously with, instead of following, that impulse. A hard life of constant peril had brought this coordination of mind and muscle to the acme of perfection in the *Spider*. The automatic reaction of any man in his position would have been to draw a gun and shoot at the juggernaut of destruction that was leaping at him across the room in the shape of this huge giant wielding the deadly crowbar.

But the *Spider* wanted that man alive. He crouched, then threw himself in a low tackle that caught the leaping giant almost in mid-air, while the crowbar descended with a murderous thud upon the floor at the spot where the *Spider* had been.

The impact of the *Spider's* shoulder against Silvestro's legs sent the giant tumbling to the floor, and the crowbar flew from his hand. Silvestro rolled over and over, toward the table near the wall, upon which stood the single candle that gave light in the room. Silvestro jack-knifed to his feet, and his huge arm swept across the table, hurling the candle to the floor. Its sputtering light was snuffed out.

The shack was plunged into darkness, and the *Spider* crouched, waiting tensely, his ears pitched to catch the slightest sound of motion. He heard Silvestro's labored breathing, heard the man's cautious footfalls on the floor, and prepared to tackle him in the darkness.

But instead of moving toward the door, Silvestro leaped suddenly toward the far corner of the room. In a flash the *Spider* understood what he was doing, and leaped after the man, but he was too late. Silvestro had jumped clear through the trapdoor.

From below came a sound of a dull thud as Silvestro's body landed.

With swift fingers the *Spider* drew his flashlight, sent the beam of light stabbing down through the open trapdoor. He was just in time to glimpse the shambling figure of Silvestro leaping along a dark passageway at the bottom of a ten-foot drop. The *Spider* leaped down unhesitatingly, landed on hands and knees, then scrambled up, sent his light down the corridor in which he found himself.

This was a long passageway which had been cut

234

into the ground underneath the shacks, and it ran east and west. The beam of light outlined Big Harry Silvestro racing around a curve in the passage, and the *Spider* dashed after him. Big Harry's footsteps echoed hollowly through the dark corridor, as they took one turn after another. The sides of this passageway were lined with rock, and the *Spider* noted that it had apparently been cut through the point of least resistance—that is, where the rock ended. This was the reason for the curves and twists in the corridor.

The *Spider* began to gain on Silvestro again, aided by the flashlight. Big Harry's footsteps sounded louder and louder, but he remained out of sight because of the turns in the passage. Suddenly, as if he had stepped into a void, the sound of Big Harry's footsteps ceased.

The *Spider* stopped short, listening carefully, but could hear no sound. Cautiously he advanced, throwing the light ahead of him, until he came to a point in the passageway where it forked. The *Spider* hesitated.

Big Harry had gone down one of these, but it was strange that his footsteps had ceased to echo. Cautiously, the *Spider* sent his flashlight flickering down the left hand passage, saw that it was lined with gravel, like the one in which he was standing. He swung his light to the right hand passage, and the answer to Big Harry's disappearing footsteps lay there before him.

The floor was a bed of oozing mud instead of gravel. Big Harry must have gone this way, the mud accounting for the sudden cessation of footfalls. The man's big footprints were clear.

The *Spider* had lost valuable time at the fork. He hurried through the right hand passage, his shoes *squishing* each time he took a step. He progressed more slowly now, for perhaps a hundred feet, until the passage began to rise in a sharp slope. He could hear the lapping of water, and in a moment he came out of the passage, to stand almost at the bottom of the slope of the mud flats, with the waters of the river not six inches below him. Big Harry Silvestro was not in sight.

The *Spider* clicked off his flashlight, so as not to make a mark of himself in the night for gunfire, and stood silently, listening for sounds. There were none, except the soft lapping of the water. Out in the middle of the river, several barges and a couple of company tugboats were anchored. Aside from that, there was no sign of life here. Big Harry Silvestro had disappeared as if into thin air.

For a moment the *Spider* let his gaze wander from one to another of the boats anchored in the river. There were two tugboats, and each of them carried riding lights. The barges were dark, deserted. The *Spider* clicked on his flashlight once more, let the beams play across the tugboats, and a hail came from one of them.

"Who's that with the light?" a jittery voice asked.

"I'm looking for someone," the *Spider* called back. "Did you see a man on shore here just now?"

"Not a soul, until you came along," the man on the tugboat replied. Then, with a note of suspicion: "What are *you* doing there? Who are you? Speak up!"

The *Spider* did not reply. He did not wish to

indulge in lengthy explanations now. His flashlight had told him that the nearer of the two tugboats was called the *Miss Susan*, and the one further down the river, the *Miss Nellie*. Both were owned by the Keystone Steel & Iron Corporation, as were the barges.

The man on the *Miss Susan* clicked on a powerful flashlight which he directed toward the shore. "I got a gun here!" he shouted. "You better speak up, or I'll shoot!"

The man's voice was nervous and high-pitched. He could not be blamed, considering the conditions in the city.

Wentworth quickly slipped back into the passageway, began to retrace his steps toward the shack. He had had Silvestro within his grasp, and had let him go. Now he must start all over again, to seek some clue, some answer to the weird events that were taking place here in Keystone. Grimly he retraced his route toward the shack. . . .

CHAPTER FIVE

Aboard the *Miss Susan*

For several minutes after the *Spider* had reentered the tunnel, there was utter silence along the shore and out in the river. Nothing stirred; even the dim, shadowy figure of the watchman on the *Miss Susan* was motionless.

Then a dark shape rose slowly out of the water, clinging to a rope that hung from the gunwale of the tugboat. Water glistened from the man's naked torso as he scrambled agilely up on the deck. The man with the searchlight went to the rail and helped him over.

A light went on in the cabin, and momentarily illuminated the face of the watchman. He was no ordinary tugboat employee. Fair-haired, with an ugly scar across his left cheek, anyone in Keystone would have recognized him as the leader of the vicious band of criminals in their assaults upon the steel workers.

He scowled at the dripping man who had climbed

out of the water, and said: "That was the *Spider* on the shore, wasn't it, Silvestro?"

Big Harry Silvestro loomed a head taller than the fair-haired man with the scar; but it was apparent that he feared him thoroughly. He spoke in a subdued voice, haltingly: "Yes, Gregory—"

The fair-haired man's open hand came up in a sharp slap to the side of Silvestro's face, rocking the big man's head. Big Harry cringed.

"Do not be so familiar," the fair-haired man said coldly. "You will call me Mr. Bayer."

"Yes, Mr. Bayer." Big Harry lowered his eyes before the other.

"That is better. Now, tell me what happened."

"The *Spider,* he see me at the shops, and he chase me. I knew you and the men be coming back here through dat shack, so I not go there. I lead *Spider* around in circle, to give you time to get on board boat, then I run to shack. I t'ink he no see me in the night, but that damn *Spider,* he too clever. You leave candle burning there, and he see the light, break in the door. We have big fight."

Gregory Bayer was watching Silvestro closely. "Yes? You fought? And you did not kill the *Spider?*"

Big Harry uttered an oath. "Me bigger man than him. Me strong man. But that damn *Spider*—he's a devil. I got big crowbar, see, but even that no good. I punch, he dance away. Then he smack me. Cut up my face, sock me in belly, till I almost can't get up no more. So I knock over candle and jump through trapdoor. Then I swim out here and hang on rope till he go away. We fooled him, no?" Big Harry grinned

239

through split lips. Gregory Bayer looked thoughtful. "I wonder if we did. That *Spider* is very clever; too clever. We will have to do something about him. We must not allow one man to spoil our plans."

He waved a hand. "Go to your quarters, Silvestro. Fix up that face of yours. It's badly damaged."

Silvestro started across the deck. "Wait till I meet that guy again. I smash in back of his head. He no know what hit him!"

Big Harry scrambled down the companionway into the hold. Here some seventy men were packed closely together, sleeping on mattresses on the floor. These were all that was left of the gang of desperadoes who had attacked the company plant that night, after slaughtering steel workers and their families during the week. Machine guns and automatic rifles were stacked in one corner of the hold.

These men, like Big Harry, wore queer, pinched expressions. Criminals they were; murderers they were. But there was something else about them— something that was almost inhuman—which set them apart from other men. That strange something was the look of bestial ferocity that glowed in their eyes. Looking at them thus closely in the smelly, crowded hold, one might have sworn that every vestige of human emotion had been removed from their souls— if they had any souls—by some mysterious process of chemistry or black magic.

They paid no attention to Silvestro. Big Harry moved among them surlily, picked a spot on the floor, and plopped himself down. He felt gingerly of his face, and one of the criminals, seeing his battered features, guffawed loudly. Big Harry swung around, glared at the man, who subsided at once.

Big Harry grunted: "You laugh, huh?"

"No, no, Harry, not me!"

"Hah!" Silvestro lumbered to his feet, started toward the man. The fellow screeched, tried to scramble out of the hold. But Silvestro's huge foot lashed out, caught the man in the temple with a sickening thud, sent him crashing into a bulkhead where he slumped in a limp heap.

Big Harry turned away from the unconscious man, callously, and glowered around the hold. "Anybody else vant to make laughing at me?" he demanded truculently.

Nobody answered him. . . .

Above decks, Gregory Bayer had thoughtfully watched Big Harry's broad, naked back disappear down the companionway. Then he turned and stared for a long time out over the river toward the shore where the *Spider* had stood at the mouth of the underground passage. The ugly scar on his cheek glowed redly in the darkness.

From a sheath under his coat he drew a thin, silver-like knife, with a bone handle. He hefted the vicious weapon in his hand, then ran the keen edge along his thumbnail. A chuckle sounded far down in his throat. With a swift motion he *swished* upward through the air, holding the knife like a sword. It was a practice thrust. Had an antagonist stood before him, that thrust would have disemboweled the man.

Again Gregory Bayer chuckled, replaced the knife and walked quickly across the deck toward the cabin.

This was no ordinary tugboat. On the bridge, the wheel was lashed, but a seaman stood guard, and saluted smartly as Bayer passed him, stepped into the chart room. The chart room was equipped as no tugboat had ever been equipped before. There were maps, and a multitude of instruments, such as might have been found upon a seagoing yacht. It was apparent that this tubby craft could navigate the Great Lakes if necessary, in spite of its awkward appearance. In a rack on one wall of the chart room hung a row of the newest type of Browning rapid-fire machine guns, capable of firing a steel-jacketed bullet that could pierce armor-plate.

Two officers in the chart room saluted Bayer as he went through, and he returned the salute carelessly.

Within the cabin he seated himself at the desk, and reached for an open box of candy at his elbow. He ate half a dozen pieces of the confection, smacking his lips in evident enjoyment. It was strange to see this heavy-set, hard-faced man eating bonbons with such relish. Gregory Bayer had killed many men in the course of his career, and had not hesitated to inflict torture upon countless others. And always he had managed to have a box of candy near him.

He was a Russian. He had been a spy for the Russian Imperial Secret Police before the collapse of the Czar's government. Skillfully he had managed to ingratiate himself with Kerensky, then with the Soviets, and had risen to the position of Commissar. His ruthlessness and his cruelty had become a proverb. Finally the man's excesses of atavistic sadism had become too much for the government. An investigation revealed his past as a Czarist spy, and Gregory

Bayer had been forced to flee. His knowledge of languages helped him to live on the Continent for a number of years, until he found the various capitals of Europe too hot for him. America was his next port of call. The craving for candy followed him.

He stuffed a large chocolate-covered cream into his mouth, and swung the swivel chair around to a sending and receiving radio set, built into the wall of the cabin. He fiddled with it for several moments, then spoke into the mircophone.

"Number One. Number One. Number One. Number Two calling. Number Two calling Number One. . . ."

He repeated the call several times, then waited, with earphones clamped to his head. At last he caught a reply. "Number One answering Number Two's call. Make your report quickly. I have little time to spare."

Gregory Bayer answered respectfully: "Our attack on the company plant was a total failure, sir. We failed to reach our objective due to interference from a well-armed body of steel workers under the leadership of the *Spider*."

"The *Spider!* You say the *Spider* is there?" Number One's voice grated through the ether, rasping into Bayer's earphones. "It's impossible. He couldn't have come so soon!"

"I'm sorry, sir," Bayer replied, "but I'm sure it was the *Spider*. No one else could have beaten Big Harry Silvestro in a rough-and-tumble fight. Even I couldn't do it—bare-handed. Silvestro's face is almost cut to ribbons. The *Spider* must have brought guns in with him, too, because all those steel workers

243

were armed. My men weren't prepared for anything like that, and the steel workers shot down almost half of them. Mayor Gaylord must have sent for the *Spider* in spite of the warning note. What will we do with his daughter? Shall I have her nose cut off, as we threatened?''

Gregory Bayer's voice was as cool as if he were discussing the weather instead of proposing to cruelly disfigure a beautiful, innocent girl.

''No, no,'' Number One rasped. ''Do not harm the girl unless I give the word. I am sure Gaylord wouldn't have sent for the *Spider,* knowing that his daughter is in our hands. The *Spider* must have come on his own. We need the girl, alive and healthy, to prevent Gaylord from asking the Governor to establish martial law.''

''Then what'll I do next, sir?''

''You will leave Keystone at once, with all your men. We have no time to make another attempt at our objective here. The plan is too accurately timed to delay any longer. You will steam down the river to Croton City. Our operation at the Croton Steel Plant must begin tomorrow. I will personally take charge of the campaign in Keystone.''

''But the State Police are guarding the river and the road—''

''You must pass them, Bayer. It is imperative that you and your men be in Croton City by tomorrow. How you do it is your concern. You understand, Bayer—'' the voice coming over the ether became silky, dangerous ''—what happens to a Number Two man who must be replaced?''

244

"I—understand, sir. I'll get through somehow, depend on it."

"As for the Gaylord girl, you will keep her on board with you. I think it best that she should be taken out of town, out of reach of this *Spider*. But remember that no harm be done her. As long as she remains alive and in good health, we can depend upon it that Gaylord won't call on the Governor to declare martial law here in Keystone. You have your instructions. Communicate with me tomorrow, when you reach Croton City. Now sign off."

As Gregory Bayer removed the earphones and shut off the radio, there was a half-cunning, half-savage smile on his thin lips. "So you're riding high, Number One! And Gregory Bayer is expected to lick your boots, eh? Well, what you don't know won't hurt you!"

Savagely he pressed a button, at the same time stuffing a couple of pieces of candy into his mouth. To the man who answered his call he ordered: "Bring that Gaylord girl in here—quick! And tell the first officer to get up steam. We're leaving at once—down the river for Croton City. Pass out the Brownings to the men below, and call me five minutes before we reach the State Police barricade."

The man saluted and left. In a moment he was back, leading Susan Gaylord.

The dark-haired, slender girl sank back against the wall, watching Gregory Bayer with half-frightened eyes. The man who had brought her in saluted, and left the cabin, closing the door softly behind him.

Gregory Bayer's eyes burned hotly as he let them

wander in lascivious enjoyment over her slender body.

"You are very beautiful, Miss Gaylord," he said softly.

She made a visible effort to repress her fear of the man, and forced a smile. "Thank you," she replied. Her lower lip was trembling. "W-what are you going to do with me?"

"We are going out of town, my dear," Gregory Bayer told her. "I thought that perhaps you would provide a little entertainment for me on the trip."

Slowly he got up from his chair, his eyes still fixed on the girl.

Susan Gaylord whispered: "No, no—"

Gregory Bayer lunged at her, and she screamed, twisted out of the way. He swung after her, and his big hand reached out, gripped her dress. Hysterically she pulled away, and the dress tore in Bayer's hand. Susan screamed again, leaped toward the door, and tripped. She fell, her head striking the door jamb, and lay still.

Gregory Bayer stood over her, frowning. Under his feet the boat began to tremble as it got under way. They were moving down the river. Bayer scowled. He turned to the water cooler, seemed to change his mind, then shrugged and opened the door, stepped out of the cabin. He went up on deck, leaving Susan Gaylord to lie unconscious on the floor.

In the chart room, the first officer was passing out the Browning machine guns to the men, who had come up from the hold. They were spread out on the deck, along the rail, with the guns so placed as to be hidden from view of the bridge tenders along the

246

river. As the boat progressed down stream, bridge after bridge opened for it without question. None of the bridge tenders entertained any suspicion of one of the company tugboats.

Gregory Bayer strode up and down along the deck, cautioning the men to silence.

"We'll reach the State Police barricade in a half hour," he told them. "You will do nothing to attract attention. Don't shoot unless I give the word. If we can pass the state troopers without a fight, so much the better."

Silence descended upon the *Miss Susan* as she worked slowly down the river with her crew of desperate killers.

Neither Gregory Bayer nor any of his men noticed the coupé which drove along Main Street, parallel with the river, slowly pacing their tugboat. The coupé contained two men. The face of one was shrouded by a broad-brimmed black hat, and he wore a long cape about his shoulders. He was driving. Beside him sat broad-shouldered, stubborn-jawed Mike Foley, president of the local Steel Workers Union.

The *Spider* had not been entirely fooled by Silvestro's ruse. He had worked his way back through the passageway, into the shack where the fight with Silvestro had taken place. There he had stood for ten long minutes, watching the boats on the river. At last he had seen the *Miss Susan* get into motion. And the *Spider* had nodded his head in satisfaction. By a process of elimination he had deduced that the only place where Silvestro could have taken refuge was in one of the boats anchored in the river. The fact that the *Miss Susan* was getting into motion at this late hour of the night convinced him that his deductions had been correct.

Swiftly the *Spider* hurried off across the railroad tracks, retraced his steps past the company plant where ambulances were already picking up the dead and wounded to be transported to the Keystone General Hospital. He did not stop here, but made his way back to where he had left the parked coupé. The armed steel workers were waiting outside the union headquarters, talking excitedly among themselves in groups. Mike Foley was waiting beside the car. When he saw the *Spider* he hurried over to him, smiling broadly.

"We put it over on them that time, *Spider!* That's the way to handle them all right!"

Wentworth gripped Foley's arm. "Quick, Foley! Give orders to your men to await us here. You're coming with me. Have somebody on the telephone all the time, in case we need them. There may be another fight within the next half hour!"

Foley's eyes glowed with excitement. He asked no questions, but immediately issued instructions to the gathered steel workers, and assigned two men to stay at the telephone at all times. Then he got into the car, and the *Spider* drove swiftly away, crossed the Broad Street Bridge long before the *Miss Susan* had reached it on its way down the river. They drove back up Broad Street until they came abreast of the *Miss Susan,* then turned around and paced it. Twice during the tugboat's progress, they crossed small bridges just ahead of it, and Foley leaned far out over the car to peer down upon the deck of the moving boat.

"I think you're right, *Spider*," he said eagerly. "It's kind of dark down there, but I think I can see a lot of men on the deck. What do you think they're up to?"

"They must be trying to get out of town. How far is the next city from here?"

"Croton City," Foley told him. "It's a steel town, a little bigger than Keystone. The Croton Steel Works are located there."

Slowly the *Spider* nodded. "I think I see the idea. We've got to stop them. This is the second phase of their plot. If they are not hamstrung now, this thing will spread to every steel town in the country. Whoever is behind it is playing for very big stakes, Foley."

The union president was tense with excitement. "Let's phone the boys, *Spider*. They can head this boat off before—"

"No. Not yet. As long as your steel workers confine themselves to the other side of the river for the protection of their homes and their women and children, nobody can have any quarrel with them. But if they should attack a company boat, that would be a different matter."

The *Spider* slowed his coupé down, allowed the tugboat to pass them in the river. Then he said to his companion: "Get back to union headquarters, Foley. Have the men ready to start at once. Commandeer as many cars as you can. I'm going to see Mayor Gaylord, and try to get him to deputize all of your men. I'll phone you from the Mayor's office, and if

I put it over, you can start for the river to head off the tugboat."

"Okay," Foley said. He got out promptly, started across the bridge toward the mill district. The *Spider* swung the car around in another turn and drove back toward City Hall. Before reaching City Hall, he turned into a dark side street, pulled the coupé up to the curb, and removed his hat and cape. A few moments' work with his make-up kit expunged the features of the *Spider,* replacing them with those of Dr. Elias Benson—the disguise which Wentworth had used upon entering Keystone.

He sat more sedately behind the wheel, and his every action was that of a dignified physician. He drove swiftly to Broad Street, and parked before the City Hall building. Descending from the coupé, he made his way up the broad steps, finding his way easily to Mayor Gaylord's office. He had been in this very building, in the very office of the Mayor on his last appearance in Keystone.

He rapped upon the door, and entered when a voice within called out: "Come in."

CHAPTER SIX

Slaughter on the River

Wentworth recognized two of the four men in that room. On his last visit to Keystone he had met Mayor Gaylord. Jonathan Spencer he had seen only a little while before at the union headquarters. The other two men in the room were young Charley Hendrix and Dr. Arvin MacLeod.

All four men regarded him questioningly. He stepped up to the desk, bowed in a dignified manner, and placed a card on the glass top before Mayor Gaylord.

"Permit me to introduce myself, Mr. Mayor," he said. "I am Dr. Elias Benson from New York."

Gaylord raised his eyebrows. "Quite so. You phoned for permission to enter Keystone, Dr. Benson. I want you to meet Mr. Jonathan Spencer, the General Manager of the Keystone Steel & Iron Corporation, Dr. Arvin MacLeod, the Coroner of Keystone County, and Mr. Charley Hendrix, a close friend."

Wentworth shook hands in turn with each of the men. Although his appearance was entirely casual, his keen eyes were appraising every one of them. He could see that Mayor Gaylord was visibly under a great strain. The man's face was almost yellow in texture, his hair was disarranged, and his collar wilted. He had the appearance of not having slept for several days. Young Charley Hendrix was also distraught, nervous, and manifestly at his wit's end. Jonathan Spencer seemed to be in a towering rage about something. He glared at Wentworth as if the interruption were most unwelcome. There was no sign in his eyes to indicate that he recognized in the dignified Dr. Elias Benson the man who, only a short while ago, had saved him from the rage of the steel workers at union headquarters. He shook hands brusquely, and stamped away to the other end of the room, where he stood with his back to the others, looking out of the window.

Dr. Arvin MacLeod shook hands with Wentworth a little more cordially, but there was a slight trace of suspicion in his voice as he said: "I am extremely glad to meet you, Dr. Benson. I somehow recall having seen your photograph in the newspapers some years ago, but your appearance is quite different from the picture, as I remember it—"

"That was a number of years ago, Doctor," Wentworth said easily. "Perhaps you confuse the photograph with that of someone else."

MacLeod shrugged. "Perhaps. However, my memory for faces is ordinarily very good."

The name of Dr. Elias Benson was a famous one among the diagnosticians of New York. Wentworth

252

had assumed it to enable him to gain easy access to the city. He had deliberately taken the risk of meeting someone here who might know Dr. Benson. It was a risk that was absolutely necessary. He saw that MacLeod's suspicions were not entirely quieted, and welcomed the change of subject as Mayor Gaylord broke it.

"I want to tell you, Dr. Benson, how much I appreciate your coming here. It has been almost impossible to get anyone to enter the town since the epidemic of madness broke out. Even the state police won't come across their barricade. Luckily, the epidemic does not seem to be spreading very rapidly, although we have a few new cases every day—just enough to keep the quarantine strictly in force."

"From what I hear," Wentworth said, "this must be a very rare disease indeed. Have you progressed very far in your work of identifying it, Dr. MacLeod?"

"No, I'm sorry to say. I find some fine substance present in the blood of every individual who has been stricken, but there is no category within my knowledge of medicine into which that substance fits. I shall be glad to have you conduct any examination you care—"

"Thank you," Wentworth broke in. "Tomorrow I shall be glad to visit the hospital with you. Tonight, I think there is a matter of even greater importance, in which I am sure you will all be interested."

Jonathan Spencer did not turn from the window. But Charley Hendrix took an eager step forward, while Gaylord pursed his lips.

Wentworth had wanted to approach the subject of

253

the tugboat in a less abrupt manner, but time was precious. Soon the *Miss Susan* would be at the barricade, and once they passed the State Police guard, the men would scatter from the boat without difficulty.

"I understand," he went on, "that Miss Gaylord was abducted—"

Charley Hendrix exclaimed: "Yes! She was taken right out of this room, from under our noses. We scoured the city, but there's not a trace of her!"

"Can you assign any reason for the abduction?" Wentworth asked.

"A very good reason," Gaylord told him bitterly. He opened the top drawer of his desk, extracted from it the note he had received, and handed it across to Wentworth. "There you are, Benson. I haven't given this note out to the newspapers. Only a few of us know about it. That's why I haven't asked the Governor to declare martial law here."

Wentworth read the note carefully, inspected the fool's bauble which was drawn at the bottom of the sheet of paper. The evil face of the jester, drawn with an uncanny ability, stared up at him with its ugly, slit mouth.

"If I could only get Susan back," Gaylord explained, "I could be my own man again. I dare not ask the Governor for troops while Susan is in their hands!"

Dr. MacLeod said dryly: "I doubt if you could get troops in here anyway, Gaylord. The Governor wouldn't want the responsibility of sending the militia into a town with an unknown epidemic. Imagine what havoc would be wrought if the troops should

254

be taken with the same kind of madness that seized Silvestro and the others!"

"What I can't understand," Charley Hendrix said, "is where they could have taken Susan. They must have some hide-out in the city. They escaped after they slaughtered the steel workers at the river bank, and they escaped again after that attack on the company plant this evening. But there isn't a place in the city that hasn't been searched. They seem to have disappeared into thin air!"

"Not quite thin air," Wentworth told him. "Have you given thought to the idea that they might have made their headquarters on board one of the boats in the river?"

Jonathan Spencer swung around from the window where he had been standing, as if he had been stung by a bee. "That's ridiculous!" he exploded. "The only boats in the river, inside the city limits, are company-owned boats, and they're all in charge of trustworthy, reliable men.

"I don't know who you are, Dr. Benson, but I *will* say—" and he glanced significantly around the room, letting his gaze rest for a long minute on Charley Hendrix "—that we certainly have a lot of meddlers in this city now. First our friend Mr. Hendrix, then the *Spider,* and now you. For anyone to claim that a company boat is being used as headquarters for these criminals is absolute idiocy!"

"I'm sorry if I have given offense," Wentworth said mildly. "However, it is possible that these desperadoes have overcome the crew of one of your boats. I did not mean to imply that the company had any part in this conspiracy."

255

Gaylord grunted. "Don't mind him, Benson. Spencer is just interested in one thing—keeping the shops going. And he doesn't care how many people die, or what happens to my daughter—" Gaylord's voice grew caustically bitter "—as long as he can fill his contract!"

Charley Hendrix was impatient. "You were talking about Susan, Dr. Benson. What about her? You think she's on one of those boats?"

"I do. Upon arriving in the city this evening, instead of coming directly here, I drove across one of the bridges into the mill district. I talked with many of the workers, including the president of the Steel Workers Union. I wanted to get some first hand information on the symptoms of this epidemic of madness. On my way back, I happened to notice one of your company tugboats—the *Miss Susan,* if I'm not mistaken—steaming down the river. There were men with guns on the deck, and I am sure I saw a young woman on the bridge."

Wentworth was deliberately lying about having seen Susan on the tugboat. He was doing it in order to make sure that the *Miss Susan* would be stopped before reaching the barricade. He waited to see what reaction his words would have upon the four men in the room. Upon that reaction he would base his deductions as to the head of this conspiracy.

He entertained no delusions that this campaign of terror might be an abortive attempt on the part of some second-rate criminal. Thus far nothing had been stolen, no definite aim accomplished by the spread of the epidemic or by the attack against the

256

steel workers and the company plant. There was something behind this campaign that was far deeper than the hope of immediate gain. And the person behind it must be a man of intellect, holding a high position in the city; otherwise it would have been impossible for him to lay the groundwork secretly for such a major operation.

Dr. MacLeod frowned. "You are sure of this, Benson? You're sure your eyes didn't deceive you in the night?"

Charley Hendrix was almost shouting in his excitement. "Let's stop that tugboat, Mr. Gaylord! Order the police after it. Phone the state troopers at the barricade. Quick, do something, for God's sake! That boat will be at the barricade soon!"

Gaylord seemed uncertain just what to do in this crisis. "Susan!" he murmured. "Susan, aboard that tug! And with all those criminals!" He groaned. "Why didn't we think of searching the boat before!"

Jonathan Spencer sneered. "I'm sure Dr. Benson must be mistaken. Why don't you send a couple of city patrolmen to stop the boat while it's still in the river? They can satisfy themselves that the boat is moving on a legitimate errand, and that there are no captives on board."

"Yes, yes," Gaylord said eagerly. "That's the thing to do. I'll have a couple of men go on board—"

"If I may be pardoned for intruding," Wentworth broke in, "I would suggest that it may be necessary to send more than just a couple of men. If this tugboat is really manned by the desperadoes who have massacred the inhabitants of this city, they will make

257

short work of one or two patrolmen. You must concentrate as many men—"

"But I can't move them all at once, and leave the rest of the city unguarded," Gaylord protested.

"I have thought of that," Wentworth replied. "I notice that the steel workers across the river have all been armed. There must be more than a hundred of these armed men, ready and willing to fight. They've already beaten those criminals once, at the company's plant. Why don't you deputize them, and let them stop the tugboat?"

"I won't do it!" Gaylord exclaimed stubbornly. "Those men have no right to carry arms. Why, I'd be the laughing stock of the country if it became known that I deputized a gang of steel workers to attack one of their own company's tugboats."

"But what about your daughter?" Wentworth demanded. "How would you feel if your daughter should be carried out of town by Silvestro and those others?"

Jonathan Spencer barked: "Hah! You don't have to worry about that. The tugboat will never pass the police barricade."

Charley Hendrix was glancing from Gaylord to Spencer. Suddenly he pounded the desk with a frantic fist. "My God! Are you two going to sit there bandying words all evening while they're carrying Susan off? Why don't you do something? Aren't you going to do *anything*?"

Gaylord's voice sounded like that of a broken old man. "I'm afraid there's nothing we can do, Charley. If we send the steel workers against that tugboat, and if those desperadoes are really on the tugboat, a pitched battle will result. Susan may be killed. Our best bet is to let the state troopers stop the *Miss Susan.*"

"Of course," Dr. Arvin MacLeod broke in suavely, with a sharp glance at Wentworth, "this all depends on whether Dr. Benson here really saw what he says he saw."

Wentworth glanced sharply at MacLeod. He detected that same note of suspicion in the Coroner's voice that had been present when he mentioned the photograph in the newspaper. He shrugged, with an assumption of carelessness.

"Well, it's none of my business how you handle this situation. I'm a stranger in the city, and my only interest is a scientific one. However, I should think you would take some action about it, as young Mr. Hendrix here suggests."

Charley Hendrix gripped Wentworth's arm in desperation. "Look here, Dr. Benson, you seem to be the only sensible man here. Will you come with me? I'm going to try to stop that tugboat!"

"With pleasure," Wentworth told him.

The two of them hastened from the room, leaving Spencer, MacLeod and Gaylord staring after them.

Outside, Wentworth got into the coupé with Hendrix beside him and drove swiftly down Main Street. He was reproaching himself bitterly now for having gone to see Gaylord at all. He should have ordered the steel workers to attack the tugboat without consulting the Mayor. It would have been a drastic thing to do, but the more he thought of it, the more he felt that he would have been justified in imperiling the lives of the steel workers in such an attack.

Even now he hesitated to call Mike Foley. If the tugboat were manned by the criminals, they could mow down the steel workers with their machine guns from behind the security of the deck rails. The steel men would not have a chance against them.

Wentworth had to drive almost to the edge of town before he caught sight of the *Miss Susan*. She was chugging slowly through the night, and was now less than twenty yards from the barricade. Wentworth raced his car down darkened Main Street, while Charley Hendrix urged him to more and more speed. But he was too far away to beat the tugboat to the barricade.

Ahead, he could see one of the state troopers step off the road to the edge of the river and raise his hand in signal to the tugboat to stop. The *Miss Susan* was almost abreast of the barricade on the road, but she gave no sign of slowing down.

Charley Hendrix shouted into Wentworth's ear: "You must have been right about that tugboat! Look, she's not even slowing down for the state troopers!"

Four or five other state troopers had run to the edge of the river, and they were all waving to the tugboat to stop. But there was no sign that anyone on the tug had seen or heard the troopers. She continued serenely on her way.

Wentworth could see Sergeant Murphy standing at the edge of the shore, could see the Sergeant draw the revolver from the holster at his side and fire into the air across the tugboat bows.

Almost as if that had been a signal, red flames

lanced out from machine guns all along the rail of the *Miss Susan*. The staccato bark of the deadly Brownings beat a terrible tatoo of death, riddling the bodies of the unfortunate troopers with steel-jacketed slugs. Sergeant Murphy and the other men on the edge of the river fell at the first volley, their bodies almost cut in half by the vicious barrage. Other state troopers rushed to the edge of the river, only to be met by a continuous hail of lead.

Wentworth drove furiously, recklessly, with Charley Hendrix hanging out of the window, peering ahead. Hendrix suddenly pointed at the tugboat, and screamed against the whistling wind: "There's Susan! There's Susan!"

They could see her clearly now, her torn dress flying behind her as she raced across the deck of the tugboat toward the rail. They did not know that she was half dazed from the blow she had sustained in the cabin. They did not know that she had regained consciousness only because of the rattling volleys from the machine guns. She was running, not knowing where she wanted to go, but half frantic with hysteria and fright. Behind her lumbered the burly figure of Gregory Bayer.

Susan reached the rail, tried to leap over into the water, but Bayer caught up with her, threw a thick forearm around her slender waist, and heaved her backward.

The Brownings were still chattering, sweeping the shore clear, beating again and again into the dead and wounded bodies of the unfortunate state troopers on the road. And the tugboat was slowly passing the barricade.

Wentworth brought his car to a halt with its nose touching the barbed-wire barricade across the road. He ripped open the door, leaped out, just as Charley Hendrix jumped out from the other side. The machine guns had stopped their rat-tat-tat, and Wentworth watched with bleak eyes while the *Miss Susan* moved, unmolested down the river. Charley Hendrix pointed frantically.

"That big brute caught Susan! See him? He's dragging her into the cabin! God! What'll we do about it?"

There was no one here with them now, except for the lifeless bodies of the state troopers. Wentworth's mind was made up in a moment.

"The two of us can't stop that tug, Hendrix," he said swiftly. "But are you game to board her with me?"

"Board her?" Charley Hendrix asked blankly.

"Of course!" Wentworth snapped. "It's dark. There are no lights on the tugboat deck. See that hawser dangling from the gunwale? We could swim out in the darkness and climb aboard, mingle with the other men. Quick, before she gets too far away from us. What do you say?"

Charley Hendrix looked at Wentworth with sudden suspicion. "Either you're crazy, or you're playing a trick to get me on board. Why, man, you could never get away with that! We'd be discovered in a minute. Our clothes would be dripping wet and they'd notice us. Who are you, anyway? Dr. MacLeod seemed to have some doubts about you."

Suddenly, Charley Hendrix placed both hands on Wentworth's arms, gripped them tightly, pressing them to Wentworth's side. "I think you're a fake! You're just posing as Dr. Benson. You're in with those criminals!"

From down the slope leading toward the city Wentworth could hear the sound of shouts and running feet. People were quickly coming to the scene of the shooting. If they were to go on board the *Miss Susan,* they must act at once. It was imperative to allay young Hendrix's doubts. He could see that the young man was wrought up, almost hysterical with worry about Susan Gaylord. He would have to trust Hendrix with his secret. He had been in town only a few hours, and he did not know whom to trust as yet. But he must take a chance with Hendrix.

Slowly, without apparent effort, he twisted his arms out of Hendrix's powerful grasp. Young Hendrix strained against the pressure of Wentworth's arms, but it was no good. Wentworth twisted his arms slowly inward, then up and out, and Hendrix was forced to let go. Charley stepped back, with an expression of wonder in his eyes.

"Good God!" he exclaimed. "You're strong! I used to play basketball, and fence. I have strength in my wrists and my fingers; yet you broke my hold without trying. Who—are you?"

Wentworth stepped close to the young man, met his gaze squarely. "Were you in Gaylord's office when he phoned to Commissioner Kirkpatrick in New York?"

"Y-yes. I was there. Why—"

"That was when Susan Gaylord was kidnapped, wasn't it?"

"Yes. Why—"

"Gaylord was asking Commissioner Kirkpatrick to get in touch with a certain person, wasn't he?"

"Yes. How do you know—"

"I am that person!"

Charley Hendrix's jaw dropped open in amazement. "You—the *Spider!* I should have known—"

"Now—" Wentworth pursued his advantage "—will you follow me?"

"Yes, *Spider—anywhere!"*

Wentworth nodded, turned and raced back toward the coupé, with Hendrix behind him. He slid back the bolt of the gate in the barricade, swung it open, then leaped into the coupé. Hendrix joined him, Wentworth had the car started almost at once. He raced through the gate, sped down the road after the tugboat.

His eyes were glued to the *Miss Susan,* and he did not notice the small car which had been approaching the city, and which pulled over to the side of the road as he sped by. He, therefore, did not see the young woman who was driving that car, nor did he see what she did after he passed her. Had Wentworth seen that car and its occupant, the events of the next few days might have been materially altered. But whoever it is that directs the fate of men ordained that Wentworth should speed by without noticing either car or driver.

He raced down the road, with lights out, until he had gotten well past the tugboat. The men on the *Miss Susan* were paying little attention to what was occurring on shore. They had successfully passed the barricade, and that was all they cared about. Wentworth pulled the coupé up to the side of the road about a hundred yards beyond the tugboat. He leaped out, followed by Hendrix, and raced down the sloping side of the river bank, to the edge of the water. It was pitch dark here, and there was no chance of their being observed by the men on the boat.

The two of them waited tensely until the tug had come almost abreast of them in the middle of the stream, then Wentworth buttoned his coat tight about him and plunged into the water in a clean dive that made no sound. Hendrix followed him, and the two of them swam silently toward the boat.

Sounds of shouting and wild jubilation came to them from the deck of the *Miss Susan*. Those desperadoes were celebrating their bloody victory over the state troopers. Gregory Bayer had disappeared into the cabin with Susan Gaylord. The watch on board was relaxed, and in the dead darkness no one noticed the two dripping figures that hoisted themselves over the side of the boat and swung on to the deck. Many of them were tilting bottles of liquor to their thick, bestial lips. Others were merely standing about or shouting with the mad joy of victory.

The figure of Big Harry Silvestro loomed above the others on the deck.

Silently, Wentworth and Hendrix stole across the deck and ascended to the bridge. Their dripping clothes left a wet trail behind them. The man at the wheel glanced suspiciously at them, but said nothing.

Wentworth whispered to Hendrix: "Are you armed?"

Hendrix nodded. He produced a gun, and Wentworth said: "Okay. Let's go."

*   *   *

They entered the chart room, where there was only a single man. This was the First Officer. He looked up, saw their dripping garments, and frowned in puzzlement. He took a step toward them, and Wentworth came in at the man, brought up a smashing blow to his jaw. The First Officer crashed backward, uttering a shout of warning which was cut off as the back of his head struck a chair. The man collapsed in a limp heap on the floor, unconscious.

Outside, the man at the wheel turned to see what was the trouble, and Charley Hendrix covered him with the revolver. The door at the far end of the chart room, leading into the cabin, was suddenly swung open, and Gregory Bayer appeared.

He began to bellow: "What's happening—"

Then he saw Wentworth, and his hand went for the gun in his shoulder holster.

Wentworth's draw was a thing of miraculous swiftness. He had Bayer covered almost before the other's hand had touched his shoulder holster. Wentworth would have pulled the trigger without mercy at that moment, but just then Susan Gaylord leaped out of the cabin from behind Bayer.

She had seen Hendrix, and she ran across the cabin, directly in the line of fire. She was shouting: "Charley! Charley! I knew you'd come!"

That action of Susan Gaylord saved Gregory Bayer's life. The Russian stepped quickly into the cabin and slammed the door.

Susan Gaylord had run across the cabin, and Charley Hendrix, forgetting everything, took her in his arms, trying to cover the patches where her torn dress showed her bare white skin. "Susan darling!" he said softly. "My dearest Susan!"

Wentworth scowled, then shrugged. These two young people were truly in love with each other.

The man at the wheel had seen what was happening in the cabin, and now he bawled out in a loud voice to the men on the deck below: "Quick, boys! The boat's attacked! Up there!"

Wentworth streaked out of the cabin like a thunderbolt, launched himself at the quartermaster. The man swung away from the wheel, brought up his hands to defend himself, but Wentworth forged through with scientifically pistoning fists. He landed two blows, smashing through the man's defense. One went to his stomach, the other to the side of the jaw, and the quartermaster dropped like a log. Wentworth swung away from him without even waiting for the man to hit the deck and sprang to the companion ladder, up which half a dozen of the desperadoes were swarming, guns in hand.

Orange streaks of fire lanced through the night as the men shot at Wentworth. Wentworth's two guns sprang into his hands with the speed of legerdemain and his answering fire swept the attackers off the companion-ladder. Screams of agony from the wounded men who had been hurled to the deck below came up to them.

Wentworth sprang away from the head of the companion-ladder, called to Hendrix: "Over here, Charley. Hold this ladder for a minute!"

Wentworth raced back to the engine room signal box and pressed the button marked "Stop." It would be a few minutes before the engineer below learned of what was happening above deck. In that time, he would still obey signals from the bridge. Almost at once the throbbing of the engines ceased as the engine room obeyed Wentworth's order.

Now, other men were swarming up the ladder, and Charley Hendrix was firing at them. Wentworth sprang to his assistance, slipping new clips into his automatics. In a moment his guns were blazing down at the attackers once more, and they fell away before the deadly fire.

Someone on the deck below shouted: "Let's jump! We can't stay on the boat!" Big Harry Silvestro, who stood out head and shoulders above the others, yelled: "To hell wit' dat!"

He snatched up one of the Browning machine guns, raised it to his shoulder, his finger on the trip. In a moment that machine gun would spray the bridge with deadly lead. Wentworth raised his left arm, rested his automatic on his forearm, took careful aim, and fired once. The slug caught Silvestro square in the forehead, sent the huge man hurtling backward, to trip over the rail and plunge into the river.

The death of Silvestro sent panic into the hearts of the other desperadoes. There was a concerted scramble for the rail, and they leaped over the side into the river as fast as they could. In almost no time the deck was deserted. From the engine room, the engineer and his crew of two men appeared on deck, saw what was happening, and likewise ran to the rail, leaped over.

Wentworth uttered a short laugh. These killers were all the same. They had no courage. They were brave only when faced with defenseless men or

268

women. He swung around, leaped past Susan Gaylord, who had been standing on the bridge, leaning against the wall of the cabin, with both hands pressed hard against her breasts. Wentworth threw her an encouraging smile, then went through the chart room and tried the door of the cabin. It was locked.

"Better come out of there!" he shouted to Bayer. "The boat is taken. You might as well give up."

From outside came the sound of Susan Gaylord's shriek.

Wentworth twisted about, leaped out of the chart room onto the bridge in time to see Susan pointing at a dark figure which had emerged from the side window of the cabin, onto the bridge. It was Bayer. Bayer saw Wentworth and jumped from the bridge, landing down on the deck on all fours.

Wentworth might have shot Bayer even as he crouched there on all fours, for he knew by now that the man was without conscience and without human instinct, an enemy of society and a peril to the city of Keystone while he was alive and at liberty. But he had emptied his automatic at the attackers coming up the companion-ladder, and his guns were useless for the moment. Bitterly he watched Bayer look up from the deck, then saw the Russian leap across to the rail, and dive into the river.

"That man should have been the first to die!" he said bitterly.

Later on, he was to realize only too well the truth of his words. . . .

The engines were silent, and the tugboat was drifting toward the west bank. Wentworth paid no attention to the drifting boat, but walked somberly around the side of the bridge, and climbed into the cabin through the window by which Bayer had escaped. He looked around, studying the room, and noted the radio set alongside the desk. A light went on and off just above it.

Wentworth stepped over to it, put on the ear phones and depressed the receiving key.

A voice rasped in his ears: "Number One calling Number Two. Number One calling Number Two. Number Two, why don't you answer? Number One calling Number Two!"

Wentworth's eyes glittered with sudden inspiration. He threw on the sending apparatus, spoke into the transmitter: "Number Two standing by. Number Two standing by."

The same rasping voice replied: "Number Two! Where have you been? I've been calling you for five minutes!"

"I'm sorry, Number One. I wasn't in the cabin—"

"You should have stood by for my messages! Have you passed the state police barricade yet?"

"We are past it."

"Good. Keep a sharp watch. You are suspected. A Dr. Benson, together with young Hendrix, are driving out to intercept you. So far, no armed force will attempt to attack the boat. Try to capture Benson and Hendrix without disturbance. Proceed at once to Croton City."

Wentworth asked cautiously: "Whom shall I get in touch with in Croton City?"

"Get in touch with? You will get in touch with

no one. You know what you are to do. You will receive instructions from me by radio—"

Suddenly the rasping voice ceased for a moment, then went on with a note of suspicion. "What is the matter with you? Is this Number Two talking?"

Wentworth savagely clicked off the transmitter. "Compliments of the *Spider,* Number One. The boat is past the police barricade, but your men have fled from it. Your plans are slightly disarranged, I'm afraid. I don't know who you are yet, Number One, but you have the *Spider's* promise that you will die within twenty-four hours!"

Wentworth savagely clicked off the keys controlling the set, and ripped the ear phones from his head. If Number One had not been so keen, Wentworth might have had an opportunity to learn his identity.

For several minutes he paced up and down in the cabin, his mind racing over the situation. Only three men had known that he and Hendrix were going to intercept the *Miss Susan.* Those three were Mayor Gaylord, Jonathan Spencer and Dr. Arvin MacLeod. Number One must be one of those three.

Wait! Mike Foley had also known. But Foley had not known that Hendrix was going along. That should eliminate Foley, except that he might have spied upon Wentworth, watched him come out from the City Hall building with Hendrix. So Foley must still be included among the list of suspects. But he had definitely narrowed it down to those four men.

He tried to recall every movement, every word, every gesture that they had made during the time he had been in contact with them. Some slight thing that they might have said or done might give the clue. Spencer's quick hostility, MacLeod's open suspicions, Gaylord's vacillation—all those things might have been cloaks for their real intention. Mike Foley too, had been ardently urging the steel workers to go on strike, but had changed with abrupt suddenness when the *Spider* entered the picture.

Of course, the attitude of each of those men could easily be explained. Gaylord's vacillation pointed naturally to the fact that he knew his daughter to be in the hands of the ruthless criminal who controlled the mad men; Spencer's hostility might be due to his anxiety to keep the mills going; MacLeod's open suspicion had foundation in fact; and Mike Foley's quick change of heart could be attributed to the fact that he had supreme confidence in the *Spider*.

But *one* of those men must be acting a part. *One* of them was the head of this conspiracy.

Wentworth sighed. He had risked his life over and over again tonight, he had rescued Susan Gaylord from her captivity, he had beaten back the master of the madmen on every front tonight, but he was still no nearer a solution than when he had arrived in town.

Wearily, he climbed out through the window again, just as the tugboat bumped gently against the concrete abutment at the river bank. Charley Hendrix and Susan Gaylord were waiting for him.

"Let's get off," he said. "We'll go back to the city. I made their Number One man a promise that he would die within twenty-four hours. I mean to keep that promise!"

CHAPTER SEVEN

A Trap for Nita

Back at the unguarded barricade, past the dead bodies of the state police lying in gruesome silence along the river bank, a horde of men and women and children was pouring through the gate. They were fleeing from the city.

Word had spread everywhere that the south road was open, and the residents of Keystone seized the opportunity to escape from the reign of terror which had engulfed them for the last week.

The thought that they might spread the epidemic to other parts of the country failed to halt them. They wanted only to get away from the danger of slaughter and pestilence. They plodded on foot, they rode crowded in autos and trucks, and some went on bicycles. The great exodus from the town of Keystone had begun.

The young woman whom Wentworth had failed to notice as he pursued the tugboat continued to drive her car toward the city, against this outflow of traffic. She was forced to hug the edge of the road, riding half in and half out of the ditch. Her progress was slow, and she eyed the fleeing throngs with wonder and apprehension. It was almost three quarters of an hour before she finally arrived at the corner of Main and Broad, opposite the City Hall. Setting out from her car, she crossed the street swiftly, and ascended the steps. She was tall, graceful and lithe, with a lively, vivacious beauty that caught the eyes of all who passed.

In the broad corridor of the City Hall building, she stopped for a moment, uncertain which way to go. A tall, middle-aged man who was just leaving the building noted her perplexity, and bowed, saying: "Can I help you?"

She flashed him a quick smile of gratitude. "If you can direct me to the office of Mayor Gaylord—"

The man bowed. "Glad to. You will have to wait, because he is in conference. Perhaps I can be of assistance to you. My name is Jonathan Spencer. I am the General Manager of the Keystone Steel & Iron Company."

"Oh, yes, Mr. Spencer. You—you are working with Mayor Gaylord to fight this dreadful calamity that has struck your city?"

He nodded. "I am doing everything I can. You are a stranger here?" Spencer's eyes were studying her carefully. "How did you get into the city?"

"The barricade was open. The state troopers were killed. I stopped a number of people to ask about it, but they all seemed in such a great hurry to leave

274

town that I couldn't get a satisfactory answer. The people are trooping out of here in hordes."

"You have—business here?"

"Yes, Mr. Spencer. Since you are associated with Mayor Gaylord, I feel that I can tell you what I am here for. Naturally, it is to your interest to fight this thing. My name is Nita Van Sloan."

Spencer started perceptibly. "I've heard of you, Miss Van Sloan. You were associated with Commissioner Kirkpatrick in New York, at the time that he was fighting Tang-akhmut."

"That's true," she said eagerly. "I induced Commissioner Kirkpatrick to tell me—"

She stopped suddenly, as if she had said too much.

But Spencer smiled knowingly. "To tell you—what?"

"I mean," she faltered, "I mean, I got Commissioner Kirkpatrick's permission to come here. I want to help."

"You mean, don't you, that you induced Commissioner Kirkpatrick to tell you—where the *Spider* had gone?"

Nita's face assumed a poker expression. "The *Spider?*" she asked, as if she had never heard the name before.

Spencer laughed lightly. "You needn't worry, Miss Van Sloan. I know all about the *Spider's* coming here. In fact, Gaylord and I were anxious to have him help us. We shall be glad to have you with us, Miss Van Sloan. Come now, and I will introduce you to Gaylord."

Nita Van Sloan followed him down the corridor.

275

She was thrilled with a sense of adventure, and of having done wrong. She knew very well that she should not have come. But where Wentworth went, she must also go.*

Spencer entered the Mayor's office without knocking. Gaylord was sitting at his desk, conversing in low tones with Dr. MacLeod, who was bending over him. Gaylord frowned as he saw Spencer, then looked quizzically at Nita.

Spencer said: "I haven't abandoned the sentiments that I expressed to you a few minutes ago, Gaylord. The only reason I am returning is to escort

---

*AUTHOR'S NOTE: Readers of previous *Spider* stories have met Nita Van Sloan in the past. Beautiful and wealthy, she might have found herself a husband among the socially elect of the country and lived her life in the gilded boredom of a society matron. Instead she chose to follow Richard Wentworth along the road of peril and imminent death which he had chosen as a career. To live fully, swiftly, in the breath of daily adventure was the epitome of happiness for Nita Van Sloan when the fullness of life was achieved in company with the man she loved—Richard Wentworth. In the career of crime-fighting which he had chosen, he was stopped from offering Nita the quiet happiness of marriage and a home—and motherhood. But he gave her fully of the things which make life sweet to those who have been endowed with a high heart and shining courage; he gave her the privilege of participating in a game of danger, daring, excitement and thrill. Neither could have loved the other had they not both been constituted with a love of peril. Like gamblers staking their whole fortune on the carnival wheel, these two gloried in staking their lives. And if Wentworth would have preferred to see Nita Van Sloan safely at home while he risked life and limb, he had long ago given up hope of attempting to keep her out of the game. As was seen in a previous chapter, he had asked Kirkpatrick to keep from Nita the secret of where he was going. But he might have known that she would wheedle it out of the Commissioner.

this young lady here. I met her outside. She is—a friend of the person you sent for. You know whom I mean.''

Gaylord grew taut. His eyes travelled over Nita, searching her face. "You mean—the *Spider?*" he asked of Spencer.

The General Manager of the Keystone plant nodded. "I didn't want to mention the *Spider's* name, because I didn't know whether you had let Dr. MacLeod into the secret. Apparently you have.''

"Of course," Gaylord said petulantly. "Dr. MacLeod is the County Coroner. He is entitled to know what is going on." Nita stepped forward quickly. "Please, let's not argue and bicker." She stretched forth an appealing hand to Gaylord. "Now that you know what I've come here for, can you help me?"

Gaylord hesitated, glancing significantly at Jonathan Spencer.

Spencer bowed stiffly. "I understand." He turned to Nita. "You see, Miss Van Sloan, Gaylord and I don't see eye to eye in certain things. I insist that we must keep the shops open at all cost, while he feels that they should be closed.''

He waved his hand apologetically. "But I mustn't bother you with things like these. I'll leave now, so that Mayor Gaylord can tell you whatever he wants to, in confidence." He threw a scornful glance toward Gaylord and MacLeod, turned and stalked to the door. "Perhaps Dr. MacLeod is more to be trusted than I am.''

When the door had closed behind Spencer, Nita took an impulsive step toward the desk. "I've been

277

rash in coming here this way, Mayor Gaylord, but I couldn't rest until I knew whether the *Spider* was here. You must tell me—have you seen him?''

Gaylord shook his head. ''I am sorry to say, Miss Van Sloan, that I haven't. But I know he's in town. He rescued Mr. Spencer, who just left, from an angry mob of steel workers. Since then he hasn't been heard from.''

Dr. MacLeod came around the desk, put an arm on Nita's shoulder. ''You shouldn't have come here, Miss Van Sloan. It's bad enough for those people who must remain in town. But for someone as beautiful as you to thrust yourself into the danger of epidemics and riots and slaughter—it's unthinkable. Come with me. I'll give you comfortable quarters in the hospital, and you can wait for news.''

''Thank you,'' Nita said abstractedly. She was penitent, already regretting her hasty action in coming here, and thus disclosing her connection with the *Spider*. She would have given much to take back the things she had disclosed in the last ten minutes. But after all, her interest in the *Spider* did not necessarily implicate Richard Wentworth in any way. Though some might suspect his true identity, suspicion was not proof.

She allowed herself to be conducted from the room, and down the corridor where Dr. MacLeod showed her into a small waiting room. The door of the waiting room was open, and through it she could see the desk sergeant seated in the corridor.

Dr. MacLeod said: ''If you will wait here a few

moments, Miss Van Sloan, I'll finish up my business with Mayor Gaylord, and conduct you to the hospital.''

He bent lower, and his voice dropped. "I may mention to you in passing, that I think I know where the *Spider* is. There was a gentleman here who gave the name of Dr. Benson. Somehow, I recollect Dr. Benson as looking differently from what this gentleman did. It may be that he is your friend, posing as Benson. In that case, I fully expect that he will visit the hospital. He will want to see the men who have been stricken with the epidemic of madness, whom we have under observation there. Your best chance of meeting him, therefore, will be to come with me.''

Nita thanked Dr. MacLeod, and he left her in the waiting room. Nervously, she lit a cigarette. Her mind was filled with a thousand conflicting ideas, and she was reproaching herself for doing the thing she had done. While she waited, she could see the desk sergeant busy over his phone, sending out hurry calls to patrolmen in other parts of the city, ordering them to rush to the South Road and set up the barricade once more before the city was emptied of its population.

Out on Main Street, people were excited, milling about, exchanging wild comments as to the nature of the events that had taken place within the last half hour. A steady stream of inhabitants was moving south on Main Street toward the south barricade.

Among the crowds, the small group of individuals whose clothing dripped water as if they had recently emerged from the river went unnoticed. These men drifted by twos and threes across the various bridges, over into the mill section. They all seemed to be converging upon an old, unused railroad shed alongside the siding. Soon there were almost a hundred of them closely packed in the old shed. These men were the ones who had escaped from the tugboat, *Miss Susan*.

They waited about in silence, a silence more ugly than any shouted threats might have been. Many of them held the small, compact Brownings which they had taken from the boat. They had carried these through the streets under their coats.

Now, as they waited a last figure vaulted up into the shed. The men stirred expectantly. It was their leader, the Russian, Gregory Bayer.

It could be seen that Bayer was in a towering rage. He pushed men aside indiscriminately, growling at them, and made his way across to the far corner of the shed. Here he bent and raised a trap-door, climbed down a short set of steps into a compartment underneath the floor of the shed.

"Two of you men come down here," he called up, "and get some of these bombs!"

Two of the men nearest the trap-door descended, and Bayer stepped over to a row of boxes snugly stuck into a corner. He pried the lid of the boxes open with a crowbar, revealing that the contents consisted of rows of grenades, packed closely together in straw. The men carried up four of the boxes under his direction, and then Bayer was left alone in the basement compartment. He stepped across to a radio set which had been installed in one corner, and set the dial, then spoke into the transmitter: "Number Two calling Number One. Number Two calling Number One."

He repeated the call several times, until suddenly that same rasping voice replied: "Number One on the air. Number Two, you have failed. You allowed the *Spider* to rout you from the tugboat. Now our plans are wrecked as far as Croton City is concerned. The epidemic has been planted there, and we were all ready for your men to come in and take charge. Where are you?"

"We are at sub-headquarters Number Four, sir," Bayer replied. "I am sorry that we failed, but I couldn't control the men. I was locked in the cabin. They swam ashore, and I figured they would come to this headquarters, because it's the only other one they know. Most of the men are here, and if there is anything we can do—"

"Yes. But you must act quickly. There is a young woman in the City Hall building now. Her name is Nita Van Sloan. She is five foot, five and a half, very beautiful, brown hair, a small nose. She is dressed in a grey tailored suit and a grey hat. You will take as many men as you need and proceed to the City Hall at once. Use whatever means you must, *but I want that girl captured!* Understand?"

"I understand, sir." It was one of Gregory Bayer's virtues, that he could grasp an order at once, and not ask unnecessary questions. "I'll start at once, sir.

281

I expected action, and I distributed the gas grenades to the men.''

"Very good. You will take her back to sub-headquarters Number Four, and then proceed with Alternate Plan Two. You know what that calls for?''

"Yes, sir. With the Brownings and the gas grenades, we should be able to carry out Alternate Plan Two. I'll report to you as soon as we reach our objective.''

"All right, then. But do not fail this time, Bayer. I cannot excuse or overlook two failures in a row. Sign off.''

The rasping voice went off the air, Bayer removed the ear phones from his head.

He climbed up into the shed, and the men, who had begun to whisper among themselves, stopped and faced him expectantly.

"I want fifteen men.'' Bayer counted off the men that he wanted. "You will follow me. We'll have to commandeer a couple of cars on the way. The rest of you, wait here for my return. Be prepared for action.''

Bayer and his fifteen men marched out into the night, while those who remained behind closed the sliding door of the shed. That shed had been gone through twice during the city-wide search for the hidden desperadoes and the kidnapped Susan Gaylord. But nobody had been inside, and none of the searchers had thought to look for a hidden trap door. All was silent along the river bank as Bayer and his men trickled across the Broad Street Bridge in the direciton of the City Hall building, each with a couple of the gas grenades in his pocket, while half of them carried Browning sub-machine guns under their coats. . . .

CHAPTER EIGHT

The Attack on No. 3

The *Spider*, with Charley Hendrix and Susan Gaylord, had been compelled to halt at the barricade in the South Road. The crowd of fleeing residents was so thick that it was virtually impossible to get through. It was fifteen or twenty minutes before the city police arrived on the scene. They immediately closed the gate again, and set up a guard. But hundreds of people had already left the city, and hundreds of others gathered in a solid, compact mass, yelling and shouting to be permitted to leave.

Wentworth worked his coupé inside the barricade, and drove slowly through the milling throngs until he got out into Main Street.

Charley Hendrix sat with his arm around Susan, and the girl snuggled close to him. All three of them were wet and cold, and Hendrix had given Susan his coat, which was little comfort because it was still soaking wet from its immersion in the river.

Wentworth stared grimly ahead. He was trying to figure out logically what would be the next step of Number One in this campaign against the city. Thus far he had not been able to work out any tangible theory as to the motive behind the entire conspiracy. What could this Number One man possibly have to gain by spreading terror and madness through the town, and by slaughtering the steel workers *en masse?*

As the *Spider,* Wentworth had met many criminals of a high order of intelligence; and he had arrived at the conclusion that the basis of any criminal conspiracy lay generally in a very simple scheme. The cleverer the criminal, the more devious would be his way of attaining that simple goal. This was a perfect example of that thesis.

There was no question but that the Number One man at the head of this conspiracy was a very clever person. This so-called epidemic of madness and these unwarranted massacres of innocent steel workers and their families were, Wentworth was convinced, only smoke-screens to cover the true objective of Number One. The devilish part of it all—the clever part of it—was that Wentworth's activities must all be directed to combating these smoke-screen activities, whereas he would much have preferred to be free to delve deeper into the matter of the criminal's motive. One thing was certain—Number One was striking hard and fast, on the old theory that if you keep your enemy on the run he won't have time to organize.

Even now, as Wentworth drove up Main Street he

was wondering where Number One would strike next. His answer came dramatically, startlingly. From the direction of the City Hall building there suddenly came to their ears the sharp, high-toned explosions of gas grenades, mingled with the quick, vicious rat-tat-tat of sub-machine guns. Once more the night was abruptly filled with sounds of battle.

Young Charley Hendrix pressed Susan Gaylord closer to him. "Good God!" he exclaimed, "they're attacking the City Hall! They've come across the river for the first time!"

Susan Gaylord moaned: "When will this murdering end?"

Wentworth said nothing. He stepped down on the accelerator, raced the coupé down Main Street, regardless of traffic obstructions.

The shooting continued, growing in crescendo. They were still some ten or twelve blocks from Broad Street, and as Wentworth kept his foot down on the accelerator he could imagine what was taking place there. Now he could glimpse the white City Hall building down the street and could see crowded masses of panic-stricken people fleeing in every direction, could see clouds of smoke pouring from the City Hall building, while above everything could be heard the continuous staccato barks of the sub-machine guns.

Abruptly, a compact group of men dashed out of the City Hall building. It was too far yet to see their faces, but Wentworth could guess who they were. He could see a man in the lead carrying an inert form over his shoulder. It was the figure of a woman.

Wentworth's lips tightened. Whom were they abducting this time? He could not guess that it was Nita Van Sloan. He had not seen her come to the city, and he was relying on the fact that Kirkpatrick had promised not to divulge his whereabouts.

Hendrix gasped: "Hurry, *Spider*. Hurry!"

"This is as fast as we can go," Wentworth told him. "I'm afraid we can't make it."

He was right. The compact group of men had spread, and were entering three automobiles at the curb. Sprays of machine-gun bullets swept the crowd in the streets, mowing them down, clearing the way for the three cars as they sped into the night directly across the Broad Street Bridge.

The whole thing was over almost as soon as it had begun. Wentworth raced down Main Street, swung to the left over the Broad Street Bridge, a good four blocks behind the fleeing sedan.

Charley Hendrix, looking behind, said with bated breath: "They've killed dozens of people! And they must have used gas grenades in the building. Look at that smoke coming out of it!"

Wentworth sent his coupé speeding after the sedan, twisting in and out of dark, deserted streets in the mill district. The rear car of the three suddenly braked to a stop, and the snout of a sub-machine gun was poked out through the rear window, smashing the glass. At once, slugs began to rip down the street at Wentworth's coupé. They beat against the shatterproof windshield, cracking it into a thousand crisscross lines; they smashed into the radiator, ripped the tires, and both of the front shoes went with a great explosion. The coupé veered, swerved. Wentworth fought the wheel madly but before he could bring the car to a stop it had skidded in a complete turn. The fleeing gunmen did not wait to finish their job. Apparently they were satisfied to stop pursuit. The sedan lurched forward after the first two, disappeared into the night even while Wentworth was leaping out of his coupé.

No one came out to see what was the matter. Farther east, the blast furnaces and the open hearths sent up their streaks of fire into the night, accompanied by the incessant clanging of the huge hydraulic presses. The mills were working, and the slight flurry of machine-gun fire was drowned by the noise of the steel manufacture.

Grimly, Richard Wentworth stared into the night after the fleeing sedan. "Come on," he called to Hendrix and Susan Gaylord. "We're going to the union headquarters. I think this thing is heading for a show-down!"

He started off, walking at a brisk pace, leaving the other two to follow him. His mind was working swiftly, coping with every angle of the problem.

An attack upon the City Hall building was the last thing which he had expected the Number One man to order. Such an attack would force the hand of Gaylord, would arouse public sentiment throughout the state to such a pitch that the Governor would step in whether he was requested to do so or not. It seemed to him that things must be drawing to a head, or else that the Number One man had been driven to a desperate measure by the loss of the tugboat.

Whatever the situation, Wentworth was convinced that a crisis was approaching. In such a crisis he

288

wanted the cooperation of the steel workers whom he had armed. He left Hendrix and Susan Gaylord far behind as his long, swinging stride carried him through the night.

In the meantime, the three fleeing cars containing the gunmen had swung off to the south and cut back in a wide circle toward the railroad shed.

Gregory Bayer climbed down from the first car, carrying the inert figure of Nita Van Sloan across his shoulder. A red gash at the side of her temple indicated how she had been treated.

At a signal from Bayer, the sliding door of the shed was pushed open, and the desperadoes crowded within climbed out.

Bayer handed Nita's body to two of his men, and they placed her in the back of one of the cars. Then the Russian issued swift orders. The gunmen crowded into the three cars, hanging on running boards and clinging to spare tires on the back. Those who could not be accommodated formed into a group and set off on foot behind the three slowly moving cars. They cut across the mill district toward the north end, where open hearth shop Number Three was situated.

They stopped in the shadow, about a hundred yards from the entrance to the shop, shrouded by the night from the view of the small guard of policemen at the entrance. Bayer issued further orders, and twenty of the men, each armed with a sub-machine gun, crept forward. The others followed at a short distance, one of the men carrying Nita. When the advance guard was within fifty feet of the gate, one of the police spotted them and called out a nervous challenge: "Who goes there?"

Bayer rapped out a quick order, and the guard challenged was answered by a hail of machine-gun slugs that swept the police guards off their feet, cutting them down mercilessly. The night reverberated with the vicious spitting of machine guns. Bayer issued another order, and the entire contingent of desperadoes rushed forward. One of the men hurled a bomb at the gate, and it exploded with a shocking detonation, shattering the obstruction and clearing the path for the charge.

The desperadoes raced through that gate, and were met by three more policemen within the grounds. The three were also armed with sub-machine guns, but they could not stand against the superior force. They were mowed down before they could fire a shot.

Bayer's ruthless gunmen swept over their dead bodies and stormed the entrance of open hearth shop Number Three. The steel workers were taken by surprise. The desperadoes swept into line just within the entrance, their Brownings covering everybody in the huge room. The Russian's eyes were glittering avidly.

"Kill! Kill!" he shouted.

The gunmen pressed the trips of their machine guns, and the echoes of the chattering bursts rebounded from the high ceilings of the shop, as steel workers fell before that hail of slugs. Here and there an isolated worker ran in panic-stricken dread, seeking safety; but they were all cut down by the Brownings before they could get out of the big room. The shop was in the hands of the gunmen.

Gregory Bayer's thin lips twisted into a wicked smile. He raced across the shop to a door marked "Office." He ripped open the door, and his revolver spoke three times in quick succession. Three slugs crashed into the body of the white-faced shop manager who had arisen from behind a desk. The manager was hurled backward into his chair and sat there, head thrown back, blood spurting from the three great wounds.

Bayer did not vouchsafe a second glance for the man he had killed. He reached across the dead body, snapped up the telephone, and spoke a number into the transmitter. He waited a moment, then when he got his connection, he spoke triumphantly.

"I guess it's all right to call you on the telephone now, Number One. This is Number Two reporting. Alternate Plan Number Two is a complete success. We have the girl, and we have complete control of open hearth shop Number Three."

Over the phone came that familiar rasping voice of Number One: "Good, Bayer. You will hold the shop as long as you can. There is enough food and ammunition in the store room to hold you for a week. But you need remain only another day or so. Our operation should be completed within twenty-four hours. Do not use the telephone again. You will find complete radio equipment hooked up in the store room. Use that."

"Very good, sir," Bayer replied. "Do you want me to proceed with the other element of Alternate Plan Number Two?"

"Yes, yes, by all means. You will send out small raiding parties to bomb the other plants. You must cause as much havoc and destrction within the next two days as you possibly can."

Bayer asked: "What about our getaway when we're through? You're sure the underground passage is open?"

"It's open all the way through to the South End Bus Terminal. There will be two big buses at the terminal, capable of taking you all out of town. Now hang up. Report to me by radio hereafter."

Bayer replaced the instrument on the hook, went out into the shop. His men had spread around in the huge room and were callously carrying the bodies of the dead steel workers and dumping them in a corner. The open hearth furnaces were glowing redly, with the molten steel ready to pour, but there were no workers to tend them. Their temperature was rising swiftly, threatening to burn through the stoppers in the vents. But none of the desperadoes paid any attention to that. They had laid Nita Van Sloan upon the floor, and she was stirring with returning consciousness. Bayer strode across the room, picking out three groups of ten men each.

"Go down to the storeroom in the basement," he ordered, "and supply yourselves with bombs. You will find them stored there in boxes marked 'Machinery.' You will form into three raiding parties and spread out through the mill district. Each group will take one of the cars outside and make a swift raid. Do as much damage as you can, then return here at once."

While they were obeying his instructions and getting ready to leave on the raid, Bayer stepped across to Nita Van Sloan, watched her dazedly trying to focus her gaze upon the strange scene. His forefinger stroked the ugly scar on his cheek.

"So you are the *Spider's* woman, eh?" he said softly. "Maybe the *Spider* won't like what we're going to do to you, lady; but it'll be fun. Ha, ha. Plenty of fun!"

CHAPTER NINE

No Quarter Asked!

Richard Wentworth reached Union headquarters far ahead of Hendrix and Susan Gaylord. In fact, he had walked so fast that the two young lovers were blocks behind him. Wentworth had removed from the wrecked coupé the hat and cloak of the *Spider,* and he donned these before turning the corner. There were four steel workers on guard at the headquarters' entrance, and upon seeing him they all stood to attention, like trained soldiers.

Wentworth smiled. Mike Foley must have been working on them in the short time since they had acquired weapons, trying to whip them into shape to meet organized crime with organized vigilance. And Foley had done a good job. Upstairs in the big meeting room where Jonathan Spencer had almost been mobbed a short while ago, the main body of the steel workers were sitting about, conversing in groups.

Mike Foley had rigged up a desk on the platform, and he was transacting his business from there.

It was strange to see the twisted, caped and hatted figure of the *Spider* walk through a room full of men, unmolested. Even Wentworth felt the novelty of the situation. Hitherto, he had always been hunted by the law, as well as by the underworld. It was a novelty to him to enjoy, in the identity of the *Spider*, the respect and admiration of law-abiding men.

A low cheer went up from the steel workers as Wentworth passed down the aisle, and mounted the platform. Mike Foley leaped up, smiling broadly. "We were worried about you, *Spider*. We almost decided to go out and see did you need any help."

Wentworth waved a hand. He spoke brusquely. "I think things are coming to a head, Foley. The Number One Man has been driven into the open at last. Apparently he must strike swiftly now, or all his plans will crumble. I want you to send out scouts to cover every section of the mill district. Keep the main body of men in readiness to go wherever trouble breaks—"

He was interrupted by the distant sounds of machine-gun fire, carrying fitfully through the night above the noises of the shops.

Foley exclaimed: "That sounds like they've started already! It's from the east—right from Open Hearth Shop Number Three, where the trouble originally started!"

The *rat-tat-tat* of continuous machine gunning continued, rising in intensity. Abruptly it ceased, and after an instant there was a terrific detonation, as of a bomb.

Wentworth said crisply: "All right, men, we needn't wait any longer. Let's go!"

He leaped down from the platform, raced to the door, and down the staircase, with the steel workers trooping after him. In the street, they once more heard the quick sharp bursts of Brownings.

"It's Number Three Shop, all right!" Foley shouted.

Wentworth broke into a swift lope in the direction of the shooting, followed by the now eager steel men. They were anxious to come to blows with the desperadoes who had terrorized the town, and who had killed friends and relatives of theirs. Brownings or no Brownings, these men were ready to fight.

Open Hearth Shop Number Three was only a few blocks north of where they were. The main company plant was located at Broad Street, almost directly across the river from the Keystone City Hall. The open hearth shops and the blast furnaces were spread out over the North End, and as Wentworth and his men ran through the night, their numbers were augmented by workers from other shops, who had heard the firing.

Now, as they approached Number Three, they were suddenly met by a blaze of machine-gun fire from the grounds outside the shop. Luckily, the gunmen under Gregory Bayer had opened up just a little bit too soon, and the steel workers were still out of range.

Wentworth shouted: "Spread out! Keep your distance. Get down!"

The men dropped to the ground, taking cover wherever it was afforded, while steel-jacketed slugs from the Brownings whistled harmlessly in the street. Wentworth knew that his men, with their automatics, were no match for the gunmen armed with their high-powered Brownings. If they were to charge, they would be cut down mercilessly.

Foley wriggled over to him, where he lay hugging a hydrant. "What'll we do, *Spider?*" Foley shouted. "Do we go in and smash 'em?'

"No. You'd be cut down before you could reach the gate!''

From where he lay, he could see the breach in the fence, where the gate had been blown away by the bomb. "Those men have bombs as well as machine guns. We'll have to try taking them in the rear. You stay here with half the men. I'll take the other half and work around to the back.''

With the machine-gun slugs still ripping down the street, Wentworth crawled about among the men, picking his contingent. "When you hear firing from the rear,'' he told Foley, "you begin your advance on this side. Crawl forward, firing as you go. But don't get reckless. If the machine-gun barrage gets too strong for you, stop.''

"Like hell we'll stop!'' Foley growled. "The boys are good and sore now. They're bent on cleaning these guys out for good!''

"Let's hope we can do it,'' Wentworth said. He raised his arm in signal, and began to run, crouching, around the side of the fence. The men he had selected followed him.

Around on the west side, there was another narrow gate in the fence, through which ran the single gauge track upon which iron ore was hauled up from the river. This track ran east and west, serving seven or eight open hearth shops along its route.

Just as Wentworth rounded the corner, he saw a small group of the gunmen running toward the narrow gate, dragging two prisoners. He recognized those two at once—Charley Hendrix and Susan Gaylord. They had been picked up by one of the raiding parties that had gone out at Bayer's order. They had fallen so far behind Wentworth that they had lost him and had wandered around in the mill district till they were caught.

Now, Wentworth called to his men: "Don't shoot. That's Mayor Gaylord's daughter and her fiancé that they've got there!"

He crawled forward, watching while the gate over the narrow gauge track was opened to permit the entry of the raiding party. They could see that a strong guard was posted here as well as at the front, armed with the Brownings. It would be folly to attack in the face of those machine guns.

Swiftly Wentworth went over the situation in his mind, while the steel workers crowded around him in the night. From the front of the shop they could still hear sporadic firing. The gunmen had realized that Foley's men were still out of range, and they were merely sending an occasional burst in their direction to make them keep their distance.

Wentworth frowned, puzzled. He couldn't understand why the Number One Man, whoever he was, should have ordered his desperadoes to seize and hold one of the mills. A thing like this would surely bring down martial law upon the town, whether Gaylord asked for it or not; and since the Number One

Man knew that Susan Gaylord was out of his hands, he must know that Gaylord would hesitate no longer about calling on the Governor for assistance. He could not have known that Susan would be recaptured. Wentworth could only assume that the next few hours meant everything to the plans of Number One. Therefore, the shop must be captured, and the desperadoes driven out. But how? They were too well armed.

One of the men crowding around him asked: "What do we do now, *Spider?* Say the word and we'll rush the gate—"

Wentworth laughed harshly. "And be slaughtered like cattle! No, we've got to find some way—"

Suddenly he snapped his fingers. "By God, I've got it!" His eyes, travelling through the darkness, had spotted the bulk of an electric locomotive hooked up to half a dozen freight cars, standing idly on a siding some two hundred yards away.

"Follow me!" he shouted.

As they began to run toward the locomotive, the gunmen inside the gate spotted them and opened fire with the Brownings. Slugs whined through the air, bit into the ground at their feet, and four or five of the steel workers fell, mortally shot, before they got out of range. The gunmen inside the gate yelled derisively after them.

Now Wentworth was close to the train. He climbed up into the locomotive, with the steel workers swarming up after him.

"Spread out through the train," he ordered, "and be ready for the shock when we crash the gate!"

The men grasped the idea with enthusiasm. Half

a dozen of them volunteered to drive the engine, and Wentworth assigned two for that honor. He posted himself in the cab, made sure that all of his men were aboard, then gave the word. The engine started, dragging the freight cars behind it.

"There's only about two hundred yards to go," Wentworth told Harry Sellers, the man at the throttle. "Get up as much speed as you can."

Sellers nodded, sent the engine rolling forward. "I don't know if I can get up enough momentum to crash the gate, *Spider*, but I'll try."

The train rumbled down the narrow gauge track with dreadful slowness. Wentworth groaned. They would never get up enough steam in that short distance. The gunmen inside the gate had become aware of what was taking place, and they were firing systematically at the engine. Bullets whistled around the cab, *spanging* against the metal of the locomotive.

Wentworth reached over and pressed the button which controlled the headlight. The powerful beam cut through the night, illuminated the interior of the grounds behind the fence, showed them the gunmen kneeling and firing their Brownings, and other gunmen running out from the building to support them. The narrow gauge track ran up close alongside the shop, where a loading platform jutted out to receive the shipments of ore.

Now the engine was almost upon the gate. Suddenly, under Harry Sellers' manipulation, it spurted forward, smashed ponderously into the iron framework. That last spurt was what did the trick. The gate crumbled under the impact, and the train rolled into the yard!

300

The gunmen were on either side of it, firing up at the cab and at the freight cars. Wentworth and his steel workers returned the fire with their automatics. Battle raged in the night, and the flashes of the guns followed each other so swiftly that one might have thought them a continuous blast of flame. The headlight was shot out by a spray of machine-gun bullets, just as the train rolled to a stop against the loading platform.

The steel workers, from the protection of the freight cars, swept the yard with a continuous barrage from their automatics, sending the gunmen to cover.

Wentworth leaped from the cab, landed on all fours on the platform. A man with a Browning gun, just inside the shop, saw him and raised the tommy to his shoulder. Wentworth shot the man through the forehead, sprang forward into the shop. He raced through the receiving rooms, which were deserted, then entered a corridor where two of the gunmen were running toward the loading platform. Both men had machine guns, but before they could use them in the cramped quarters, Wentworth's automatics spoke twice, and the two men fell away before him as if blown down in a gale.

Wentworth kicked the Brownings out of the way, ran on. Another man might have stopped to pick up one of those sub-machine guns. Not the *Spider*. He knew that if there was going to be shooting in the big shop, it would have to be close shooting, for he knew that the gunmen had prisoners. A machine gun is all right when you are facing a massed enemy; but it's no good when you have to shoot carefully, when you have to avoid hitting friends among the enemy.

301

He didn't bother to see whether his men were behind him, whether he was cut off from them. Now the *Spider* was in his proper element, fighting the kind of fight that he gloried in—one man with blazing automatics against many.

He burst into the great shop honey-combed with the tracks of its overhead travelling cranes, with the heat of the open hearths spreading its hot breath to every corner. Swiftly he gazed about, summed up the situation. He saw the pile of bodies in a corner—the dead bodies of the workers who had been massacred when the gunmen seized the shop. He saw the desperadoes massed at the door, fighting back a group of steel workers who had stormed the front entrance while Wentworth created his diversion at the rear.

The *Spider* smiled grimly. Now he could have no more doubts as to Foley's integrity, for he saw the big union president locked in hand-to-hand struggle in the doorway with one of the gunmen.

And then his smile faded. There, across the vast room, he saw something that sent a chill of horror up his spine in spite of the heat of the place. . . . Nita Van Sloan was lying on her face on the floor, directly in front of one of the open hearth furnaces!

Near by, the big Russian, Gregory Bayer, was supervising four of his men who were trundling a flat conveyor toward the open door of another of the furnaces. Upon that conveyor were tied two figures—Charley Hendrix and Susan Gaylord!

The conveyor was intended for trundling ore into the furnaces. When the conveyor entered the furnace, its slab-like top could be raised to an angle which would cause the ore to slide into the furnace. But instead of ore, the conveyor now carried the figures of Susan Gaylord and Charley Hendrix.

The four gunmen under Bayer's direction were pushing the conveyor toward the furnace. Charley and Susan were tied hand and foot, on their backs in such manner that they could not move. The open door of the furnace irradiated a heat so intense that the faces of the two captives as well as the four gunmen appeared supernaturally ruddy to Wentworth from where he stood, across the vast room. Nita Van Sloan, too, as she lay on the floor, gave the impression of a sun bather lying on the broiling beach in Miami—except that the peacefulness of the southern beach was lacking from this scene of terror and confusion.

Bayer, his ugly scar showing red in the glow from the furnaces, was ordering the men to shove the conveyor into the oven. In a moment the bodies of Susan and Charley would be shrivelled, consumed, reduced to ashes. They were straining against their bonds, twisting their heads in frantic terror.

And Wentworth raised his two automatics, fired carefully and accurately four times in swift succession. His shots mingled with the explosions of other automatics outside, and with the shouts and curses of the embattled men in the doorway. The four desperadoes at the conveyor fell away from it ludicrously, one after the other, as the four slugs found their marks unerringly. Abruptly, the conveyor ceased moving. Molten steel squirmed like live lava within the furnace, seeming to writhe in impotent wrath at having been cheated of its prey.

Susan and Charley could not seem to understand what had given them a respite from the dreadful death toward which they had been moving. They twisted their heads to get a better view, and their eyes opened wide as they saw the *Spider* at the far end of the room.

Other desperadoes came running toward the conveyor at the shouted command of Gregory Bayer. They stooped to push the conveyor. The Russian had raised his gun to fire at the *Spider,* but appalled at Wentworth's uncannily accurate aim, he leaped to one side, seized Nita Van Sloan by the hair, and dragged her up from the floor, holding her as a shield in front of himself. Nita was only half conscious, and the fiery flames from the open hearth threw a weird, ruddy glow over the soft white skin of her body, which was exposed where the Russian had ripped her dress away.

Bayer held her up, his thick fingers twisted in her glorious hair. She was just conscious enough to feel the pain of that tugging against her hair. She swayed on her feet, with her dress ripped open at the breasts. Bayer rasied his gun again, fired at Wentworth from behind her body.

Now Wentworth glanced behind him, saw that his own men were storming through the corridor toward the shop. Apparently the fury of their rage had prevailed against the Brownings, at close quarters. They had broken through the gunmen at the loading platform. At the front door, the desperadoes and the steel men were still locked in deadly conflict, neither side

304

yielding an inch. They were too close for shooting now, and they were slugging with clubbed revolvers, gouging and kicking. No quarter was being asked or given in this grim battle.

A slug from Bayer's gun ricochetted from the floor, almost at Wentworth's feet. Wentworth raised his gun to answer, but held his fire. At that distance, not even he could hope to hit Bayer without endangering Nita's life. Wentworth glanced desperately about, saw a crane directly above his head, suspended from tracks that ran directly to the open hearth before which Bayer stood, and into which Susan and Charley were once more being trundled.

Bayer's shots were coming closer now, and several of the gunmen had detached themselves from the fight at the doorway, had spotted the caped and cloaked figure, and were shouting: "It's the *Spider!* Get the *Spider!*"

They opened up with their revolvers, and one of them raised a Browning, placed a finger on the trip.

Wentworth leaped backward, to where a switch in the wall controlled the power of the travelling crane. Ordinarily these cranes were controlled from a main cubbyhole, but each crane had its own emergency switch, which could operate it in case of necessity. If only the power had been left on in the line! . . . Wentworth threw the switch.

Bullets thudded into the wall beside him as the Browning opened upon him. He paid them no attention, but eagerly watched the crane.

It began to move. The power was on!

Wentworth bent his knees, went into a flying leap,

and grasped the hook of the crane, drew his knees up and rode with it across the room!

The man with the Browning swung the muzzle of his machine gun to cut Wentworth down. But the crane was moving swiftly enough to delay his aiming. Wentworth snapped a shot with his free hand, and the machine gunner toppled backward with a gaping hole in his chest. Now Wentworth concentrated his fire upon the four men trundling the conveyor, regardless of the slugs that whined past him from Bayer's gun. He brought down two of them, firing with almost miraculous accuracy from the now swiftly moving crane. The other two let go of the conveyor and turned to run, at sight of the fate which had overtaken their fellows.

Ordinarily, one man attacking them would not have meant anything to these hardened gunmen. But they had all heard of the *Spider;* and that caped figure, riding the overhead crane and shooting with deadly marksmanship, reminded them of the grisly stories they had heard in the dark corners of the underworld—how no man could hope to escape the vengeance of the *Spider;* how the *Spider's* blazing guns had brought death to the boldest and the most dangerous of criminals. And the *Spider's* reputation, as much as his uncanny shooting, won the day. Those two turned and fled toward the doorway rather than trade shots with the man the underworld dreaded.

But not Gregory Bayer.

Safe behind the protection of Nita's body, he raised his gun once more, aimed carefully, coldly. His finger compressed on the trigger, and Wentworth could see that the Russian had a dead bead on him, was following him with a steady hand. Bayer's shot could not miss, and Wentworth dared not try to fire at him, shielded behind Nita. The *Spider*, hanging by one arm from that travelling crane, stared death in the eye, and could do nothing about it.

But just as Bayer was about to pull the trigger, Nita intervened. The pain of Bayer's grip on her hair had brought her back to full consciousness, and she saw what was happening. She twisted about, clenching her hands against the excruciating pain at the roots of her hair, and sank her teeth into Bayer's wrist.

The Russian screamed with the sudden pain. The gun was deflected, exploding into the floor. Nita kept her teeth in his wrist, and he dropped the gun, let go his grip on her hair, and slugged her on the top of the head with his knotted fist. Nita gasped, and her jaws opened, fell away from Bayer's wrist. The Russian hit her again, stepped back as she sagged to the floor. He glanced up in sudden terror at the black figure of the *Spider*, which had come directly over his head on the travelling crane.

Wentworth's gun was empty. He flung it away, leaped down at the Russian. Bayer's hand slid inside his coat to the sheath strapped at his chest, and came out with the flashing, keen-edged knife that he always carried.

Wentworth landed on his feet, and he launched himself at the Russian. Bayer lunged upward with his knife, in the blow he constantly practiced. With that lunge he had often disembowelled an antagonist. But this antagonist was different from the others. Wentworth was experienced in the deadly methods of waterfront fighting as well as in more conventional methods. He had seen men disembowelled by that stroke, in street fighting in Singapore, and in riots in Canton and Shanghai.

Instead of retreating before the deadly blade, he stepped forward and to one side. The knife swished past him, stabbing up into empty air; and he caught Bayer's knife hand in a powerful grip, twisted abruptly, mercilessly. The Russian howled with sudden agony as his wrist snapped like a dry shell. The knife dropped from nerveless fingers, and Wentworth rocked him back with a hard blow to the jaw. Bayer tottered, taking two involuntary steps backward. He brought up against the white hot surface of the open hearth, and screamed, began to dance on the floor.

Now Wentworth's face paled under the make-up of the *Spider*. He saw that a stray bullet had struck the vent of the furnace, and the molten steel was pouring out, on the floor. Usually a huge cylindrical bucket was placed at the mouth of the vent to receive the hot flow of wriggling metal. Now the bucket was not there, and the liquid steel was spreading in a small, seething, white-hot lake over the floor. It was this that Bayer had stepped into. The steel had bitten right through his shoes, and he screamed with agony, leaped away, but tripped and dropped full in the river of steel.

He squirmed, twisted, screaming, flailing with his broken wrist. His agony lasted but a moment, for no living organism can survive the shock of a first degree burn administered by molten steel. In an instant he stopped flailing the air, and lay still in the

308

fiery bath of metal, his flesh sizzling terribly. He was dead!

Wentworth glanced at the conveyor, saw that Susan and Charley were far enough from the furnace to be safe, then swung toward where Nita lay.

He uttered a cry of dismay. She was dazedly struggling to her knees. The edge of the lake of molten steel was slowly oozing toward her, barely a foot away. In a moment it would be lapping at her limbs. Wentworth leaped toward her, lifted her bodily, and carried her away from the sizzling river of fire.

"Nita, darling!" he exclaimed.

Her eyes opened and she smiled. "Dick! I'm always getting into trouble—and you're always there to get me out!"

He kissed her, set her on her feet, looked around for the automatic he had dropped from the crane. It was right in the middle of the flowing steel, beside the body of Gregory Bayer.

He shrugged, took out his second automatic and inserted a clip with swift, steady fingers. But that was unnecessary. The gunmen at the door, seeing the death of their leader, had lost heart, and were throwing down their arms in surrender. The steel workers under Foley took them prisoner, none too gently. From the rear, the men who had followed Wentworth came trooping in, also with prisoners. The victory was complete!

Wentworth walked carefully around the river of steel, reached out for the conveyor upon which Susan and Charley were tied, and dragged it out into the center of the room. Foley produced a knife and cut them loose.

The steel workers were celebrating wildly, jubilantly, crowding around Wentworth, patting his back and shaking his hand. Nita, partially recovered from her ordeal, had her arms around Susan and was comforting her, while Charley Hendrix looked on with a dazed expression, hardly believing that he and Susan had really escaped the fiery death in the furnace.

Foley said to Wentworth: "What now, *Spider?* We've cleaned up here. What do we do next?"

Wentworth said soberly: "We've cleaned up, all right. But we still don't know who the Number One Man is. That man must be eliminated!"

"But—how you going to do that?"

"I'll show you. Get your men out of here. I want to be alone with Bayer's body for a few minutes."

Foley didn't understand, but he complied, ordering the men out, sending a small party to stand guard at each gate. Wentworth had told him to do that, saying: "I'd like to keep the news of this victory a secret for another hour—long enough for me to try a little plan."

He was left alone with Nita and the body of Bayer. Even Charley Hendrix and Susan Gaylord went out.

Nita watched him while he took out his make-up case, and carefully set to work. Bayer was lying face up, and though his body was sizzling revoltingly, his face, with its ugly scar, remained untouched. Wentworth used pigment, nose plates and facial creams, turning every few minutes to study the dead Russian's features. At the end of five minutes he sighed,

310

and stood up. "What do you think of it?" he asked Nita.

"Marvelous!" she gasped. "If I hadn't seen you do it, I'd think I was looking at the Russian!"

He chuckled. "It's because you're so wrought up, Nita. No man can disguise himself to pass accurately for another. But this scar—" he touched the long streak he had simulated upon his left cheek—"helps with the delusion. It'll be good enough to serve for what I have in mind tonight—I hope!"

He raised his voice, called to Foley: "All right, Foley. I'm ready. Get me a car, and four men to drive into town. We're going to pay a call—on Number One!"

Half an hour later, Wentworth, minus his cape and hat, emerged from a sedan at the back entrance of the City Hall. Inside the car were the four men he had brought with him, as well as Susan Gaylord and Charley Hendrix.

"Come with me, Charley," he said. "I think I'll be needing you."

On the way into the City Hall building, Wentworth asked Charley: "You're connected with Hendrix, MacIntyre & Hendrix, aren't you?"

Charley nodded. "My father and my uncle own the firm. We've had seats on the stock exchanges of every large center for almost thirty years."

"Do you carry stock trading accounts for any of the executives of the Keystone Steel & Iron Corporation?"

"Of course. We have Spencer's account, Gaylord's, and almost every other director and executive."

311

"How is the stock of the Keystone Corporation these days?"

"Well, it's fallen off about fifty percent since this business started. But all the stock that's being dumped on the market is being absorbed by the directors. Gaylord and Spencer are using every nickel of their personal fortunes to buy all the stock that's offered, in order to keep the bottom from dropping out of it."

"I see," Wentworth said softly.

They walked through the wide corridor leading to the executive offices.

Charley Hendrix threw a side glance at Wentworth. "God!" he said in a hushed voice. "If I didn't know you were the *Spider*, I'd almost swear I was walking alongside of that Russian. That scar looks just like his. I can't believe it's only paint."

Wentworth squeezed Charley's arm. "Quiet. Here comes Spencer. Duck around the corner. I want to talk to him alone."

Charley Hendrix saw Jonathan Spencer coming down the corridor, and he quickly stepped away from Wentworth, slipped around the corner. Spencer was apparently walking toward Mayor Gaylord's office, and there seemed to be something weighty on his mind, for he was gazing abstractedly at the floor. He did not see Wentworth until the *Spider* said: "Good evening, Mr. Spencer."

Spencer looked up startled, then his brow furrowed. He stepped back in alarm. "You—you're the man that led those murderers on the raid tonight! Help—"

He raised his voice to shout, but Wentworth

stepped in quickly, placed a hand over his mouth. "Silence! You won't be hurt!" He placed a gun against Spencer's ribs. "Move back around the corner!"

Spencer hesitated, and Wentworth poked him again with the gun. "No harm will come to you if you obey!"

Spencer stuttered: "W—what are you going to do? Haven't you done enough damage? God—"

"That's enough!" Wentworth hustled him around the corner to where Hendrix was standing. "Take care of Mr. Spencer, Charley," he ordered. "Keep him out of circulation for ten minutes. And you can explain to him while you're waiting, that I'm not the villain he thinks I am!"

Charley nodded, drew his own gun and covered Spencer.

Wentworth left them, walked down the corridor to the Mayor's office, turned the knob and entered without rapping.

Gaylord and Doctor MacLeod were sitting at the desk, and Gaylord was talking into the telephone: "Your son is all right, Mr. Hendrix. Now about that stock. I want you to buy everything that's offered. It'll drop some more tomorrow, I'm afraid—"

He stopped, his eyes staring as if at a ghost, fixed upon the apparition of Wentworth in the doorway. MacLeod followed his glance, uttered a startled oath, and sprang up.

Gaylord said into the phone: "Excuse me, Hendrix. Something important has come up. I'll call you later." He hung up, got to his feet, and asked coldly: "What brings you here?"

*   *   *

Wentworth grinned, and simulated the voice of Bayer. He was glad that there was only a single light on the desk, for it helped his disguise. "I had to come," he said. "I tried to get you on the radio, but there was no answer. We were attacked at Number Three Shop, and all my men are killed or captured. The game's up."

Gaylord glanced at MacLeod, then looked at Wentworth. "How—how did you know to come here? How did you know—"

"That you are the Number One Man?"

Gaylord nodded weakly.

Wentworth laughed harshly. "You don't think Gregory Bayer is a fool, do you? I like to know whom I work for. And it's a damn good thing I did, because otherwise I wouldn't have been able to get in touch with you now. I tried that telephone number that I used earlier in the night, but it didn't answer."

"That's right," said Gaylord. "That was Doctor MacLeod's phone. He has it tapped into a public telephone, so it can't be traced. He hasn't been there tonight, because we expected to hear from you on the radio. But quick—why did you fail?"

"That damn *Spider*. I have to admit he's too clever for me. I'm afraid the game's up, Gaylord!"

"No, no!" Gaylord shouted. "We're in too deep now. MacLeod and I are buying every bit of Keystone stock on margin. By tomorrow we'll control the whole corporation—with stock bought at bargain prices. We've got to keep up this terrorization for another twenty-four hours at all costs!"

MacLeod broke in: "But how can we, Gaylord? Isn't it risking too much—"

Gaylord turned on MacLeod furiously: "Risking too much! You fool! Haven't we risked everything already? Didn't I risk my own daughter in the hands of Bayer, so that Spencer would think I was being forced into standing by supinely? Didn't you risk your reputation when you injected that coma-producing drug into the men you vaccinated, and then hypnotized them so they'd go berserk at a certain time? What more have we to lose?"

Just then the door was pushed violently open, and Jonathan Spencer strode in, followed by Charley Hendrix, who looked crestfallen. Young Hendrix spread his hands apologetically to Wentworth. "I couldn't hold him after I'd explained who you were," he said. "Spencer dared me to shoot, and of course I couldn't kill him in cold blood."

Spencer smiled warmly at Wentworth. "By God, *Spider*, you're clever! I want to thank you for everything you've done for the town!" He turned to Gaylord and MacLeod. "Look here, Gaylord, this man is perfectly all right. Charley Hendrix told me all about it. He's the *Spider*, and he's disguised himself as that damned Russian in order to trap the criminal behind all this. I'm sure we'll all help him—"

Wentworth sighed. "You're an honest man, Spencer, but you certainly know how to put your foot in it. *These two are the criminals!*"

Gaylord and MacLeod had been listening almost with stupefaction to Spencer's innocent disclosure. Gaylord was the first to recover. Suddenly he was a snarling beast at bay as he reached into the open drawer of his desk and brought out a long-barreled forty-five.

"The *Spider!*" he snarled. *"Kill them, MacLeod, and our secret remains safe!"*

MacLeod was not slow to grasp the situation, and his own hand flashed in and out of his shoulder holster, came out with a snub-nosed automatic. But before either of them could fire, Wentworth's two automatics had appeared in his hands miraculously. They spat spitefully twice, and a round, black hole appeared in the forehead of each of the two super-criminals.

Richard Wentworth stood stiffly while MacLeod and Gaylord sank to the floor, dead.

Then, while Spencer and Hendrix watched open-mouthed, he stepped forward, manipulated with a platinum cigarette lighter, while bending over the two still-warm bodies. When he arose, Spencer and Hendrix could see that the forehead of each, alongside the black bullet hole, bore the scarlet imprint of—a spider!

Slowly Wentworth walked from the room. At the door he said wearily: "I think this will be the end of the Keystone massacres. I'll leave it to you, Charley, to tell Susan about—her father."

And while the two men watched in silence, the *Spider* stepped out of the room.

FINE MYSTERY AND SUSPENSE
TITLES FROM CARROLL & GRAF

- [ ] Allingham, Margery/NO LOVE LOST — $3.95
- [ ] Allingham, Margery/MR. CAMPION'S QUARRY — $3.95
- [ ] Allingham, Margery/MR. CAMPION'S FARTHING — $3.95
- [ ] Allingham, Margery/THE WHITE COTTAGE
  MYSTERY — $3.50
- [ ] Ambler, Eric/BACKGROUND TO DANGER — $3.95
- [ ] Ambler, Eric/CAUSE FOR ALARM — $3.95
- [ ] Ambler, Eric/A COFFIN FOR DIMITRIOS — $3.95
- [ ] Ambler, Eric/EPITAPH FOR A SPY — $3.95
- [ ] Ambler, Eric/STATE OF SIEGE — $3.95
- [ ] Ambler, Eric/JOURNEY INTO FEAR — $3.95
- [ ] Ball, John/THE KIWI TARGET — $3.95
- [ ] Bentley, E.C./TRENT'S OWN CASE — $3.95
- [ ] Blake, Nicholas/A TANGLED WEB — $3.50
- [ ] Brand, Christianna/DEATH IN HIGH HEELS — $3.95
- [ ] Brand, Christianna/FOG OF DOUBT — $3.50
- [ ] Brand, Christianna/GREEN FOR DANGER — $3.95
- [ ] Brand, Christianna/TOUR DE FORCE — $3.95
- [ ] Brown, Fredric/THE LENIENT BEAST — $3.50
- [ ] Brown, Fredric/MURDER CAN BE FUN — $3.95
- [ ] Brown, Fredric/THE SCREAMING MIMI — $3.50
- [ ] Buchan, John/JOHN MACNAB — $3.95
- [ ] Buchan, John/WITCH WOOD — $3.95
- [ ] Burnett, W.R./LITTLE CAESAR — $3.50
- [ ] Butler, Gerald/KISS THE BLOOD OFF MY HANDS — $3.95
- [ ] Carr, John Dickson/CAPTAIN CUT-THROAT — $3.95
- [ ] Carr, John Dickson/DARK OF THE MOON — $3.50
- [ ] Carr, John Dickson/DEMONIACS — $3.95
- [ ] Carr, John Dickson/THE GHOSTS' HIGH NOON — $3.95
- [ ] Carr, John Dickson/NINE WRONG ANSWERS — $3.50
- [ ] Carr, John Dickson/PAPA LA-BAS — $3.95
- [ ] Carr, John Dickson/THE WITCH OF THE
  LOW TIDE — $3.95
- [ ] Chesterton, G. K./THE MAN WHO KNEW
  TOO MUCH — $3.95
- [ ] Chesterton, G. K./THE MAN WHO WAS THURSDAY — $3.50
- [ ] Crofts, Freeman Wills/THE CASK — $3.95
- [ ] Coles, Manning/NO ENTRY — $3.50
- [ ] Collins, Michael/WALK A BLACK WIND — $3.95
- [ ] Dickson, Carter/THE CURSE OF THE BRONZE LAMP — $3.50
- [ ] Disch, Thomas M & Sladek, John/BLACK ALICE — $3.95
- [ ] Eberhart, Mignon/MESSAGE FROM HONG KONG — $3.50

☐ Fennelly, Tony/THE CLOSET HANGING		$3.50
☐ Freeling, Nicolas/LOVE IN AMSTERDAM		$3.95
☐ Gilbert, Michael/ANYTHING FOR A QUIET LIFE		$3.95
☐ Gilbert, Michael/THE DOORS OPEN		$3.95
☐ Gilbert, Michael/THE 92nd TIGER		$3.95
☐ Gilbert, Michael/OVERDRIVE		$3.95
☐ Graham, Winston/MARNIE		$3.95
☐ Griffiths, John/THE GOOD SPY		$4.50
☐ Hughes, Dorothy B./THE FALLEN SPARROW		$3.50
☐ Hughes, Dorothy B./IN A LONELY PLACE		$3.50
☐ Hughes, Dorothy B./RIDE THE PINK HORSE		$3.95
☐ Hornung, E. W./THE AMATEUR CRACKSMAN		$3.95
☐ Kitchin, C. H. B./DEATH OF HIS UNCLE		$3.95
☐ Kitchin, C. H. B./DEATH OF MY AUNT		$3.50
☐ MacDonald, John D./TWO		$2.50
☐ Mason, A.E.W./AT THE VILLA ROSE		$3.50
☐ Mason, A.E.W./THE HOUSE OF THE ARROW		$3.50
☐ McShane, Mark/SEANCE ON A WET AFTERNOON		$3.95
☐ Pentecost, Hugh/THE CANNIBAL WHO OVERATE		$3.95
☐ Priestley, J.B./SALT IS LEAVING		$3.95
☐ Queen, Ellery/THE FINISHING STROKE		$3.95
☐ Rogers, Joel T./THE RED RIGHT HAND		$3.50
☐ 'Sapper'/BULLDOG DRUMMOND		$3.50
☐ Stevens, Shane/BY REASON OF INSANITY		$5.95
☐ Symons, Julian/BOGUE'S FORTUNE		$3.95
☐ Symons, Julian/THE BROKEN PENNY		$3.95
☐ Wainwright, John/ALL ON A SUMMER'S DAY		$3.50
☐ Wallace, Edgar/THE FOUR JUST MEN		$2.95
☐ Waugh, Hillary/A DEATH IN A TOWN		$3.95
☐ Waugh, Hillary/LAST SEEN WEARING		$3.95
☐ Waugh, Hillary/SLEEP LONG, MY LOVE		$3.95
☐ Westlake, Donald E./THE MERCENARIES		$3.95
☐ Willeford, Charles/THE WOMAN CHASER		$3.95

Available from fine bookstores everywhere or use this coupon for ordering.

FINE WORKS OF FICTION AND NON-FICTION AVAILABLE FROM CARROLL & GRAF

☐ Amis, Kingsley/THE ALTERATION   **$3.95**
☐ Borges, Jorge Luis/THE BOOK OF FANTASY   **$10.95**
☐ Brown, Harry/A WALK IN THE SUN   **$3.95**
☐ Buchan, John/JOHN MACNAB   **$3.95**
☐ Chester, Alfred/THE EXQUISITE CORPSE   **$4.95**
☐ Crichton, Robert/THE CAMERONS   **$4.95**
☐ Crichton, Robert/THE SECRET OF SANTA
    VITTORIA   **$3.95**
☐ De Quincey, Thomas/CONFESSIONS OF AN
    ENGLISH OPIUM EATER AND OTHER
    WRITINGS   **$4.95**
☐ Farrell, Henry/WHAT EVER HAPPENED TO
    BABY JANE?   **$3.95**
☐ Farrell, J.G./THE SIEGE OF KRISHNAPUR   **$4.95**
☐ Farrell, J.G.] THE SINGAPORE GRIP   **$4.95**
☐ Gresham, William Lindsay/NIGHTMARE
    ALLEY   **$3.50**
☐ Gurney, Jr., A.R./THE SNOW BALL   **$4.50**
☐ Higgins, George V./COGAN'S TRADE   **$3.50**
☐ Hilton, James/RANDOM HARVEST   **$4.50**
☐ Johnson, Josephine/NOW IN NOVEMBER   **$4.50**
☐ Kipling, Rudyard/THE LIGHT THAT FAILED   **$3.95**
☐ Masters, John/BHOWANI JUNCTION   **$4.50**
☐ Masters, John/THE DECEIVERS   **$3.95**
☐ Masters, John/NIGHTRUNNERS OF BENGAL   **$4.95**
☐ Mitford, Nancy/THE BLESSING   **$4.95**
☐ Mitford, Nancy/PIGEON PIE   **$4.95**
☐ O'Hara, John/FROM THE TERRACE   **$5.95**
☐ O'Hara, John/HOPE OF HEAVEN   **$3.95**

☐ O'Hara, John/A RAGE TO LIVE		$4.95
☐ O'Hara, John/TEN NORTH FREDERICK		$4.50
☐ Proffitt, Nicholas/GARDENS OF STONE		$4.50
☐ Purdy, James/CABOT WRIGHT BEGINS		$4.50
☐ Rechy, John/BODIES AND SOULS		$4.50
☐ Reilly, Sidney/BRITAIN'S MASTER SPY		$3.95
☐ Scott, Paul/THE LOVE PAVILION		$4.50
☐ Taylor, Peter/IN THE MIRO DISTRICT		$3.95
☐ Thirkell, Angela/AUGUST FOLLY		$4.95
☐ Thirkell, Angela/CHEERFULNESS BREAKS IN		$4.95
☐ Thirkell, Angela/HIGH RISING		$4.95
☐ Thirkell, Angela/MARLING HALL		$4.95
☐ Thirkell, Angela/NORTHBRIDGE RECTORY		$5.95
☐ Thirkell, Angela/POMFRET TOWERS		$4.95
☐ Thirkell, Angela/WILD STRAWBERRIES		$4.95
☐ Thompson, Earl/A GARDEN OF SAND		$5.95
☐ Thompson, Earl/TATTOO		$6.95
☐ West, Rebecca/THE RETURN OF THE SOLDIER		$8.95
☐ Wharton, Williams/SCUMBLER		$3.95
☐ Wilder, Thornton/THE EIGHTH DAY		$4.95

Available from fine bookstores everywhere or use this coupon for ordering.

Carroll & Graf Publishers, Inc., 260 Fifth Avenue, N.Y., N.Y. 10001

Please send me the books I have checked above. I am enclosing $_____ (please add $1.25 per title to cover postage and handling.) Send check or money order—no cash or C.O.D.'s please. N.Y. residents please add 8¼% sales tax.

Mr/Mrs/Ms _____

Address _____

City _____ State/Zip _____

Please allow four to six weeks for delivery.